Through Adversity to the Stars

Squadron Leader Roy Handley
and Denise Lunt

Grosvenor House
Publishing Limited

All rights reserved
Copyright © Squadron Leader Roy Handley and Denise Lunt, 2023

The right of Squadron Leader Roy Handley and Denise Lunt
to be identified as the author of this
work has been asserted in accordance with Section 78
of the Copyright, Designs and Patents Act 1988

The book cover is copyright to
Squadron Leader Roy Handley and Denise Lunt
The book cover was designed by Imagine Design & Print Ltd

This book is published by
Grosvenor House Publishing Ltd
Link House
140 The Broadway, Tolworth, Surrey, KT6 7HT.
www.grosvenorhousepublishing.co.uk

This book is sold subject to the conditions that it shall not, by way of
trade or otherwise, be lent, resold, hired out or otherwise circulated
without the author's or publisher's prior consent in any form of
binding or cover other than that in which it is published and
without a similar condition including this condition being imposed
on the subsequent purchaser.

This book is a work of fiction. Any resemblance to
people or events, past or present, is purely coincidental.

A CIP record for this book
is available from the British Library

ISBN 978-1-80381-449-0
eBook ISBN 978-1-80381-450-6

This book is dedicated to the men and women who have served, and continue to serve, in the Royal Air Force. The oldest and finest in the world. In particular, those who gave their lives without question defending this great country.

Through Adversity to the Stars.

Chapter One

Missing Presumed Dead

"Hello Mr Jenkins, how are you feeling today." I asked my housekeeper's husband Bob Jenkins, who had been suffering from a really nasty cold and had taken to his bed. At last, it was so nice to see him up and about once again, even if he did still look a little on the pale side.

"Much better thank you Mrs Davenport." Bob Jenkins answered.

Mrs Jenkins, Bobs wife of nearly thirty years, then interrupted and said, "Off you go Bob my dear, and thank you for bringing the parcel up; I will see you at home shortly."

"Goodbye Mrs Davenport, give my best to the Air Commodore." Bob Jenkins said in a cheerful voice. He then proceeded to give his wife a peck on the cheek, stopping long enough to wait for my reply before he left.

"I will, and thank you Bob. I know Guy has been waiting for this particular parcel."

Bob and Rosie Jenkins were such a lovely couple, always smiling and happy to help no matter what we may ask of them. They have been with us for many years once we moved into this wonderful cottage.

The estate agent had actually informed us, it had always been known as. A Gentleman's Pink Cottage, which Guy eventually decided to buy. Having Mr and Mrs Jenkins come up each day, Guy and I regarded them as real treasures, making our lives so much easier.

"Mrs Davenport, are you and the Air Commodore ready for your afternoon tea?" Mrs Jenkins asked.

"Yes, thank you Mrs Jenkins. I am sure a cup of tea will be most welcome this afternoon, as Guy has been tinkering most of the day with his baby." I then asked Mrs Jenkins laughing.

"Tell me Mrs Jenkins, how does one call a 3.8 Jaguar; a baby? Though the way Guy looks after it, I am sure it is better looked after than most children."

Mrs Jenkins looked at me, then joined in by chuckling for a moment or two, before she said.

"I am sure you are right; the Air Commodore does spend a great deal of time with his car. Bob tells me it is a classic, unfortunately Mrs Davenport, I am afraid I know very little about cars."

"Quite honestly Mrs Jenkins, that makes two of us." I replied, then informed her. "Now we must not keep Guy waiting any longer, we will take tea this afternoon on the small terrace." As Mrs Jenkins gently laid the tray down on the serviceable round garden table, then after thanking her, I asked. "Mrs Jenkins, maybe you would like to go home as I am sure we can manage now, and I rather suspect Mr Jenkins will indeed be pleased to see you."

"Thank you, Mrs Davenport, that is very kind of you. Enjoy your tea and I will see you tomorrow," Mrs Jenkins replied. She then turned and made her way back to the kitchen to pick up her coat and personal belongings.

Sitting for a few moments waiting for Guy to join me, I can remember the first time I saw him driving the Jaguar up towards the house. At the time, he was working in London at the Ministry of Defence, but felt he needed a change of environment at the weekends and stated he would very much like a place in the countryside. After discussing his feelings at some length with me, we decided to spend some lovely long weekends looking for houses by driving through various areas of the countryside reasonably close to London, including Suffolk.

As we drove through the lovely hamlet of Aldeby, quite by chance we found our dream home. Guy instantly insisted we drive into Beccles; (which is the nearby town) to find the agency the cottage was advertised with. Once there, Guy spoke to the man who greeted us, and requested to speak to the main agent. The man in fact, was the main agent. Guy then immediately told him he agreed to rent the property at the asking price, and asked if we may view the cottage the following day.

I remember thinking how funny it was as Guy was not normally so impetuous, in fact by nature far from it. Amazingly here we were, as Guy had fallen in love with the whole place. Later Guy told me, not only did he love the cottage, it was actually the double garage that had really attracted him.

The agent had happily agreed to join us and would take us around the property first thing the following morning. This information left Guy to practically gobble down his breakfast, as he felt very excited and could barely wait until we eventually drove over to join the agent, at the time that had been arranged.

As we entered the small drive, the warm pink painted exterior of the cottage came into view, and made one feel so very welcome. I could not resist a smile, as Guy insisted the agent allowed him to first take a look inside the double garage obviously having already planned what he was going to use it for. Once Guy was satisfied with what he saw, it was then we took the few steps needed in allowing us to enter and take a look around the cottage itself.

The kitchen one could only describe as a little on the small side, also very old fashioned. Instantly spotting the Aga which took up most of one wall, my thoughts were. I simply loved it, knowing how cosy the room would be once it was lit. At the far end of the kitchen there was a small utility room, which like the kitchen was very basic but serviceable. We then entered the sitting room which was quite well lit, the light coming from the two medium size windows set in two of the walls. The room also having a fairly new wood burner, giving this room also a cosy atmosphere, especially during cold winter days.

Upstairs were two reasonable sized bedrooms. The main bedroom having French doors overlooking the rear lawn, but sadly no balcony. Glancing out of them, I decided in that instant; a flower bed needed to be added. The second bedroom, Guy decided we should use as a dressing room for the time being. As we were just about to go and take a look at the bathroom, Guy whispered in my ear, stating. "I promise you Annabelle my darling, one day I will own this property and enlarge it, enabling you to have a room to use as you wish."

We then took a quick look at the bathroom, which though in good order, indeed really needed refurbishing. We then re-traced our steps and made our way back downstairs. On reaching the ground floor once again, the agent asked if we would like to see the rest of the property.

"Absolutely." Guy replied delighted, and with that we followed the agent back through the front door. I could not help but notice there was actually no back door, which I found rather unusual. The agent decided we should first go and see the swimming pool, which was situated to the right of the cottage.

Guy and I were quite surprised at the size of the pool, as one could only describe it as being fairly large and in perfect working order. The pool had been set in an immaculate lawn. Taking a look at Guy's smile, I could already visualise him swimming in it, especially during warm evenings. On leaving the pool area, we continued walking to the right of the property. This in turn lead to the rear of the cottage. Once there we were amazed, in fact quite stunned to see the natural beauty of the countryside all around us stretching out as far as the eye could see, and looked simply wonderful.

After allowing Guy and I a few moments to enjoy the view, the agent suggested we should continue to make our way back to the front of the cottage where another surprise awaited us. Once there, we were delighted to find a small orchard which had obviously been planted many years previously, now containing apple trees of every description. I was very impressed at the manicured lawns and how well they were kept, considering they were vast. The cottage actually stood in just under two acres of land, and luckily for us; at the moment stood empty.

Guy and I loved everything we saw. So much so, Guy went ahead and asked the agent." Where do I sign."

The agent laughed pleasantly, and proceeded to ask Guy. "Would you like to follow me back to the agency, once there we could complete the paperwork."

"My pleasure to do so." Guy replied in haste.

Before leaving, I wanted to know who tended the lawns so beautifully. The agent informed me that a local couple who went by the name of Bob and Rosie Jenkins, normally looked after the cottage and would probably be more than happy to continue should I like them to. With the paperwork completed, the agent handed Guy the keys. After receiving them and leaving the agency, we decided to drive immediately back to London.

After talking it over, Guy and I, decided we would return the following weekend, also making the time to drive over to Lowestoft. Once there, we hoped to purchase various household items we would require for the present, rather than remove things from our home in London; which we normally used on a daily basis. Straight after breakfast the following morning, my first job was to make a few phone calls. I needed to know how quickly I could arrange for various pieces of furniture to be delivered to the cottage. This would at least enable me to make the cottage as comfortable as possible under the circumstances. From the very first weekend of seeing the cottage, we have been so happy here ever since.

Guy gave his hands a quick wipe and then stood back, while admiring the superb piece of engineering he had the joy of tinkering with at every possible opportunity. Mostly by keeping the engine of his treasured Jaguar, in a pristine condition. He would spend an untold number of hours polishing the dark navy-blue coachwork until it glistened, especially in the sunshine. I loved the smell of the pale blue leather seats, and the carpets that were fitted through the car, all matching in exactly the same colour of the seats. The dashboard and trims were in a highly polished walnut veneer, making the whole appearance of the interior as wonderful to look at, as the car looked from the outside.

After Guy had driven up in the Jaguar for the very first time, I can remember I was making a pot of tea. He came into the kitchen and insisted that I stopped whatever else I may have wanted to do and sit with him. Once having offered him a cup of tea, he related to me every tiny detail about his precious car, starting by saying.

"The Mark 2 S is a fast mid-size luxury sports saloon with a 3.8 litre engine, and that Sir William Lyons' advertising slogan had been Grace... Space... Pace." Guy continued on, practically drooling about the design of the engine, which I did not have a clue about or anything else he was telling me meant. He then went on to inform me about the windows, describing how the front windscreen had been made wider and how the rear window almost wrapped around to the enlarged side windows. He also mentioned the chrome frames. By this time, his enthusiasm seemed to getting the better of him, as he continued informing me about how the radiator grill had been changed, allowing for larger side tail and fog lights etc etc. To be honest, though I tried patiently to understand everything he was describing, I still did not have a clue what in the world he was talking about. I tactfully decided to bring the conversation to an end by telling him I needed to go to the bathroom.

Hearing Guy's voice, brought me back to reality. "Hello darling, I am now ready for my cup of tea," he said, as he bent down to kiss me on the cheek.

As I recoiled in mock horror, I told him. "Don't you dare touch me Guy Davenport with those dirty hands, no matter how much I love you." I then laughed and went on to hand him a packet of wet wipes. Guy firstly pulled a face, then laughed, going on to reply as he gently smudged my nose with an oily finger.

"Just wait Annabelle Davenport until I have cleaned my hands, then we will see how much I love you; and now please pour my cup of tea."

Guy sat his tall frame down on one of the comfortable garden chairs, while his attention was still drawn across to the double garage. Not only did it house the Jaguar, it also housed his Kawasaki 1100 cc motorcycle, which together with the Jaguar provided him with his passion for speed.

As I offered Guy his afternoon tea, I could not help but notice the tinges of grey now appearing in his wonderful head of auburn hair. Beside the amazing colour of his hair, one of the other things that had first attracted him to me as a very young girl, were his overly large blue eyes. They had prompted the powerful emotions I felt, which until then I had never experienced. Guy was the epitome of a character in an old movie who had been described as having, eyes like chips of blue ice and wrists like bands of steel. Something he still quotes today when having fun in company.

The next hour we spent discussing various things, while enjoying the lovely afternoon tea which Mrs Jenkins had prepared, including Guy's favourite cucumber sandwiches. Having removed my straw hat and popping it on one of the two spare chairs, all of a sudden Guy burst into uncontrollable laughter. Asking him what he was laughing at, I had to wait for a few moments until he managed to say.

"Your hat darling, has just reminded me about Toby's RAF hat when we were stationed at Lossiemouth. Members entering the Officers Mess, would leave their hats on a side table in the foyer. For some reason, Toby's hat would frequently be taken by persons unknown. Tired of retrieving his headgear from various places, Toby finally decided to place a note inside his hat, which read, 'Caution! The owner of this hat suffers from a serious, incurable, and contagious disease, affecting the growth of hair on the scalp. This message was rather incongruous. As you know darling, to put it kindly; Toby is somewhat thin on top. Strangely Annabelle he never had any problems after that.

"Oh, Guy how funny," and with that both Guy and I started laughing all over again.

"Well, my darling, must get back and finish off what I was doing" Guy said as he rose from his chair. He took one step to reach me, then bent down and gave me a loving kiss. "I love you Annabelle Davenport, just as much as I did on the day I realised how much you meant to me."

With that statement I watched him walk away back in the direction of the Jaguar. Pouring myself another cup of tea thinking to myself. I really loved this time of day, especially on sunny afternoons such as this. The birds happily singing in the trees, constantly flying down to the feeders we had put up in various parts of the garden and the world seemed at peace. Slowly my thoughts drifted back to when my father had phoned and asked. "Annabelle would you please come over and see me immediately."

"Yes of course daddy," I replied; then asked. "Are you and mummy alright?" As I was now deeply concerned at the urgency in my father's voice.

"Yes darling, we are both well. Please Annabelle, I would appreciate it if you would come without any further delay. I will explain everything to you when you arrive." With that my father replaced his receiver. When my father intimated, he wanted something done quickly, he actually meant right now, immediately and at the double and yet, I cannot remember him ever saying those words to me, so naturally I wondered what the urgency could possibly be.

Slipping my coat over my arm, then quickly picking up my purse and car keys; I drove over to my parent's home. As they lived outside of London, in Berkshire, it meant it would take a little while to get through the London traffic.

As I drove up the drive, I could see my father's batman who had been with him for many years, waiting at the bottom of the steps to greet me. "Good afternoon, Lady Annabelle, your father is waiting for you in his study. I hope you will forgive me for saying so my lady. Sir John is in a bit of an agitated state which is very unlike him, I hope all is well."

"Thank you, Smithy, so do I." Came my answer, I then said. "Quite honestly Smithy, it is so unusual for him to demand my presence the way he has; in fact, he never has; and that is what is worrying me."

With that I ran up the steps and made my way to my father's office. Gently knocking on his door, on opening it and saying hello as I normally did. I found my father looking out of the window which overlooked the garden he loved. As he turned around, I could not help but notice how pale he looked, something again which was very unusual. Before he had time to say anything, I asked him if he and mummy really were alright."

"Yes darling, we are perfectly well, but thank you for asking. Please Annabelle come and sit down as I do have some very serious news to import, in fact my darling, some pretty dreadful news to sadly tell you about."

My father pointed to the two very comfy armchairs either side of the window. Between them, a small round table had been placed, and covered by a beautiful hand embroidered tablecloth my mother had purchased while on their travels. Also on the table, was a small crystal vase with sweet peas which smelt so lovely. My father remained standing until I chose one of the chairs and sat down, he then walked over and joined me. Sitting himself down in the opposite chair, I could not help but notice my father looked very nervous and took his time, even that look was somewhat strange. After what seemed a lifetime, even though it was only a few seconds, he went on to tell me what was on his mind. His tone of voice, one could only describe as being very grave as he said. "Annabelle, I have some pretty awful news to convey to you, and I wanted you to hear it from me before you heard it from anyone else. Annabelle it is with the deepest sadness that what I am about to tell you, I am sure will upset you terribly."

My father was silent once again, until a further moment or two had passed before he gently said. "Annabelle my darling, Guy Davenport has been killed. The plane he was flying in is missing, it is believed to have crashed at sea, and so far there is no trace of any wreckage. Darling I am so deeply sorry to be the one to give you this dreadful news, as I know he has been a friend of yours for such a long time."

As I sat there, I could feel the blood draining from my face. I looked intently at my father and could see the sadness in his eyes. My father then quietly told me what he knew about the accident. "Darling, a friend of Guy's on his course at Cranwell, was fortunate enough to own a Cessna 175 aircraft and a private pilot's license. As there was a mid-term recess due, his friend had invited Guy to join him on a long weekend away in France. All I know so far, is the aircraft crashed en route into the English Channel. Until now my darling, neither bodies or wreckage, have so far been recovered. I am truly very sorry Annabelle, unfortunately we must fear the worse. Tactfully my father then said.

"Darling will you excuse me; I will ask Smithy to bring in a pot of tea or maybe you would prefer your own company for a while."

"Thank you, daddy if you will forgive me for the moment, I would just like to go to my room."

With that I practically ran from my father's office leaving the door ajar. As I reached the hallway, I could feel tears welling up, and desperately needed the privacy of my old nursery. Running up the stairs as fast as I could, by the time I reached the nursery door the tears became like a waterfall I could not stop. From being a tiny child, I had always loved this room. At its medium size windows, hung lovely Chintz curtains. There were lots of scattered cushions that matched on the overly large settee and comfy armchairs. Nanny had ensured the nursery was not only warm and welcoming, it was also spotlessly clean. Using the tiny china tea set I had been given one Christmas, I would have afternoon tea with my dolls and teddy bears, while sitting around the small beautifully made wooden table and tiny chairs that had been made for me. The toy cupboard which had been built from floor to ceiling, contained every type of toy and games any child could have desired. This included many beautiful dolls from overseas countries, some double jointed. My favourite teddy which still had place of honour on the settee, I immediately picked up as I continued to cry. How long I sat there, I have no idea. I felt thoroughly dreadful, perhaps the word decimated would be a better way to describe emotions I was now feeling. Eventually, I did manage to stop the cascade of tears that could have filled the basin of the Trevi Fountain. Slowly, I started to remember the past by taking a walk down memory lane.

I had known Guy Davenport most of my life. His parents Sir Richard and Lady Rosalind Davenport are very close friends of my parents. Our fathers when duty allowed, would frequently play golf together. Our mothers were very firm established old friends. Guy's father and mine had also been close friends as boys, and together, both having been to public school and university. While my father joined the army following in his father's footsteps, Guy's father decided he quite fancied the Royal Air Force. Both men eventually reaching the high rank they now held.

Also part of our circle, were the parents of my closest friend Amanda. Her father Sir Hugh Barrington Sandford was a diplomat, currently serving as the United Kingdom's Ambassador to France, which suited Lady Lucille, as she was French and loved Paris. Lady Lucille, Guys mother Lady Rosalind and Deri Langton, who was now married to the American Ambassador to the United Kingdom, Craig Langton. All were close friends of my mother, as all had been great friends through school and university. As the families were very close, we would join each other during the Christmas or Easter holidays. Sometimes, Lady Rosalind would hold a birthday party for Guy outdoors if the weather of course permitted; due to the fact his birthday is in early spring. During the summer recess, my mother would hold a garden party. We were then joined by other friends, along with their children who we knew from school, but there always seemed a special relationship between Amanda and Guy's parents the Langton's, and mine.

Amanda, Guy, and I, followed our parents; by attending public school in England. At public school the three of us were all academically above average, Guy though surpassed all of us. He was also extremely popular, eventually becoming Head Boy and Captain of Cricket. Having obtained the requisite grades at A level, and after the required interview, we all gained places at Cambridge University. Guy to read economics and Chinese, whereas Amanda and I had chosen to read Law. Guy's love of cricket continued at university. Having played in the Inter Varsity match against Oxford at Lords, he gained a Cambridge blue. At the end of his studies, he gained a "First" and after selection, Guy entered the RAF College at Cranwell in Lincolnshire. His aptitude and ability were soon evident to staff during his elementary flying training.

Now he will never become a pilot, and I have lost one of my closest friends. The tears started to well again and I suddenly realised, not only have I lost my friend. I have lost the man I have loved from being a little girl.

The following morning, I phoned one of my colleagues who worked at the law company I was employed at. With great difficulty trying not to shed further tears, I informed him of what had taken place and then asked for his advice. "Ross would it be expected of me to phone later and speak to one of the senior partners."

"Not at all Annabelle," he replied, and then continued. "I am sure everyone will understand how you must be feeling; I will inform Jeffrey Hatton myself. As you may have heard, he is an extremely understanding man, which in due course, you will come to find out. I hope Annabelle they are able to find the bodies very soon, it must be simply awful for his family and friends. Annabelle, do please let me or any member of the staff, know if you require any further help, we are all here for you."

"Thank you, Ross, that is so kind." I answered, then told him. "I have no idea at the present what will happen next. I just know his parents must be devastated as we all are. Guy was not just their son; he was their only child. Naturally, they loved him to bits and are... I should say, were so very proud of him." I stopped for a moment, trying to control further tears, before continuing to say.

"Ross, I will keep in touch, thank you again for your kindness. Would you please now excuse me for the moment, as I want to join my parents for breakfast and see if they have any further news?"

"Of course, Annabelle, just remember I am here if you wish to talk. Give my regards to your family and we will speak shortly."

"Thank you again," I replied, and with that replaced the receiver; then ran downstairs to join my parents in the morning room.

"Hello darling," my mother greeted me. She looked so tired and drawn but continued with what it was she wished to say, before I could answer her. "Oh Annabelle, this is all so dreadful. I spoke to Rosalind last night, as you can imagine she is absolutely heartbroken. When I spoke to her this morning, she told me Richard has barely spoken a word to anyone and remained in his study most of the night. Guy was everything to them, especially after Rosalind found out she was unable to have any more children. I have no idea how they will now live without their incredible wonderful son. Richard had such high hopes for him becoming a fighter pilot in the RAF."

My father then interrupted. "Damn it all Arianna, it is the blasted situation of not knowing where they went down that is bothering me. So far there is not even a trace of any wreckage. No wreckage, no bodies and no one seems to know a damn blasted thing."

"Calm down dear," my mother told my father, before she further said, "we all understand John, how upset you must feel. I know as we had no sons, you were always very fond of Guy."

I then looked from my father to my mother, and wondered if I should reveal how I felt about Guy. Maybe this was not the right time to tell them, and so held my own council. I did though ask.

"Daddy, how long do you think Guy's parents will have to wait, until there is a memorial service?"

"At the moment darling, I have no idea. The authorities will do their level best obviously to try and find the wreckage of the aircraft, or at least part of it. Maybe the boys will still be inside the cockpit, I just do not know. All I do know my darling, I would not like to be part of that team, as it is a frightful thing to find a body once it has been in water a great length of time."

"John, please stop." My mother pleaded; her face now quite pale. She then told my father in a firm voice. "I feel so distressed dear; I cannot bear to hear any more gruesome details. We are just going to have to try and sit this out, at least until we are better informed about the whole dreadful situation. I am driving over to the Davenports later, would either of you like to accompany me?"

"Yes, of course I will join you," my father replied, he then turned to me and enquired.

"What about you Anabelle, would you care to join us

"No daddy, not this trip, but thank you for asking, I answered, trying hard not to cry once again.

My father then commented. "Very well darling, now do eat up. We will need all our strength to get us through the next few days."

The following few days were simply dreadful. Guy's parents had slowly come to accept he would never be returning home, and preparations had begun to be put in place for his memorial service. The weekend dragged on unmercifully, leaving everyone drained and desperately unhappy as each long hour and day passed, and the continuation of there still being no news.

By Monday morning, the enormity of losing Guy was becoming unbearable for everyone. My father was like a bull in a China shop, should anyone have said anything he did not wish to hear. Mummy and I sat very quietly trying not to say a word during breakfast. Just as we were close to finishing the last of many cups of tea, the phone rang out in the hall. Smithy as normal answered it. Without knocking on the door, which is something he never did, he entered the morning room in what can only be described as in an over excited state; and in a matching over excited voice he said, "Sir Sir, you had better come to the phone quickly, it is Air Vice Marshall Davenport on the other end."

Without another word, Smithy practically ran from the room and returned back to the hall, but first he watched as my father jumped to his feet and then followed him out. Mummy and I sat there, not daring to think what Guy's father would be saying to daddy. After a few minutes, daddy returned to the room and ran over to mummy planting a kiss on her cheek and then mine. Mummy and I looked at him in astonishment, as we had never seen him do this at breakfast before, or for that matter at any other time.

"My darlings, I have the most marvellous news to tell you. Guy, thank the good Lord, is not dead after all, he is at this very moment on his way home. We do not have any other details at present, but I am sure all will be revealed once Guy arrives back."

"Oh daddy, that is wonderful, simply wonderful news to hear." I said excitedly. I still decided that for the moment, I would keep my feelings towards Guy to myself. Mummy just sat and clapped her hands; we even observed a few tears of relief escape from her lovely eyes.

"I am over the moon," my father said, in a tone of voice which now, not only mirrored his inner sentiments of happiness, but that of mummy and I. He then informed us. "Damn shame about the time though, as I would have opened a bottle of my finest Champagne." Mummy laughed at daddy's sentiments even though she was now feeling incredibly happy as I did. I should say, as we all did!!

We found ourselves laughing and talking about all sorts of things, occasionally the three of us all talking at once, then laughing some more. Most of the conversation being in regards to Guy and his family. I am sure not only Guy's family, but the whole staff at Davenport Hall would be celebrating. By this time we were all so desperate to know exactly what had happened, but of course would have to wait a little longer, our patience now being terribly tried.

The following morning a taxi drew up outside of Davenport Hall, the driver looked inquisitively at the man who alighted from his cab. Even though Guy's clothes had been laundered, they were not up to the standard one would have expected of a guest who may be visiting such an establishment as the Hall, most notably was the fact that Guy had no luggage either.

"Thank you." Guy said to the taxi driver.

He was just about to pay him; Hopkins though had already spotted the taxi on the Halls security cameras and ran out to pay the driver. Guy thanked Hopkins, then walked briskly into the entrance, and into the waiting arms of his parents.

"Oh, my darling boy, how wonderful to see you," his mother said, as she embraced him fondly.

His father then hugged him, his words began to tumble out, first asking. "How are you? Oh, my precious son, you have no idea how happy your mother and I are to see you. Would you like a cup of tea or something a little stronger, maybe you are hungry and would like to eat, and then my boy you must tell us everything that has happened?"

Guy could not help but laugh, hearing his father asking so many questions at once, giving him no time to answer even one question. Eventually he did manage to say. "Thank you; I would love some tea."

As all three turned to walk towards the small cosy sitting room, which Lady Rosalind regarded as the one that had become her most favoured room in the vast, though very beautiful and historic Davenport Hall. Hopkins who had quietly stood by the door winked and at last said, "Nice to see you home young Sir."

"Thank you, Hopkins, nice to be home." Guy replied.

His father then asked, Hopkins, if he would please bring some tea. "Certainly Sir." Hopkins answered, wearing a broad smile which was quite unusual. As Hopkins walked towards the kitchen, Guy and his parents entered the small sitting room.

Within a matter of minutes, Hopkins returned carrying a large silver Queen Anne tray, laden with beautiful heirloom Paragon fine bone China, plus a plate of Guy's favourite chocolate biscuits as requested.

"Now my boy; I want to know every detail of what has happened to you since last Thursday. Damn it all Guy, you have certainly given your mother and I a pretty awful scare."

Guy poured himself a cup of tea, then proceeded to say how sorry he was they had been so distressed. He then went on to explain to his father about the events that had taken place, starting with prior to the mid-course recess.

"My friend Paul Charlesworth, who was a fellow student; approached me and asked if I would care to accompany him on a short trip to France. He suggested we might fly and visit La Rochelle, on the Cote Sauvage in the Charente Maritime; which of course as you know is very lovely.

Paul owned a Cessna 175 aircraft, which his father had bought him as he had a Private Pilot's Licence. Delighted at the thought, I readily agreed. We departed from Cambridge Airport and flew south. After an uneventful flight, we reached the south coast close to Brighton.

Leaving England, we then headed south east towards France. Nearing the coast of France, the single engine misfired and stopped. Despite our efforts we could not re-start the engine, so we both agreed that our only option was to ditch the aircraft in the sea. Fortunately, the English Channel was relatively calm, and Paul was an accomplished pilot. He made a remarkable landing, as the aircraft did not overturn or disintegrate and landed in a horizontal position. Unfortunately, Paul's head appeared to have struck the control column, causing him a severe head injury, which unfortunately left him barely conscious. I unfastened our seatbelts and managed to get both of us out of the cockpit. Once we were outside the aircraft, I inflated our life jackets.

The Cessna as you know is a high wing monoplane, therefore it was impossible for us climb up onto the wing. As the aircraft was in a slightly nose down position, we managed to reach a degree of safety on the aircraft's tailplane.

The aircraft came to rest near the entrance to St Valery en Caux, close to a small fishing port. Luckily, a French trawler happened to be leaving port at the time and had witnessed the aircraft crash. The vessel rapidly drew alongside us, and the crew helped us on board.

The French skipper sensibly took us to Le Havre, which thank goodness has a modern hospital. Sadly, on arrival Paul was pronounced dead. The staff took great care of me and made arrangements for Paul's body to be transferred home. The doctor insisted I stayed in the hospital, as he was treating me for shock. Not just because I had been involved in a plane crash but having lost one of my closest friends.

By Sunday I told the staff it was time for me to return home, in fact I insisted I did so. I am so sorry to have caused you a number of unnecessary days of distress by not phoning, but quite honestly at the time I felt pretty rough. I asked the hospital if they would get in touch with the British Consul for me, who in turn provided the papers and funds I required, ensuring I could return home without further worry. On leaving the hospital I caught the first available ferry back to Dover, and then picked up the taxi which brought me home. Must admit this is the best cup of tea I have enjoyed in days.

Sir Richard with a huge smile on his face told his son, "I cannot express to you Guy; just how happy your mother and I are to see you; we really thought we had lost our precious son. You do know you mean the world to us, and we could not be more proud of you. I am assuming you are returning to Cranwell tomorrow."

Guy gave his father a smile lighting up his face, before he replied. "Yes Sir, I must return there tomorrow, as I have already taken enough time out from training."

Sir Richard answered his son by saying, "in that case your mother and I will drive you there, at least it will allow you a little more time to rest and allow us a little more time in your company."

"Thank you both." Guy replied and then continued, "I deeply appreciate it, and now if you will please excuse me, I must get in touch with Paul's family. I would then like to rest, take a shower and change. I will see you for dinner."

As Guy left the room, his father turned to his wife, and said, "Will you excuse me darling Rosalind, I have some phone calls to make as everyone will wish to know Guy is home safe and sound."

Chapter Two

Sword of Honour

On his arrival at Cranwell, Guy received a message asking him to report to the College Commandant at 0900 in his office. Promptly as requested, Guy entered the outer office of the Commandant. His secretary stood up and greeted him, then invited Guy to sit down while he informed the Air Commodore of Guy's arrival. Minutes later Guy was ushered into the inner office.

On entering, Guy marched smartly up to the front of the large desk, going on to salute Air Commodore Godfrey Harrison. The Air Commodore, stood up from his office chair and greeted him by saying. "Good morning, Davenport." The Air Commodore, then walked around his desk to shake Guy's hand saying as he did so. "Damned delighted to see you back, I am of course very sorry about your accident, and my condolences about the death of your friend." He further went on to say, "Do you feel fit enough to return to flight training?"

Guy could hardly contain himself at the thought of flying once again and replied. "One hundred percent sure Sir."

"Excellent, delighted to hear it. Dismissed Davenport." With that the men shook hands once again. Guy saluted, turned smartly and left the office, now feeling greatly relieved and happy at how the meeting had gone.

After six months of intensive flying training in the Shorts Tucano aircraft, a Brazilian aircraft built under licence by Shorts in Belfast, Northern Ireland. With the course nearing its end, preparations were in hand for the Passing Out Parade to take place. By sheer coincidence, the Reviewing Officer, was to be Air Vice Marshall Sir Richard Davenport KCVO. ADC DFC, who of course was Guy's father.

On the chosen date with the parade assembled, it was announced that Flying Officer Guy Davenport had won the Sword of Honour.

From his position in front of his Entry, Guy marched smartly to the dais on which his father and the Commandant were standing. Guy stood at attention in front of the dais then saluted. His father bent forward slightly and proudly handed Guy the coveted Sword of Honour, as he did so, he said quietly, "Well done Guy, your mother and I as always; are so proud of you."

Guy smiled and replied, "Thank you Sir."

Guy then performed the correct salute with the sword held proudly in his hand, after which he turned about and marched back to his position in front of his Entry. What followed, was an inspection by the Reviewing Officer, accompanied by the College Commandant of graduates and students. With the inspection and the ceremony completed, Guy once again approached the dais, saluted, and formally requested to march off. His father proudly gave his son permission to do so.Guy returned to his position and gave the required orders for the parade to perform the traditional march past in front of the Reviewing Officer and the College Commandant, accompanied by music from the RAF College Band. The Band played the Royal Air Force March, which would then take them off the parade ground.

Once off the parade ground, the new graduates and students were dismissed. Everyone then made their way into the college for a formal luncheon. Once there they were joined by VIPs, guests, family and friends. To make it a special day for Guy, his father had invited their friends, including Amanda's parents. Lady Lucille and Sir Hugh Barrington Sandford KCMG, along with another of their oldest friends. The American Ambassador to the United Kingdom; Craig and Deri Langton, and of course my parents and myself.

Before taking their places, Guy's guests lined up and proceeded to shake hands with him, along with offering their best wishes and congratulations. All adding many lovely comments about how well he looked, especially after surviving such a frightful accident. Thanking each of them, it was now my turn. Guy smiled down at me and politely said. "Nice to see you again Annabelle, thank you for coming. How is work, are you finding the job all you had hoped?"

I returned Guy's smile and replied. "Thank you Guy for asking. Work is excellent, and yes to your second question. So far, I am actually finding most of it interesting, naturally, of course there is so much to learn. I am sure you can appreciate one must be most meticulous when practicing law." I could feel myself blushing a little, so quickly added. "I will not keep you any longer, it has been a wonderful ceremony and lovely exchanging a few words with you, but you do have so many other guests to engage with." With that I returned to my seat, leaving Guy to continue greeting the rest of his guests.

With a delicious luncheon over, a memorable day was to end on an even higher note. The Commandant of the College announced that, Flying Officer Guy Davenport in addition to the Sword of Honour, had also been awarded the College Flying Prize.

Pilots graduating from the RAF College, depending on their ability were selected for further training. This involved Fast Jet, Helicopter or Multi-Engine Aircraft training. Not surprisingly, Guy having impressed his instructors at the college was selected for fast jet training.

Guy returned home enabling him to enjoy two weeks leave, during which time he received orders to report to 4 Flying Training School at RAF Valley for advanced training.

After saying goodbye to his parents, Guy got into the new E-Type Jaguar his father had bought for him, allowing him to drive to North Wales. Leaving Conwy, he travelled down the A55 and crossed the Menai Bridge onto the Island of Anglesey. As he was in no rush, he slowed the car down allowing himself to marvel at the Welsh scenery. The road at times appeared to cling to the rocky escarpments bordering the road to RAF Valley.

4FTS AT RAF Valley, was formed in 1921 at Abu Sueir, in Egypt. Later it was moved to RAF Habbaniya in Iraq in 1939. The squadron was deployed to Basra, to protect Iraqi oil resources from anti-Government rebels. Later the squadron served in Southern Rhodesia, before subsequently returning to the United Kingdom. Eventually, the squadron took over from 7 FTS at RAF Valley on the Island of Anglesey. Currently, the resident units are 25 and 4 Training Squadrons, operating the British Aerospace Hawk MK 2 aircraft.

Advanced training having commenced in the BAE Systems Hawk aircraft, with Guy very shortly feeling at home in its cockpit. The course was intended to teach Aerial Warfare and Tactics. Guy found himself particularly enjoying the low flying exercises in the Conwy Valley and Machynlleth Loop. These exercises were held in the mountains of mid-west Wales often 100 feet above the ground. Guy was looking forward to the rest of the course, which would continue for the following twelve months. During these months, the course consisted of many other various exercises including low flying, navigation, air to ground firing and deployment to other UK units.

Amanda, by now had joined the RAF, and was a Flight Lieutenant Admin Officer. She was for the present; also stationed at Valley.

Luckily for Guy on his non flying weekends, he was able to join Amanda together with myself, at the cosy cottage Amanda's father had purchased for her on his estate. Strangely as it turned out, by purchasing the cottage; he was returning another property to the estate which had been sold many years previously by Amanda's grandfather. The Estate was truly lovely and situated close to Bangor.

The weeks and months quickly flew by, with Guy thoroughly enjoying the new pilot skills he was being taught. Returning home to his family for the Christmas holidays, we girls also returned to our respective families.

Tradition had been established many years previous, allowing all of us to join up again for New Year at

Amanda's parents' home. Sir Hugh and Lady Lucille Barrington Standford, were able to make their guests feel very comfortable in their beautiful stately home, ensuring the year started off with lots of fun and laughter. After New Year, our respective parents would return to their homes or places of work.

My parents and I, would return to our London home, which we all used during the week. This was due to my father working at the MOD, and yours truly at the eminent law firm of Meredith, Drew, and Cotts, having qualified as a solicitor. Also returning to London, were Guy's parents; Sir Richard and Lady Rosalind. Guys father Sir Richard joined my father at the MOD. Amanda's parents were fortunate enough due to the weather being reasonable, to return to the British Embassy in Paris, as Sir Hugh was still the UK's Ambassador to France.

Guy continued to impress his instructors with his flying skills in the Hawk aircraft and would be well prepared when he eventually moved on to the Tornado.

At many RAF Units, the social event of the year was the annual Summer Ball. Traditionally this formal event was usually held during September. Mess members would vote on, and then choose a theme for each Ball. This year, the theme was to be a Greek Temple, which Guy thought was a brilliant idea; so offered to help out immediately. The task ahead would need a lot of thought and required a great deal of hard work. The idea was to transform various rooms into the chosen theme, which would take many weeks to complete.

Training continued both day and night during this time, and Guy would help when flying allowed.

As usual, the theme for the ball was completed on time. The rooms looking both very impressive, as well as realistic. The Mess members this year, had indeed made an exceptional job and were very pleased with the result. Three of the rooms being used, had individual bars. The smaller one, provided the Bucks Fizz. The middle room, which was the games room, provided a variety of beers. Most importantly, was the Real Ale. The third bar was situated in the main dining room. This bar provided Champagne and oysters, which would prove to be very popular.

On the night of the Ball, England was enjoying an Indian summer, with the weather being absolutely perfect. Setting off their brilliant white shirts, the Officers resplendent in their Airforce blue Mess dress, with each having gold "lace" on their sleeves; indicating their various ranks. They stood patiently in the foyer, as they awaited the arrival of the many guests that had been invited.

After Guy's parents arrived, this was to be an evening without further ceremony, and one to be enjoyed. Following Guy's parents, Sir Hugh, and Lady Barrington Standford arrived. They were greeted by Amanda, who this evening was feeling a little despondent, which was very unusual for her. Being a woman, it was naturally very understandable, as she stood and observed all the beautiful gowns the ladies were wearing, while she had to wear RAF female mess dress.

Following the Barrington Sandford's, my parents arrived a few minutes later though without me. My parents told me later. On greeting them, Guy had commented he was surprised that I was not with them.

My father explained. "You must excuse Annabelle; she will dear boy be joining us as quickly as she is able to. Unfortunately, she has annoyingly been detained on some rather important case, but, I believe she is now on her way and hopes to be with us very shortly."

Officers and guests gradually made their way into the dining room, with many commenting they felt they had indeed been transported to Zeus' Temple.

Guy escorted his guest to the suitable table he had chosen earlier. One which was not too far from the bar, yet far enough not to be disturbed by other guests. Ensuring everyone was comfortable and had their preferred drinks, Guy excused himself to see about the oysters. On reaching the bar, he was joined by his friend Daniel another fellow Officer.

With both men having their backs towards the entrance of the room, due to them having a quick drink and a chat, neither saw Amanda or myself enter. As Guy's friend turned around to go, he just stood silent for a few seconds without moving, and quickly he turned to Guy and said."Wow, look at two o clock. I think Aphrodite has just walked into the room."

Amanda and I, had by now started to make our way towards our parents' table. Daniel immediately said to Guy, "I must ask Amanda to introduce me to that divine creature, she is absolutely stunning. I cannot wait to dance with her up close and personal."

Guy turned around to see who Daniel was talking about. Once he saw Amanda, he realised his friend was talking about me. For a moment Guy said nothing, then completely out of character he turned to face Daniel, and in a voice, cold as ice, he warned him by saying. "Daniel do not even think about it. She is off limits.

I mean it... Go anywhere near her with disrespect, and I will make you very sorry."

With that Guy walked away, leaving his friend totally speechless as he had never heard Guy threaten anyone before. He just stood and watched as Guy joined both his family, Amanda and I.

As the evening progressed, I seemed indeed to be very popular with handsome Officers who constantly came and asked me to dance. Guy by this time, had returned to the bar. Talking aimlessly to his fellow Officers as and when they joined him; but barely took his eyes off me.

Guy later he told me. "You know Annabelle, I had been thinking to himself, I had never in fact thought of you as anything more than a pale skinny, gawky girl."

I had to laugh at Guy's words though a little surprised. I must admit thinking about it. I had always kept my dark hair neatly tied back in a bun, and though my brown eyes were very large which luckily for me, were accompanied by having long double thick eyelashes; I had always regarded myself as fairly plain. Guy laughingly, also mentioned the conversation he had with Daniel, and of course he was right.

Tonight, this plain skinny girl had taken a great deal of care about her appearance, wanting to look every inch like a Greek Goddess. The gown I had chosen to wear this evening, had been very expensive and came as usual from Paris. Made of the finest white silk, which allowed it to drape so beautifully. The shoulder drape was long enough to use as a scarf, should I have wished to cover my hair. Guy was later to tell me how enchanting I looked with having only one shoulder covered. I must admit, the dress clung somewhat to my now rather curvaceous body, but I did not care as I felt so good. Guy cheekily informed me; he had not realised how well developed my bust had become. I was though thrilled at his next question when he asked. "Where Annabelle have you been hiding, as you do indeed look as if you have stepped off Olympus."

Guy returned to his family, sitting quietly and listening to all that was being discussed as well as watching the constant stream of his fellow Officers, taking both Amanda and myself onto the dance floor.

Sir Richard in the meantime was discreetly observing Guy, until in the end with a huge smile, and trying not to cause his son any embarrassment, he eventually said. "About time my boy you asked the girls to dance, you have not been up once. Bad show you know when an Officer does not dance."

"Really, who told you that Sir?" Guy asked laughing, and went on to tell his father. "Very well Sir, if it pleases you, I will ask each of the girls to allow me to tread on their toes."

Guy's father frowned, then chuckled before he stated. "I know you are a damn good dancer, chip off the old block." Guy gave a hearty laugh before replying.

"Thank you for the compliment Sir, I will endeavour to do my best."

With that, both men once again enjoyed their private joke and continued to carry on chatting, until eventually the moment I returned to the table and I sat down, Guy asked if I would care to have the next dance with him.

"Thank you Guy, how gallant of you." I laughed, then informed him. "Unfortunately, I have already promised the next dance and the following couple of dances after that to a few of your brother Officers. Maybe we could dance later?"

"Of course, not a problem." Guy answered politely, a small frown now appearing on his forehead. Apparently, he felt quite put out, and asked himself why; why was he feeling quite annoyed at having to wait? Not something that would normally ever bother him. Naturally, he had no answers, leaving him to feel irritated. As he continued to watch me dance the next couple of hours away, slowly he felt himself becoming even further agitated, and still found no reasonable answers to his emotions.

To please his father, he did ask Amanda for a couple of dances. And why not, she was after all not only a very dear friend, but a wonderful dancer. Guy revealed to me later, that dancing with Amanda, not only felt somehow very normal, but it was also as if he was dancing with ones' sister.

After having a couple of dances with Amanda, Guy returned to the bar. By this time Guy felt the evening had become deadly dull. He was not really in the mood to drink and felt he did not even want the company of his guests. Watching me dancing was not helping the situation, until in the end he desperately wanted to leave, but knew that was impossible. Looking at his watch, there was just an hour to go before the music drew to a close bringing the Ball to an end. Guy's patience had by now reached it limits.

"Damn it all." he told himself. "I am not prepared to wait any longer. I will extract Annabelle from any of my fellow Officers she may be dancing with and drag her onto the floor if I have to." Guy finished his drink and walked back to where his friends and family where sitting but remained standing waiting for me to return once again.

He did not have long to wait. As I drew alongside of him, he took my hand, then said in a determined tone of voice that I had not heard before, "My turn I think for a dance; I have after all waited the entire evening for one, and I will not take no for an answer."

I looked up at him as did his family and friends; Guy though did not notice the attention or the smiles he drew from those present.

Being as good as his word, Guy practically marched both of us onto the dance floor. Taking me in his arms and then drawing me close to him, perhaps a little closer than either he or I expected. By doing so, he was therefore unable to see the smile that now lit up my face as I was more than content being in his arms.

Little conversation took place between us, as one dance led to another until eventually, the band played the last waltz. Guy was determined no other man would take me from him, and so drew me even closer if that was possible, allowing me to feel the warmth of his firm chest. At the end of the dance Guy commented in a voice as steady as he could muster, "You dance very well; I guess your teacher found you an apt pupil."

"Thank you," I replied, and then told him, "I am sure your teacher felt the same, considering I am not suffering from any broken toes."

Guy instantly chuckled and answered, "I rather think Annabelle we had better join the others, as breakfast will shortly be served."

With that, Guy escorted me back to where our parents had unknowingly to us, been very closely observing their offspring's.

At precisely 2am, a hot buffet breakfast became available in the dining room; attended by Mess Servants for those who still remained. As the last guests left, Guy's parents made their farewells also. Giving his mother a hug, and in the process he told her he will join the family at the weekend. He then came over to where Amanda and I were also making our farewells and asked if we would join him on Saturday evening, at the local village pub for a drink. We agreed to do so, then thanked Guy for his invitation, Amanda then mentioned, she felt everyone had enjoyed what had turned out to be a perfectly successful evening. Having decided to stay with Amanda for a few days, Guy walked Amanda and I to her car, before saying a final goodnight.

Friday, found Guy driving home looking more forward than usual to the weekend, though again not quite understanding as to why. One leave normally was like any another and always enjoyable, so, what was different this time, or maybe it is just his imagination? On that particular Friday afternoon with the weather being most pleasant, Guy drove the Jaguar home with the hood down.

Before he knew where the days had gone, his week's leave indeed passed incredibly fast as Hopkins once again re-packed his suitcase.

Coming downstairs to join his parents for breakfast, quickly making his way to the morning room, Guy seemed somewhat quiet. While eating breakfast, noticing how quiet Guy was being, his father in a sober voice said. "I hope Guy, all goes well. Your results are very important, and therefore must be good enough to enable you to fulfil your ambition of becoming a fighter pilot."

Guy sat for a moment or two, before he answered by saying. "I will endeavour to do my level best Sir, keep your fingers crossed. You know I want you to be proud of me."

His mother immediately intervened and told him. "My darling boy, both your father and I are always proud of you; and have been from the day you were born."

His father then stated. "I fully agree with your mother; you know you mean everything to us Guy, no matter what the future may hold.

"Thank you, I love you both very deeply. I will always try to live up to your sentiments." After which, Guy rose off his chair and gave his mother a hug and informed them. "I really must go, please take care of yourselves and I will see you both at Christmas."

Guy's parents walked with him to his car. As Hopkins placed Guy's suitcase into the boot of the Jaguar, he wished him good luck as usual. With one final hug for his mother and a handshake for his father, Guy jumped into the car and drove away down the drive, while his parents stood and waved until at last he was no longer in sight.

On returning to RAF Valley, Guy settled quickly back again into the routine of training. With the arrival of December, the instructional staff informed Guy that his ability and progress in training, meant he would certainly continue his qualification to move on to flying the Tornado aircraft. Guy was more than delighted at this news, knowing it meant one huge step towards in his desired ambition to become a fighter pilot in a Royal Air Force frontline fighter squadron. Before commencing his Christmas leave, Guy received formal orders to report to RAF Lossiemouth to join XV (Reserve) Squadron, which was the Operation Conversion Unit for the Tornado GR4.

After saying his goodbyes to various members of the staff and then his fellow students, not forgetting to wish everyone the very best for Christmas, Guy once again headed for home. Besides trying to concentrate on his driving which for the moment he was finding rather difficult, due of course to the thought that after the New Year, he would be flying a supersonic Tornado.

By some miracle, he arrived home in one piece. Admitting later, he barely remembered how he drove all that way without luckily having an accident. Hopkins greeted him and removed his suitcase out from the boot while stating. "Welcome back Sir, nice to see you home." Hopkins then quietly informed Guy his parents were waiting for him in the small sitting room.

"Hello, my darling boy." his mother greeted him as he walked through the door.

His father then joined in, quickly saying. "Well done Guy. I must admit, I am slightly jealous; it takes me back to my days in the Harrier aircraft."

His mother allowed her two favourite men to continue talking for a few minutes, until at last she intervened and enlightened Guy of the plans that had been made. "Darling, your father and I have decided this year, to host a Christmas House Party. We have invited the Willoughbys and of course Annabelle. Amanda has informed us that her parents will be returning home from Paris and are delighted to accept our invitation. Also coming are Deri and Craig Langton before they return to Washington. Apparently, they are then flying to their home in Florida. You know darling, I will miss them terribly."

Lady Rosalind stopped in deep thought for a few moments, before at last she continued. "I do hope I will have the opportunity to pop over to America and see them later in the year, life will not be quite the same without them. We have also invited a few of my other friends who I went to university with. Darling, is there anyone in particular you would like me to invite, you know it is always a pleasure to meet your friends?"

Guy smiled, and answered politely.

"Thank you, but no mummy. I think we will settle for those you have already invited, and I am sure it will be a lovely party. I will be going into town tomorrow, as I need to do some Christmas shopping; is there anything you would like me to pick up for you?"

"No darling, I have everything I need." Lady Rosalind answered, and then told her beloved son. "You know Guy how much I love Christmas. I have been busy preparing for it and thoroughly enjoying myself for the past number of weeks, including buying lots of lovely presents for everyone."

Guy kissed his mothers' hand and replied, giving her a broad grin before telling her.

"I do indeed know; how much you love Christmas. Truthfully, I do not think I have seen the tree look as wonderful, and where in the world did you find all the mistletoe you have hanging everywhere?"

Lady Rosalind laughed and replied by telling her beloved son. "You never know darling; this year it may just become useful."

This time it was Guy's turn to laugh; as the remark his mother had just made, was a little out of character for her. He then joined his parents for one last late drink before saying goodnight. During the next couple of days, various guests started to arrive. The Barrington Sandford's arrived on the Sunday morning, and a few moments later Amanda walked in through the door.

Guy having heard of her promotion to Squadron Leader, greeted Amanda by saying, "Congratulations Ma'am," and feigned a mock salute, he then proceeded to kiss her on both cheeks leaving them and the families laughing.

After breakfast had been served on Christmas morning, everyone gradually made their way into the formal sitting room. The tree now looked even more wonderful, with the dozens of presents that had carefully been arranged around it by both guests and staff. There was a great deal of laughter and excitement in the room. Unfortunately, it was at this point, Guy seemed somewhat anxious. He told me later he wanted to retrieve the gift he had bought for me, but decided to wait patiently until his parents and other guests had theirs. At last, as the mountain of presents had by now gradually disappeared, it enabled Guy to see quite clearly the beautifully wrapped present he had bought to give me.

As Guy handed me his present, I immediately though carefully; opened it. I could not help but give a small gasp, as I recognised the beautiful box which contained a bottle of Roja Parfums Chypre Enigma. I just sat for a moment before saying.

"Oh, my goodness Guy, how incredibly wonderful. This is something I did not expect, how terribly kind of you. Thank you so much you really are spoiling me."

"Merry Christmas Annabelle, I am so pleased you like it," and with that Guy bent down to kiss me on the cheek. To Guys amazement, I took the opportunity to kiss him on the lips, lingering a moment longer than he expected. The assembled guest's suddenly fell silent and smiled, suspecting that something magical had just happened.

A formal Christmas dinner was served at precisely 8pm that evening. Sir Richard ensuring his guests had a convivial evening with superb food, each course tasting more wonderful than the last. All accompanied by several bottles of his finest vintage wines; from a wine cellar par excellence that Sir Richard was well known for. During dinner, Sir Richard recalled a couple of humorous stories, which he thought his guests may like to hear about during his service with 63 Squadron at RAF Waterbeach in 1949. Guy loved listening to his father's stories and was always eager to hear them.

Sir Richard commenced by telling his guests. "At the time when all driving tests were held in the nearby City of Cambridge. Parkers Piece was a large area of parkland in the city centre and used as the "test" course for motorcycles. The motorcyclist, a young pilot under examination, was required to complete a full circle on the road around Parkers Piece. Obviously, given the size of the test course, he or she would disappear from the examiner's view, reappearing on his side of the parkland. The young pilot was told, that once back in view, the examiner would step in front of the motorcycle; raise his hand and order an "emergency stop."

Sir Richard stopped for a moment to take a sip of his wine, and then continued. "The pilot who was taking his test, indeed disappeared as the examiner had stated. The examiner seeing a motorcycle re-appearing and approaching his position; stepped off the pavement, held up his hand saying. Halt! Unfortunately, the motorcyclist was not the young pilot he thought was taking the test with the result being, the examiner ending up in Addenbrookes Hospital with a broken leg. Annoyingly, The result of the test remains unknown."

Sir Richard was now in full swing and unstoppable, he carried on by telling another story of a Senior NCO also serving with 63 Squadron at RAF Waterbeach. "This particular NCO, had a vintage sports car and decided to take his driving test in Cambridge. As he approached the traffic lights in the centre of the city, they annoyingly turned red. Unfortunately, the brakes of the low sprung vintage MG, were somewhat suspect, and the man regrettably was unable to stop in time. Standing at the lights was a rather large Clydesdale horse, who was being led by his groom. The sportscar struck the poor animal "behind the knees" causing the horse to sit down on the car, crushing its bonnet. The horse thank goodness was unhurt, sadly the car was written off. The examiner with a wry smile suggested that the test should be postponed."

Sir Richard concluded by saying. "Must say the Squadron did have a jolly good laugh at the poor chap's expense." Everyone around the table found the tales most amusing, and dinner continued in high merriment until once again, Sir Richard decided it would perhaps be a good idea to amuse his guest, and particularly Guy by telling them about his time as a young fighter pilot...

Clearing his throat, allowing everyone to give him their attention, Sir Richard then went on to say. "Some years previous when I was flying the Gloster Meteor aircraft while serving with 63 Squadron at RAF Waterbeach. I was selected for conversion to the

Hawker Harrier fighter aircraft, of course first having successfully completed my conversion course at the 233 Harrier OCU. Renamed as you know Guy, the Harrier Operational Unit. It was during my time there I was promoted to Squadron Leader and appointed as Officer Commanding the RAF No 3 Harrier Fighter Squadron."

Sir Richard as normal stopped for a moment while he enjoyed another sip of his excellent wine, and then carried on. "The Squadron was stationed as part of the 2nd Tactical Air Force at both Gutersloh and Wildenwrath in Germany. Later in my career, came the Falklands War. This time it was a ten-week undeclared damned war between Argentina and the United Kingdom. Argentinian forces once again having invaded two British dependent territories in the South Atlantic, was simply not acceptable, also including its territorial dependency of South Georgia. As we all know, Argentina has tried to claim sovereignty over the Islands for hundreds of years.

No 3 Harrier Squadron, and the Naval No 800 Sea Harrier Squadron, joined the Task Force and sailed to the South Atlantic. They were carried on board by two requisitioned merchant vessels, the Atlantic Conveyor, and the Atlantic Causeway. Both Squadrons were eventually transferred to and operated from HMS Hermes in the war zone. As the RAF Harrier had not been designed for naval service, the aircraft had to be rapidly modified. Before departure, special sealant against corrosion had been applied and the new inertial guidance systems was installed to allow the RAF Harrier to land on a carrier as easily as the Sea Harrier. 3 Squadron was used mainly in air-to-go ground attacks against land forces. On one of my many sorties, this involved strafing Argentinian forces engaged in fierce fighting against the formidable SAS on Mount Kent.

Harrier aircraft flew a total of 145 combat sorties in the conflict. After 10 weeks and with Argentina being defeated and expelled once more from British territory, elements of the Task Force returned to the UK, and I resumed normal activities with No 3 Squadron."

Sir Richard looked at his now empty glass of wine, Hopkins having already noticed, but not wishing to disturb his boss, now approached with a newly refreshed decanter. As he did so, Lady Rosalind took the opportunity to say. "Darling, do tell everyone how you were awarded the Distinguished Flying Cross for your leadership and bravery."

Sir Richard smiled broadly and answered. "My darling Rosalind, you already have, but what I will say, and if my next words ever get out of these four walls there will be all hell to play."

The room fell silent, as no one was expecting Sir Richard to speak those words as they were so out of character for him ever to do so.

Taking another sip of his now nearly full glass of wine, Sir Richard continued. "The Harrier was developed in the 1960s, as the first operational aircraft with vertical/ short take-off and landing (VSTOL) capabilities. The Harrier is capable of both forward flight where it behaves as a typical fixed wing aircraft, as well as VTOL and STOL manoeuvres, requiring skills and knowledge unusually associated with helicopters. Most air forces demand great aptitude and extensive training for Harrier pilots. Trainee pilots are often drawn from highly experienced and skilled helicopter pilots.Now allow me to tell you, the Harrier is like a woman, and is known to be difficult to handle, but like you my darling Rosalind, she can dance beautifully on the spot and can curtsey to a Queen with all the grace you can."

The room continued to remain silent until Lady Rosalind stated. "Richard I am quite taken aback to be compared to an aircraft, but as you said that so nicely, I will take your compliment in the spirt it was given." Many comments were passed around the table as dinner continued.

Sadly, the following day, it was time to say goodbye to everyone. Lady Rosalind felt very sad as she hugged and waved the Langtons off as they had to leave directly after breakfast; promising she would do her very best to fly out to America later in the year to see them. They were driven to Heathrow airport in preparation for their long flight back home to America. Accompanying the Langton's to Heathrow, were Sir Hugh and Lady Lucille Barrington Stanford, as they were returning to Paris. Amanda decided to join her parents and then stay in London, rather than leave the following day for her flight to Edinburgh as she had now been posted to RAF Leuchars.

My parents and I, left after lunch and were driven up to London, accompanied by members of my father's staff. Sir Richard informed my father he would see him when he returned to the MOD after the holiday. Lady Rosalind and my mother hugged each other and made arrangements to meet up very shortly.

On the morning Guy was due to leave for Lossiemouth. His father asked him in a serious voice. "Would you give me a few minutes of your time, as

I wished to have a private word with you in my study straight after breakfast."

Guy looked at his father, smiled, and said, "That sounds ominous Sir." He then laughed and stated. "Actually, it sounds like a command."

"Does it really, jolly good." Sir Richard smiled broadly, and then told Guy. "I would like to have a few serious words with you, if you do not mind."

With breakfast over both men walked to Sir Richard's study. As they entered, Sir Richard walked over to the window and stood looking out for a few moments, until at last he turned to sit down. As he did so, he requested Guy to do the same. "You know Guy; I have always liked this room, as it affords me this particular outlook. Both in summer and winter, it gives me the feeling of space, enabling one to breath fresh air. Guy remained silent allowing his father to continue. "Now my boy, to business. The reports I have received so far, tell me that your progress in training to date has been exceptional."

This time it was Sir Richard who sat in silence, waiting patiently for Guy to say something. As Guy did not reply, Sir Richard then continued. "Guy, I am sure you are aware as I am, that the next stage in your training at Lossiemouth; is very important towards your ambition to be a front-line fighter pilot. From my own experience at the Harrier OCU. The training is highly competitive. Guy I am warning you in all seriousness, any decrease in your performance, or any mistakes, will certainly mean instant dismissal from training. You know your mother and I love you no matter what may occur, this is your home and you must never be afraid to return here if all does not go well. We wish you the very best of luck at Lossiemouth, and hope you have a safe journey."

With that Sir Richard stood up and proudly gave his son a hug. The two men then shook hands as Guy said. "I will bear in mind Sir everything you have said, and of course do my best not to let you down." Sir Richard looked into his son's eyes and replied. "I know you will, but always remember Guy; no matter what happens, your mother and I will never stop loving you even for a moment, and we will always be proud of you."

Hopkins carefully placed Guy's case into the boot of Sir Richard's car, while Guy said goodbye to his parents. Hopkins then drove Guy to Heathrow to catch his British Airways flight to Aberdeen. While handing Guy his case he said. "Good luck Sir, safe journey."

"Thank you, Hopkins," and with that Guy disappeared from view, full of excitement about what will unfold once he reached Lossiemouth.

Chapter Three

Tornado Training

On arrival at the OCU, at RAF Lossiemouth. Guy was delighted to meet up once again with Toby Portland, his friend from university. His father was the late Earl of Portland. Toby having inherited the title, remained totally unconcerned about using it. Guy was even more delighted to learn that Toby had been selected as his Weapons Systems Officer "WSO," for the remainder of the course. Toby had recently completed his training as a navigator, at No 1 Air Navigation School at RAF Hullavington in Wiltshire. However, a recent controversial decision by the UK Government to scrap the entire Nimrod Maritime Reconnaissance aircraft fleet, coupled with an increase in the quality of navigational aids, had seen the demise of the traditional navigator.

Like Toby, many ex-navigators were now WSOs, and required to fly in the rear cockpit of such aircraft as the Tornado. Their responsibilities included navigation, programming of weapons sensors and communication, enabling the pilot to concentrate on flying the aircraft. Both Guy and Toby, were surprised to find they would have to spend the first five weeks in Ground School, either in a classroom, or in the Tornado simulator.

Attending one of the first lectures, both Guy and Toby found to their delight that the lecturer, had decided to inform the class a little of the Tornado's history, along with other informative details. He started by asking. "Everyone sitting comfortably, then I will begin."

His comment bringing smiles all round, but wanting his men to feel relaxed and enjoy what he wished to inform them. He then stated. "Gentlemen, The Tornado is a family of twin-engine, variable sweep wing, multi-role aircraft. The aircraft was developed and built by Panavia Aircraft GmbH, a tri-national consortium of British Aerospace, MBB of Germany and Aero Italia of Italy. The aircraft was first flown in 1974 and entered service in 1979. The Tri-National Tornado Establishment was established at RAF Cottesmore, in order to maintain a level of international co-operation beyond the production phase. The Tornado was operated by the RAF, the Italian Air Force, and the Royal Saudi Air Force during the Gulf War of 1991. As you know gentlemen, Tornados of various air forces, also saw service in Bosnia, Kosovo, Iraq, Afghanistan, also in Syria and the Yemen. Gentlemen, in all 900 aircraft were built." The instructor then asked. "Does anyone have any questions so far, and if not then I will continue?"

The room remained silent for a few moments, obviously everyone wishing to hear further what their instructor had to say. The instructor then asked the class.

"No questions gentleman," and waited a few moments before saying. "Very well I will continue.

The Tornado is designed to attack enemy defences at low level. The mission during the Cold War was the delivery of conventional and nuclear devices against the forces of the Warsaw Pact countries. For the Tornado to perform as a low-level supersonic aircraft, it was required to possess both high and low speed flight characteristics. To achieve the required performance, a swept or delta wing is unfortunately, inefficient at low speeds. The solution was a variable sweep wing, which is adjustable for both low or high-speed flight. The Tornado is capable of carrying the majority of air-launched missiles in the NATO inventory, including un-guided and laser-guided bombs.

Gentlemen, this is one fearsome aircraft. May I remind you, it also carries anti-ship and anti-radiation missiles, in addition to anti-personnel and anti-runway missiles. The modern Tornado gentlemen has also been adapted to carry the Enhanced Paveway bomb and the newer missiles including Storm Shadow and Brimstone, and finally, Gentlemen. The Tornado is capable of a maximum speed of Mach 2.2 or 1500 mph at sea level. Ferry range without munitions being 2240 miles and combat range is around 800 mph with a full munition loadout. Should any of you get to fly this awesome machine, you will be bloody lucky, in fact you will be the very best of what the RAF can offer." The instructor concluded. "Approaching its 50th Birthday, the Tornado will soon give way to the Euro Typhoon and the F35B Lightning II aircraft purchased from the United States."

At the end of the five week course, the students would then have to sit a written examination with a required pass mark of 85%. While Toby managed to obtain the required mark, Guy sailed through reaching

89%. After both passing the examination Guy and Toby moved on to XV (Reserve) Squadron to commence their qualification to operate the Tornado aircraft. The training sorties were often demanding and quite difficult, particularly the air to ground bombing exercises, although demanding; Guy and Toby both found them exhilarating.

After departing from Lossiemouth, Guy and Toby flew northwest towards the Cape Wrath training range, which was located in the County of Sutherland, and is the most north-westerly point in mainland Britain. The range covers 590sq. km of peaty moorland and was first established as a Naval gunnery range in 1933. Targets included cargo containers, oil drums, scrapped military vehicles and several disused stone buildings.

The Tornado aircraft can carry both conventional and "Paveway laser-guided bombs.The Paveway bomb, is equipped with GPS technology, which is capable of destroying the majority of targets while minimising collateral damage. The bomb is also capable of being re-targeted by the WSO after release from the aircraft.

Approaching Cape Wrath, Guy called Range Control for permission to enter the range. Once entering the area, the aircraft was cleared to commence a bombing run. Toby with the aid of the Tornado's "Lightening Targeting Pod" which provided video imaging; programmed and released the Paveway bomb. After a second bombing run, Guy received permission to leave the range and return to Lossiemouth.

Normally in the OCU crew room, an unofficial list of bombing scores was posted on the noticeboard. Not unexpectedly, Guy and Toby were near the top of the list, suffering good humoured banter from the other crews.

Another exercise involved in their training, was to learn the techniques of airborne refuelling involving USAF KC 135 tanker aircraft, from an Air Refuelling Wing at RAF Mildenhall. The excellent advice Guy's father had given him on the last morning before he left, came to mind; as two of his fellow students were asked to leave after successive failures in their performance.

The weeks and months appeared to go incredibly quickly, winter turning into spring with the Scottish hills becoming a veritable panorama of multi-coloured heathers. As April approached, Guy unfortunately did not have the chance to return home that year for his birthday, knowing though he could persuade Toby to help him celebrate it, he did not mind too much.

Guy decided, it would be a good idea to also ask Amanda and myself, if we would care to come up to Scotland. He was a little concerned, that as I lived in London, I may sadly be unable to join him. Apparently, he told Toby, he would phone and see what my situation would be. He also hoped Amanda would not be on duty. Should Amanda and I manage to have the time to visit, then he would book a hotel for the four of us in Elgin. Guy informed Toby, he quite fancied Forres Hall. A beautiful stately home that had been converted into a five-star hotel a number of years ago.

After asking Toby if he would care to join him, he was absolutely delighted Toby accepted, especially as he had not seen Amanda since university days. Guy immediately phoned Amanda, who happily gave Guy the reply he had hoped, as she in turn told him. "Thank you, Guy, I would be delighted. The hotel sounds wonderful, and it will be such fun meeting Toby after all this time, by the way, have you asked Annabelle.?"

"No" Guy replied, and then told her. "I promise Amanda, I will do so the moment I replace the receiver after talking with you." They continued chatting for a little while longer before Guy ended by saying. "Take care Amanda, I shall look forward to seeing you next month."

With that Guy replaced the receiver, then immediately picked it up again and redialled, this time in the hope I would also be available. The phone rang for a few moments before I eventually managed to reach it. Once I heard Guy's voice, I must admit I was a little surprised. "Hello Guy, how are you, and what have I done to deserve you phoning me out of your busy schedule?"

With that I gave a small, pleasant chuckle. Guy made no comment about my laughter but did go on to ask. "Annabelle I was just wondering if you would perhaps like to join Toby Portland, Amanda, and myself in Elgin next month, for my Birthday?"

I was quite taken aback for a few seconds by this request, and needed a few moments to think. So instead of just simply answering his question, I inquired. "Guy, how is Toby? I have not seen him in ages. He is normally so sweet; I hope he has not allowed his new title to go to his head." For no reason other than feeling a little embarrassed, I found myself laughing again.

Guy in a firm voice answered, telling me. "No. Toby still has his feet firmly on the ground." He then continued. "Toby is still really the nicest of chaps that he always was. Must admit, I do feel somewhat sorry for him now being on his own. I hope he meets a really lovely person who will make him a wonderful wife. He certainly deserves someone nice."

I then informed Guy. "I am sure he will, and I would love to join you all. Thank you for your invite; I will book a flight to Aberdeen."

Guy immediately stopped me before I could say anything further, he then went on to inform me he would be meeting Amanda, and then pick me up at the airport and drive us all to the hotel he had decided he would book. "Then I must thank you again for your kind gesture, as I simply hate waiting for taxis. I must go Guy, but will you phone me when you are free?" Guy replied he would be more than delighted too, said goodbye, and once again replaced the receiver.

Surprised at my request for him to phone me, and obviously unable to contain his curiosity, Guy indeed phoned a few days later. After indulging in several inane niceties, he suddenly blurted out. "You know Annabelle; I am really looking forward to seeing you again."

For a man of his calibre, he must have realised how juvenile he sounded, as there was a rather long pause which must have worried him, until struggling not to laugh and to Guy's relief, I said.

"I was also thinking how wonderful it will be, especially meeting Toby again." Again, there was another pause, Guy instantly thinking maybe I liked Toby more than he had anticipated. I quickly realised what I had unwittingly said, so instantly added. "I am sure Amanda will also be thrilled at meeting Toby again, did you know she quite liked him at Uni;"

For a moment, I thought I could hear the relief in Guys voice as he answered. "Really, I had no idea that Amanda liked Toby. I hope they get on; we shall have to wait and see. Annabelle do please forgive me; but I really must go. Will speak to you soon."

"I shall look forward to your call," and with that I replaced the receiver.

As Guy walked back to join Toby, he was very surprised. Even a little intrigued to know that Amanda had fancied Toby all this time. The thought that actually Amanda would make a perfect wife for him, came to mind. Guy suddenly found himself laughing, realising that not only was Amanda senior in rank to him for the moment, but if by some chance she married Toby, she would be a Countess.

A couple of weeks later, Guy and Toby received letters from the Ministry of Defence, confirming their promotion to Flight Lieutenants. An opportunity to celebrate in the Officers Mess was not missed, with both of men consuming several gin and tonics. Fortunately for them both, the following morning they would not be flying and regarded it as a Godsend, given the size of their hangovers.

Training sorties continued for a further couple of weeks. When Guy had a free moment, he booked two superior rooms at Forres Hall. One for the girls, the other for Toby and himself, he also collected the car he had decided to hire.

By Friday morning, Toby noticed Guy had an unusual spring in his step, he simply put it down to them having a break for a couple of days, regardless they did not normally do weekend duty. Immediately after lunch, Guy asked Toby with a slight smile playing across his mouth. "Have you packed everything you need, as I rather think I would like to go now."

Toby returned Guy's smile, telling him he was indeed ready. As Guy and Toby only had around nine miles or so to drive to Elgin, Guy took his time allowing them both to enjoy the scenery.

Arriving in Elgin, Guy and Toby made their way directly to the Forres Hall Hotel. Forres Hall had belonged for many centuries to a very wealthy ancient Scottish family. The last owner having tragically lost his wife due to illness. As he never had any heirs, he decided he would like to spend the rest of his life in the sun, so had chosen to live in the West Indies. The hall had been sold as a complete estate, set in 22 acres of beautiful park land, including containing its own trout lake. The new owners having paid a vast sum of money for it, as they were a company that specialised in luxury hotels for a certain type of client.

After Guy and Toby had booked in, they were handed the key to their room by a very polite receptionist, who in turn called a porter. The porter took their cases from them and informed them he would meet them at their bedroom door. On opening the door, Toby immediately made his way to the window while Guy checked the bathroom.

"Not bad old chap, come and see this view," Toby called from across the room.

Guy stepped out of the bathroom and walked across the room to join his friend, saying as he did so. "The bathroom is up to scratch as well, not bad, not bad at all."

The two men stood at the window for a number of minutes, each keeping his thoughts to himself of the grandeur that was spread out before them. Guy was the first to break the silence, as he laughingly said.

"Come on old chap, we had better make a start. We have a drive of around 50 miles ahead of us, and I do not want to be late picking Amanda up, or she will have us both demoted."

The two men made their way downstairs and asked for their car to be brought around. As the roads were reasonably quiet, they made good progress arriving in plenty of time before the arrival of Amanda's train. Guy parked the car then tactfully asked, "Would you like to meet Amanda first on your own, or would you prefer I met her."

Toby replied with a huge smile crossing his face, "I would love to meet her on my own, that is if you do not mind. After all, it is quite a while you know since we last saw each other. Rather liked her you know at Uni, though never told her so. At least this way, with luck, I may get to have a rough idea how she feels about me."

"Fine, you go ahead, and I will wait here for you both to return," Guy answered.

With that Toby alighted from the car and disappeared into the station. He stood patiently on the platform until at last Amanda's train pulled in. Amanda alighted from the train looking stunning, being dressed in a beautiful tailored red coat, with matching shoes and handbag. Any woman could tell, it was the type of outfit that could only have come from Paris. Giving Toby a dazzling smile, Amanda proceeded to say, "Hello Toby, how lovely to see you again, it has been such a long time since we last met. How are you?"

Toby quite taken aback for a second or two at how beautiful Amanda look, and stupidly replied by asking. "How do I look?"

Amanda trying not to laugh, answered by telling him, he looked very well. Then quietly in a more sympathetic tone of voice, said, "Toby, I was very sorry to hear about your parents; it must have been very painful for you losing them both in such a horrid way."

Toby for no apparent reason, suddenly bent down giving Amanda a kiss on both cheeks, something she was not expecting, but was delighted about, he then told her, "Surprisingly I am doing well, thank you for your kind thoughts." He went on to change the subject by telling Amanda.

"Jolly nice to see you again also. Gosh you really do look so different from when we were at Uni." Toby stood for another few seconds, then quickly reverted to the subject of his parents by adding.

"As you can imagine, when I was first informed of the damned accident my parents had sustained, it left me totally devastated. Now of course, I have come to terms with the fact there is just me. Naturally, it is still very painful, especially around birthdays or Christmas time. My friends are all so kind and never allow me to spend those times alone." Amanda smiled and gently replied.

"I quite understand Toby your friends being so kind, which is very commendable of them. I will be honest with you as I still have my parents, I cannot truly imagine how you feel, as I have never experienced your emotions. You do understand what I am trying to say."

"Yes Amanda, of course I understand what you are saying. Now we really must go and re-join Guy who is waiting for us in the car, and we can talk later." Toby answered, taking Amanda's case from her.

As Amanda and Toby approached, Guy jumped out of the car to greet them, giving Amanda a peck on the cheek while Toby placed Amanda's suitcase into the boot. Toby decided he now preferred to sit in the back and keep Amanda company, which brought a private smile to Guys face. Happily chatting while making their way to the airport which was situated across town. Arriving at the airport, Guy told his passengers he would go and pick up Annabelle, unless of course they cared to join him.

"No, we will be fine," Toby informed him, then winked before he said.

"Take all the time you need." With that Guy closed the car door, smiling as he did so.

Proceeding to make his way quickly to the arrivals lounge. Unfortunately, Guy found he had a fifteen-minute wait until at long last I walked through the arrival's door.

I wanted Guy to think I looked nice, I also needed to feel comfortable while travelling. Therefore, I had chosen to wear a very well-cut, designer white woollen coat with turned back cuffs and trimmed with large black buttons. Under the coat, I wore an elegant silk white dress, with smaller black buttons that matched the coat. Wheeling my suitcase, and carrying my handbag, both matching my black high heel shoes. I hoped I looked every inch the well-bred lady I have been brought up to be. Guy, it seems surprised even himself when the next words he spoke were.

"Hello Annabelle, one would never guess you have spent the day at work as you look so beautiful."

He then bent down to kiss me on not one, but both cheeks. Something he had never done before which left me to feel delighted about.

"Do I really; how very kind of you to say so." I replied in a calm voice, giving Guy a lovely smile.

Not for the world would I tell him how thrilled I was at his statement. Guy took charge of my suitcase and wheeled it, (which I was a little surprised about) as we gradually made our way back towards where the car had been parked along, with its passengers. After greeting each other and exchanging pleasantries, Toby joined Guy once more in the front of the car, even though he would have still been more than happy to sit in the back-seat with Amanda.

Guy gradually drove back to Elgin, taking his time on the narrow road as the evening was drawing in. By the time we reached the long drive of Forres Hall, both Amanda and I could not help but pass remarks on how beautiful the place looked, as the warm welcoming glow of the lights were now clearly showing in the gathering darkness.

After checking in, Amanda and I excused ourselves and retired to our room, leaving Guy and Toby to do the same thing after having arranged to meet up at 7-30 p.m.Guy found himself pacing up and down waiting for Toby to finish off dressing, Toby could not help but notice that his friend once again seemed on edge.

"O. K. I am ready," Toby at last stated with a smile, looking at Guys stern face. Guy now laughed and replied. "Sorry, but for some unknown reason, this evening, I do feel just a little on edge." He then asked, "How do I look?"

Toby could not believe what he had just heard, as that was not a question he had ever heard Guy ask of anyone, and told him so, adding, "You look fine, normal." Guy laughed out loud at Toby's remark, then still chuckling said, "Good. Come on then; let's go."

With that, both men made their way down to join the ladies, by taking the stairs they had a chance to admire the décor as they did so. As they were a little early, Guy and Toby walked to the bar and ordered drinks, asking for them to be brought over to their table.

They did not have long to wait before Amanda and I joined them, having done our best to look as if we had stepped out of a fashion magazine. Amanda's outfit as with most of her clothes, had come from Paris; this evening of course was no different.

While visiting her parents, Amanda would take the opportunity of taking very little clothing with her, then do a great deal of shopping. Like most women, she would cleverly ensure when she returned to England; her cases were full of wonderful clothes that could only be bought in a Paris fashion house or shop.

This evening, Amanda had chosen to wear a red silk low backed sleeveless blouse, which was fastened by tiny real pearl buttons and a pair of black velvet slacks. Round her tiny waist, she wore a black kid leather belt, that needed to be fastened with the huge buckle provided. Amanda had chosen to wear very low heels also in black, which had been encrusted all over with tiny black diamantes. Her whole outfit was not only very stylish; it gave her the freedom of allowing her to feel very comfortable.

I had decided to also wear an outfit that came from Paris, and like Amanda, I too had chosen a blouse; only the colour was white, and the material being of the finest silk. The blouse though lined, still just about allowed one to see the beautiful lace of my underwear. The decollage was rather low and very feminine, the sleeves were long with large button up cuffs from the wrist practically to my elbow. Instead of slacks, I had chosen a black velvet skirt with a rather long slit up the side. Had I been getting into a car; it would most certainly have allowed an onlooker a glimpse of one of my very shapely legs.

After offering to order drinks, Guy walked to the bar and gave his order to the waiting bartender. Before walking back, I could not help but notice he stood perfectly still, taking in it seemed every detail of my appearance, and then smile to himself.

"Would anyone care to join me for dinner as I am starving," Guy asked mockingly.

"Yes," the three of us replied in unison, laughing.

As we walked towards the dining room, I noticed like the rest of the hotel, it was fitted with a superb tartan carpet which allowed your feet to sink into it. Entering the dining room, the Maître d' greeted us, and proceeded to show the way to our table. Taking a quick look around, I could not help but admire the entire room which was stunning. From the beautiful ceiling, covered in superb plasterwork, to the magnificent crystal chandeliers hanging from the heavily decorated ceiling roses, which were covered with darling cherubs and many types of flowers. I guessed the chandeliers had come from Europe, most likely Italy. Had they been switched on; the room would then have been bathed in a somewhat blaze of harsh light. Instead, the room was bathed in the calm ambience of soft welcoming light, which came from the many various wall sconces and table candles, leaving everyone to feel totally relaxed.

Dinner was superb, with all the food that was served, having been grown locally on the estate farm, and then cooked by the hotel's brilliant French chef. The four of us did a great deal of laughing, catching up with lots of tales from our days at university and of course of our lives up to date. After dinner we decided we would take coffee in the beautiful plant filled conservatory.

At this stage whether from tiredness, or perhaps it had just been the amount of wine that had been consumed, I noticed Guy became very quiet. He sat and listened to what the others and I were saying, until at last I said. "Would you mind very much if I retired to my room, it has been a lovely evening but also a very long day?"

"Of course, we do not mind," Guy answered, before waiting to see what the others wanted to do, then quickly added, "I will walk you to your room," he then turned to looked at Amanda and asked, "That is of course, if you would wish to stay a little while longer Amanda?"

Amanda smiled, and replied by asking me, Are you sure Annabelle, you do not mind me staying and talking to Toby for a while?"

"No darling of course I do not mind." I replied. With that both Guy and I stood up and said goodnight.

As I was tired, Guy escorted me towards the lift, rather than take the stairs. Arriving at our floor in a couple of seconds, quickly enabling me to reach my room. I gave Guy the key to the door which he duly unlocked. Returning the key to me, Guy stood for a moment, then in a soft beguiling voice I had not heard before, he said, "I am so pleased you came; it will make this birthday extra special."

I looked up at him and answered, "That is very sweet of you, I have actually been looking forward to coming."

"You have?" Guy answered, sounding surprised.

I tried to reply in a soft voice. "Yes, very much so."

Hearing my reply, Guy later told me his heart was pounding, it was in that moment he decided to take me in his arms and kiss me. His kisses were gentle to start with, and then one can only describe them as becoming more passionate. Time seemed to stand still as I willingly gave my lips to him, until eventually I said a little breathlessly, "I rather think Guy, we had better say goodnight."

"Must we," he said, as he gently continued to kiss my neck.

"Yes, we must. I do not trust you to behave if I allowed you to continue," I told him, softly laughing.

"Very well, maybe you are right," Guy replied, as he released me from his arms.

I then said, "Good night, Guy, I will see you at breakfast," and with that I opened my door; gently closing it behind me.

Guy decided to return to his room and wait for Toby to return. Toby was still enjoying the company of Amanda, sadly as it was becoming rather late, she eventually went on to inform Toby. "Toby, it has been so wonderful seeing you, and this hotel is really enchanting."

Toby interrupted Amanda and gently told her what was on his mind, by saying. "The hotel is indeed lovely, but not as enchanting, or as lovely as you have become." He boldly continued, "Damn it all Amanda, what I am trying to say is. Do you think it is at all possible you can fall in love with someone in seconds, regardless you have known them a very long time, but just never realised how much in love you were?"

"Yes Toby," Amanda replied. She then continued, and in a matter-of-fact way, conveyed her thoughts. "I am sure it is very possible Toby. People as you know are all so different, and of course react differently to their emotions."

Toby interrupted her again and asked, "Amanda, do you think there may be a chance for me. I know in regard to work you are senior to me, but that surely should not stop you giving us a chance."

Amanda looked into Toby's eyes as if trying to read his thoughts, then stretched out her elegant hand and gently touched his arm. With that, Toby firstly picked her hand up and went on to kissed it. He then gently proceeded to lift up Amanda's chin, enabling him to find her lips, then kiss them gently.

"Toby it is getting rather late. I think we really must retire as I do not wish to disturb Annabelle too much, though I suspect she may well still be waiting up for me."

Toby laughed and told her, "I doubt very much she is likely to be on her own in that respect. Would not mind betting, that Guy may very well also be waiting up."

"Good night darling, I am looking so forward to seeing you tomorrow." Amanda replied.

With that Amanda gave him one more kiss, they then walked hand in hand to the lift. Just before Amanda opened the door of her suite, Toby took her into his arms once again and kissed her passionately as if there was no tomorrow. Releasing her at last, Amanda quietly slipped through the bedroom door, though reluctant to do so.

After a superb Scottish breakfast, the four of us decided to act like tourists. We made our first stop the Scottish Dolphin Centre, which is nine miles from Elgin. The centre regards itself as very fortunate, as the world's largest collection of Bottlenose dolphins visit on a regular basis and are always free to return to the sea.

Not just dolphins, but many other welcomed sea mammals and creatures, along with many species of birds. Having spent an interesting morning, not just enjoying everything we saw, we also now found ourselves openly holding hands, which were accompanied by many kisses. Each of us being openly honest as to how our relationship was for the present.

Guy decided it would be nice to have lunch in a country pub, something that was not hard to find. As with the majority of Scottish hotels and pubs, the food was excellent. Guy suggested once we had finished lunch, he would drive over to the Glenranoch Distillery enabling everyone to enjoy a "wee dram" and after being given a guided tour. As he was driving, Guy made a point that he would abstain and looked forward to enjoying a glass of Scotland's finest whiskies after dinner.

Arriving back at the hotel, happy and content at having spent a lovely day. The four of us decided to have a quick coffee in the conservatory, before going to dress for dinner. Earlier, Amanda and I had secretly arranged with the hotel's manager, to arrange for one of the tables to be dressed in balloons and birthday paraphernalia, including a small birthday cake.

We had taken Toby into our confidence and asked him if he would like to join us in giving Guy this little surprise. Toby was naturally delighted, handing over to us his card and present adding them to ours. Once our car drew up, the manager having observed it on the hotel monitor, had very kindly arranged for the cards and presents to be displayed on the table.

As no one so far had intimated anything about birthday greetings to him, this naturally left Guy to think that as his friends were all having such a splendid time, they may very well have forgotten why he had invited them. Being requested to take coffee in the conservatory by the manager, which Guy thought was a little unusual. We allowed him to walked ahead of us, as we were now quietly trying not to laugh. Once he saw the balloons and the other decorations the hotel had beautifully arranged, Guy stood and laughed; no one could mistake the pleasure on his face.

Coffee was served along with a large silver decorative knife, enabling Guy to cut his cake as and when he wished. He sat and opened his cards and presents, delighted with each and every one.

"Should I cut my cake now, or leave it till later?" he asked us.

"You must do as you wish," I told him.

Toby on the other hand laughingly replied "yes." Amanda just laughed and kept her thoughts to herself. Guy decided he would wait until after dinner, as he did not want to spoil his appetite. Walking back to our respective bedrooms hand in hand, we made arrangements to meet up once again at 7-30. Each couple stealing a few kisses before changing. At precisely 7-30, all four of us were together again in the hotel's lounge bar. Amanda and I tried to look as elegant as usual.

Once again, I wore a silk blouse and a long velvet skirt, only this time both were in black. Amanda had also chosen to wear another blouse and skirt, her silk blouse though was tomato red, her straight velvet skirt similar to mine was also in black.

SQUADRON LEADER ROY HANDLEY AND DENISE LUNT

Another excellent dinner was consumed with relish by the four of us, with Guy taking the opportunity to spoil himself not having had a drink earlier in the day. As the evening drew to a close, we all agreed we still felt very full and in good spirits.

Strange how you can sense something very special had now occurred in our personal lives. Amanda and Toby were already clearly in love. As for Guy and I, it is lovely kissing and holding hands, and though I have always thought myself in love with him, for the moment I was keeping my emotions under strict control.

Guy Davenport was every girl's dream. A man born with a silver spoon in his mouth as they say. Incredibly well bred, coming from a very powerful wealthy family. Highly intelligent with a fantastic career ahead of him. I always felt the gods had ensured he was granted what every man could wish for. He was amazingly handsome, with charm oozing out of every pore. I did hope with time, things may indeed develop between us. Perhaps if I was very lucky, he may even fall truly in love with me. Whatever the emotions either of us felt during the next weeks and months, they would be severely tested.

The following morning Amanda and I had to return to both London and RAF Leuchars, Guy and Toby would be returning to Lossiemouth for further training. At breakfast the atmosphere was a little subdued, with each of us trying to make polite interesting conversation, though without a great deal of success. With breakfast over and our respective cases having been brought from our rooms, we made our way to the car which had been brought round to the front door. Guy thanked the porter while giving him a tip.

Making yours truly the first stop, Guy drove to the airport, and escorted me into the departure lounge. Kissing my cheek, we said goodbye; with Guy promising to phone as and when he could.

He told me later, as he walked away he had a lump in his throat, leaving him unable to say another word to me, or even to the others when re-joining them.

The train station was not too far away. Guy quickly drew into the parking space and jumped out, allowing Toby and Amanda a few minutes private time as they said their goodbyes.

When Toby eventually re-joined Guy, neither spoke for the first part of their journey back, each it seemed wondering when they would see us girls again.

Chapter Four

Russian Intrusion

As the weeks and months passed by, training became more demanding. For many years the Russian Air Force had entered the UK Air Space to the north of Scotland. These provocative flights by Tupolev TU 95 strategic bomber aircraft, were either en route to Russian bases in Cuba, or merely to test UK air defences.

To combat this activity, the Ministry of Defence set up two Quick Reaction Alert (QRA) units. One at RAF Lossiemouth and another in Lincolnshire, both on 24 hours standby. Several months after Guy's birthday both he and Toby were delighted to obtain relief from routine training after receiving orders to participate in a QRA sortie.

On the appointed day, Guy accompanied by Toby, taxied their Tornado aircraft into a "Q" shed which was a concrete-hardened aircraft shelter. Both men then moved into a nearby Aircrew Ready Room for the required 24-hour standby duty. As expected within a few hours Guy received a radio call from a remote Ground Radar station in Morayshire. The cryptic message was as follows. "Call to cockpit."

On receiving this message, Guy and Toby left the ready room and sprinted to their aircraft. Once in the cockpit, Guy prepared his aircraft for take-off up to the point of starting both engines. The controller at the ground radar station, then issued a second call which was. "Scramble."

Guy immediately started both engines and taxied the Tornado to the duty runway, and after clearance took off in a northerly direction. Toby of course being Guy's WSO, was receiving the required information for both the route and altitude, which would take them towards the possible intruder. This information was being provided to Toby from a Royal Air Force Sentinel aircraft, positioned many thousands of feet above them.

Arriving at a specific area northwest of Scotland, Guy immediately located the intruder which was a TU 95 Strategic bomber. The name Bear, was the codename given by NATO for this particular Russian aircraft. This remarkable Russian aircraft had first flown in 1959, and was scheduled to remain in service until 2040. The TU 95 bomber, had a maximum range of over 9,000 miles using internal fuel tanks, enabling it to reach Russian bases in Cuba. The Russians also claimed that the aircraft could if required, reach the eastern coast of the USA.

Guy endeavouring to shepherd the intruder out of UK airspace, adopted aggressive manoeuvres by flying towards the Russian aircraft. After several near misses, the Russian pilot accepted Guy's intentions and turned away. Maybe he thought, discretion being the better part of valour. As the Russian aircraft moved away, Guy received a cheeky wave from the Russian tail gunner. Guy and Toby remained in the air for a couple more hours and after refuelling from an aircraft tanker which had been scrambled from RAF Brize Norton, they eventually returned to Lossiemouth.

Once having landed, they returned the Tornado to the "Q Shed" and continued their monastic existence in the ready room. The following morning, they were relieved from the 24-hour duty and went on to enjoy a day's rest from normal training.

As the days gradually grew shorter, Scotland's climate became noticeably colder. The trees that grew around the countryside, reminded Guy of a poem he had once read as a small boy by William Allingham, which went something like. "Bright yellow, red and orange, the leaves come down in host, the trees are Indian Princes, but soon they'll turn to ghosts." He smiled to himself thinking how funny certain words or events, always stick in one's mind even from childhood.

Within a few weeks, Guy accompanied by Toby. Who he had previously asked, if he would like to join him and the family, as he would be returning home for Christmas. This year, Guy was not quite sure what arrangements had actually been made between my mother and his. While he had invited Toby, he was not sure at this stage if Amanda's parents would be returning from Paris, or if Amanda would be flying out to France to join them at the Embassy. Whichever way, this year he told Toby, he was looking forward to spending the holiday with not only his family, but also with me; and hoped I felt the same way.

The first snows appeared overnight on the mountains, turning them even more enchanting. Before long, most of Scotland that year, was covered fairly early under its first blanket of snow. Guy was a little worried in case they became locked in. Fortunately, for all personnel who had hoped to return home, the weather by Christmas chose to become a little milder, allowing everyone who was returning home to leave the base.

Guy by this time, had been informed by his mother, that the Willoughby's would indeed be joining them. Also, sadly that Amanda's parents would remain in Paris, Amanda though would still be coming, which Guy knew would please Toby no end.

Saying goodbye to their fellow officers and wishing everyone the best, Guy and Toby made their way to the airport. Within three hours the taxi they had taken from Heathrow, drew up outside the doors of Davenport Hall. Stepping into the now beautifully decorated hall with its large Christmas tree, Guy's parents waited eagerly to greet both Toby and himself. Hopkins as usual, efficiently took charge of their cases after saying, "Welcome home Sir, nice to see you back."

Thanking Hopkins and introducing Toby, Hopkins then took their cases upstairs. Guy and Toby followed his parents into the small sitting room where a late afternoon tea tray, laden with lovely goodies had very quickly appeared.

My parents shortly joined them, as I did sometime later. I must admit, I was so pleased by the time I arrived to go to my room and be able kick off my high heeled shoes, exchanging them for a pair of flat slingbacks. After re-joining the others in the sitting room, Amanda at last arrived. She explained she had a ghastly journey, due to a delay at the airport.

The following morning, once breakfast was over. Everyone gradually made their way to the main drawing room, enabling them to arrange their Christmas presents under where a magnificent Christmas tree stood. The tree having been grown on the estate, had many wonderful old as well as new decorations adorning it; many having been handed down through the generations. There were also a great number, which though sounding funny, were still regarded as new ones, even though they had been purchased over a great number of years from quite a long time ago.

Decorating the tree, was something Guy had loved doing as a child; and one it seemed he had not quite grown out of. Guy could barely control his excitement, as this Christmas was to be very different from any other Christmas's he had spent. Well at least that is what he was hoping it would be.

Having bought presents not just for his parents or very close friends. Guy, it seemed, now regarded my company to be somewhat rather special. For the first time in his life, he gave a great deal of thought and extra care in choosing what present to buy for someone who he had become fond of, even though having bought small presents for other girlfriends.

Deciding to first draw up a list which he could then add or detract from, Guy began over a period of weeks, adding to the list a number of items he thought would be suitable. Gold earrings, or even some type of necklace. At long last, and after making his final decision, he decided to settle for a wide heavily embossed gold bracelet. Before paying for the bracelet, he requested the jeweller to inscribe my name on the inside and date it.

Waking up very early on Christmas morning, knowing there was no more than a couple hours before everyone would be opening their presents, Guy was not so sure he had bought the correct present for me, telling himself. "What if Annabelle already has a gold bracelet. Damn it, of course she already as one, how stupid of me having seen her wear it many times before." His next thought being. "Maybe she will think I could not be bothered going to the trouble of choosing a present, and just bought this bracelet to save time. Oh, damn it all, it is too late for me to now do anything about it unless of course, I do not give her a present. Good grief giving her nothing, will be worse than giving her this one."

Guy came down to breakfast feeling and looking unusually tired. Later on he told me he had not slept well and felt tetchy, as he was dreading the thought of handing his present to me. As the others gradually joined us for breakfast, although noticing how tired he looked; they tactfully kept their opinions to themselves.

At last, everyone once again made their way into the main drawing room. The room which could only be described as exceptionally elegant, had been decorated in white, cream and gold. There was a pair of magnificent chandeliers, which Guy informed me, had originally come from Italy and hung from beautiful carved plaster ceiling roses. The matching French wall sconces, and the huge Aubusson carpet that one's feet sank into, surrounded by a highly polished wooden floor, all added to the ambience of this calm elegant room. The beautiful tree now standing proud, and the wonderful Christmas decorations tastefully placed around the room, just added even further to make the room feel enchanting.

Sir Richard with Guy's help, loved handing out all the presents. Lady Rosalind laughed, and then stated.

"Each year at this time, deep down both of my darling men are still small boys at heart." Her guests as well as Sir Richard and Guy, started laughing at this remark.

After opening the wonderful presents my parents had gifted me, I then carefully opened Guy's. As I sat for a few moments, looking at the contents of the box without saying a word, this left Guy to think I did not like the beautiful contents it contained. Eventually looking up at him, first giving him a huge smile, I then sweetly told him. "Guy it is simply beautiful, thank you so much, I will treasure it always. May I also thank you for going to the extra trouble of having my name engraved on the inside; that was so very thoughtful of you." The relief on Guy's face must have shown very clearly, as everyone present, could not help but notice that by this time how wound up he was.

From that moment, Guy felt the rest of Christmas day flew by, enjoying every moment including the new stories his father told around the dinner table. One of the stories Sir Richard mentioned, was about Bailbrook College. After taking a sip of the superlative wine that had been served, re-placing his beautiful crystal glass carefully back to its place on the table. He went on to relate to his eager listeners, how British Airways, had opened a new training establishment by purchasing a magnificent Georgian mansion.

Sir Richard continued by saying. "The original mansion history tells how it had been built in the late 18th century by a Royal Navy Surgeon Commander who at the time, had served in the West Indies and had built the house with money he had misappropriated... Everyone knows it had been used by various members of the aristocracy as well as William Pit the younger.

Sadly, this beautiful mansion also had a dark side to it, as it had been used as a mental asylum, which I will tell you about in a few moments. What history does not tell us; I am about to."

Sir Richard stopped, and once again picked up his glass enabling him to enjoy another few sips of his wine. Wiping his lips with his beautiful white linen demask napkin, Sir Richard further went on with his story. "After purchasing Bailbrook House in 1977 for two million pounds, as a new training establishment for Air Traffic Services and Radio Engineering, along with meteorology in 1978. British Airways changed the name to Bailbrook College. I was invited to the formal opening ceremony, along with various other VIPs. Norman Tebbit, MP was the current Aviation Minister at that time.

I was absolutely delighted that a colleague from my RAF career days; a first-class Officer by the name of Squadron Leader Roy Handley, who had after his retirement from the RAF, had been appointed as the first General Manager and Principal of the new Bailbrook College. After the opening ceremony, Roy who was always excellent company, joined me for lunch, allowing me to enjoy reminiscing about our days in the Royal Air Force. In addition to talking about the air force, Roy amused me with a couple of stories about life at Bailbrooke prior to it being purchased.

Bailbrook as we all know is set in 22 acres of beautiful parkland. The wooded site had many mature trees; many with Tree Protection Orders (TPO). Hearing a chainsaw, Roy apparently would rush out of his office, deeply concerned that someone was about to violate the (TPO) order.

SQUADRON LEADER ROY HANDLEY AND DENISE LUNT

The second incident was a little more serious. This involved a landscaping contractor who was using a bulldozer. The chap had accidently opened what appeared to be a pauper's grave, as it contained human remains, probably one of the poor devils that had been kept in the asylum. Aware that the opening ceremony was due; and fearful of a lengthy investigation by the Police, Archaeologists and others, Roy ordered the contractor (illegally of course!) to hide the site.

Sir Richard stopped once again, first chuckling at the last statement he had just conveyed. He then took another sip or two of wine from his glass, which had been discreetly refreshed by Hopkins, before further informing all those present about another very interesting fact. Roy also revealed, that shortly after arriving at Bailbrook, he had commissioned The College of Heralds to design, produce, and authorise a unique Coat of Arms at a cost of 1,200 pounds. Bailbrook of course is now a hotel, and sadly for some very strange reason, the Coat of Arms is no longer displayed in the foyer, where it once held pride of place."

Guy turned to his father as he was now quite curios as to what happened to Squadron Leader Handley. Sir Richard gave his son a huge smiled as he remembered his friend with fondness and said,

"Roy was head hunted by Westinghouse (USA) as their Personal and Training Director. Westinghouse had been awarded a franchise to provide the Royal Moroccan Air Force with an air defence system for Morocco. The appointment required him to move and live in Morocco enabling him to serve his country doing what he did best. He eventually travelled the world many times in the Queens service."

After dinner, Guy and I managed to find a little time to slip away, enabling us to have some private time together to talk. As for Toby and Amanda, I am sure they had a great deal more to do...

New Year's Eve found Davenport Hall a hive of activity. Sir Richard and Lady Rosalind were joined by a further number of other friends, accompanied with their off springs. Ensuring everything was perfect for the younger guests to also enjoy the evening, Sir Richard had asked for volunteers from the RAF band. First by tactfully having asked them, that if they had no other plans, would they care to earn a little extra by coming to play at the hall. He also informed them, that afterwards he would ensure they were driven back to the local barracks.

The entire evening was a great success, though sadly the following day, it was also time for Guy and Toby to make their way back to Lossiemouth. Amanda still had a couple of days leave before she too had to return to Scotland.

On their return, Guy and Toby resumed training which continued as intensive as ever. With the benefit of the ongoing training, Guy and Toby were becoming increasingly more competent in flying their Tornado aircraft.

On initial arrival at the OCU, students are informed that they were required to notify the staff of their choice of the RAF frontline fighter squadron they wished to join on completion of their training. Their choice would be confirmed at the traditional "Postings Party." Normally held in the penultimate week of training at the OCU.

The Postings Party is a light-hearted affair, with both staff and students attending in fancy dress. The students were required to participate in physical competitions, each one, representing a front-line Tornado squadron. Success in a chosen competition, confirmed the student's choice of the squadron they would join on leaving the OCU.

Guy and Toby with their fingers crossed, had chosen to go to 617 Squadron, the home of the famous Dam Busters. The renowned Damn Buster squadron, is of course famous for its historic magnificent heroism when the squadron participated in Operation Chastise. This raid took place in May 1943 in WW2. The raid attacked the Mohne, Edersee and Scorpe dams in northern Germany. The flood waters from the breached dams destroyed two hydro-electric plants and several factories.

Guy and Toby were both successful in their competitions and were immediately "attacked" by the staff, all being armed with large custard pies provided by the mess kitchen. This gave both the staff and students the opportunity to let off steam. After the party ended, both students and staff returned to the Officers Mess to clean up and to continue their celebrations.

The following week, Guy and Toby made their farewells to staff and colleagues, and then travelled to RAF Marham in Norfolk, the home of 617 Squadron.

On their arrival Guy and Toby were warmly welcomed by the Officer Commanding 617 Squadron, Wing Commander Penn Gibson, and other Squadron members. During the following weeks, Guy and Toby flew several familiarisation flights in Norfolk and the surrounding counties. Following a test ride, Guy and Toby were cleared for combat in the Tornado GR 4.

On receiving this news, Guy immediately telephoned his father. For a moment Guy thought there may have been a fault on the line as there was only silence, Sir Richard, obviously like any parent was in shock. Sir Richard after a few seconds, made out he was clearing his throat, and asked, "When do you go?" Sir Richard did not wait for Guy to answer him, instead he continued, "I have no idea how I am going to tell your mother; you know she will worry dreadfully about you. Maybe for the moment, I will say nothing. Guy, you know how much we love you, please be exceptionally careful, this could be a war you are flying into, not an exercise."

"We leave shortly Sir, probably for Saudi Arabia. You know I love you both very much. I promise I will try to be as careful as I can. As to mummy, whatever you feel is right, I will go along with your wise decision; I have not told Annabelle either. Should anything happen, I have posted letters to you. I would be most grateful Sir, if you will be kind enough to please ensure they are given to their respective recipients. Please give Hopkins my good wishes, I know you can confide in him about the situation. Must go, see you all on my return." With that Guy replaced the telephone before his father had time to say another word, as Guy knew how distressed his father must now be feeling.

Shortly after being cleared, the Iraqi Government led by Saddam Hussain, invaded and occupied Kuwait. His action for doing so, was to seize the oil fields, while telling the world he was concerned about production and pricing disputes. The annexation of Kuwait brought economic and military sanctions against Iraq by the United Nations Security Council; this causing the outbreak of the First Gulf War.

A coalition of 35 nations, which included the United Kingdom became involved. The largest coalition since WW2. Not surprisingly, as a front-line Tornado squadron, 617 was placed on stand-by for deployment to Saudi Arabia. A couple of weeks later, Guy accompanied with Toby, led a company of five other Tornado aircraft as they departed Marham on the first leg of their long flight to Saudi Arabia.

RAF Bruggen, 27 miles west of Dusseldorf was the first transit stop. The base was home to several sister Tornado Squadrons, numbers 9,14,17, and 31. After refuelling, the 617-flight continued to RAF Akrotiri in Cyprus, accompanied by six aircraft from 9 Squadron. The Tornado unarmed and not carrying munitions, had a ferry range of around 2000 miles and did not require in flight re-fuelling.

A 48-hour transit stop, was enjoyed by all of the crews before departure on the final leg to Saudi Arabia. 9 Squadron was due to be based at King Abdulaziz Air Base at Dhahran, which housed No 4 Wing of the Royal Saudi Air Force, while 617aircraft would operate from King Fahad Air Base at Taif, the home of the Royal Saudi Air Force No 2 Wing. Guy and Toby, plus the other crews; were grateful for the 48 hours' rest given before commencing a punishing and demanding number of sorties. Sadly, being a Muslim country, gin and tonics were not available!

The war lasted several weeks, ending when the Iraqi forces were driven out of Kuwait. Sorties by Guy and Toby were mainly concentrated on the daily bombing of RIAF air bases, including Al Asad, Wadi Al Kahir, and the remote bases of H1 and H2. On most of these sorties, their Tornado was armed with the JP 233

"Runway Denial" munitions. These bombs dispersed several hundred "bomblets." These were stage munitions, the first stage produced a hole in the surface of the runway, while the explosion of the second stage below the surface of the runway, caused significant damage preventing rapid repairs. In addition to attacks on airfields, Guy and Toby attacked oil fields armed with Paveway guided bombs. The oilfields included those at Erbil, Baiji and Kirkuk.

At last, and with the Iraqi forces retreating from Kuwait; the operations were considered successful. Guy and Toby, together with all crews safely returned to Marham.

Guy asked Toby to join him and take a welcomed rest at Davenport Hall. Receiving Toby's answer, Guy immediately telephoned his father to inform him that both he and Toby had safely returned to England, and he was looking forward to coming home on leave bringing Toby with him.

As the taxi drove up the long drive, Guy was overly eager to see his beautiful home once more, and smiled to himself knowing full well Hopkins would be the first to greet them. As the taxi stopped alongside the entrance to the Hall, Guy immediately jumped out. Wearing a very large smile, Hopkins was eagerly waiting for them. Shaking both men by the hand, he welcomed them home and then told Guy he would see to the fare, as his parents are beyond impatient to see him and the Earl of Portland. Toby chuckled and asked Hopkins, to please just call him Toby or he would feel most upset.

"As you wish your Grace" Hopkins answered with a wink and then thanked Toby. Sir Richard and Lady

Rosalind on seeing their beloved son, found themselves full of emotion.

Kissing and hugging him for a number of minutes, then offering the same welcome to Toby. Little did they realise it would be just a matter of time, before both men were sent off to another war zone.

Several months later 617 squadron were placed on standby for possible deployment to Afghanistan. To prepare for service in Afghanistan, the squadron moved to RAF Lossiemouth which Guy found rather ironic. The purpose of the move back to Lossiemouth, was to enable the squadron to practice combat tactics in Morayshire. There they would find the terrain resembled that of Afghanistan, albeit without the sand or the Taliban!!

Even though Guy had naturally kept in touch with his parents and myself, plus having had no leave at that time; Guy had to settle for birthday wishes over the phone. Now sadly, he was about to make phone calls he knew would upset both his family particularly his mother, and myself. Never being someone who made hasty decisions, Guy had given a great deal of thought whether to tell his mother himself or, allow his father to inform her that he would be seeing action in Afghanistan. He decided he would talk the matter over with his father first and be guided by what advice he gave him. The thought of telling me, apparently also worried him.

Already having been away for many months and only able to speak to me via the phone, Guy began to wonder if maybe I would prefer being with someone who I was able to see more frequently. Our relationship when together, was to say; at least warm. Guy now wanted to take our relationship to the next step, he wanted more than just warm, but marriage had still not been mentioned.

I wondered if it was the emptiness he may have felt when he was not with me, or hearing my voice laughing at his silly jokes. Either way, I was not quite sure. Guy informed me in one of his romantic moments, if circumstances were different, he would take me in his arms and ensure we travelled to the stars. Sadly, we both knew for the moment it would be unfair to make that magical journey. I was not at that time prepared to become Guy's mistress, even if I did love him.

Guy at last made the phone call he had been dreading; explaining to his father the position he now found himself in. His father listening intently at what he was hearing, allowed Guy to say all he wished to without interruption. At the end of the conversation Sir Richard informed his son he should naturally speak to his mother, he would if he wished him to; inform her first of this news if that is what is required, and went on to ask, "Guy, please ensure you phone your mother, though I feel the sooner the better rather than later. Sometime during the evening would be preferred if you could manage to do so. You must allow her the time she needs to digest your news, and once again say goodbye to you knowing how precious you are to her."

Guy and Toby remained in Lossiemouth for a month, until the squadron returned to RAF Marham. Several weeks after returning from RAF Lossiemouth, 617 Squadron were at last ordered to Afghanistan, in order to participate in the British Operation Herrick. The Squadron's role was to support the NATO-led International Security Assistance Force (ISAF.) Also, the American led Operation Enduring Freedom.

Guy and Toby departed Marham, and after airborne refuelling over southern Germany from a USAF tanker aircraft, they landed at Kandahar Air Force base. After several hours in the air, they felt somewhat tired and ready for a hot meal, a shower and bed. The Kandahar Air Force base is the largest in Afghanistan, with excellent facilities and comfortable accommodation. With American influence, the base had a board walk with a variety of restaurants and stores catering to every need, of which Guy and Toby were most grateful for.

A couple of days later 617 Squadron commenced a busy program of combat sorties. The Squadron's primary role was high level reconnaissance, using the Tornado's high tech "RAPTOR" equipment. This equipment providing high quality imagery (video) for use by ground forces in combat with the Taliban.

Several weeks after their arrival, Guy and Toby were summoned to a special briefing. Intelligence sources had discovered that two senior Taliban Commanders, were due to leave in a vehicle convoy from a Taliban compound, north of the town of Girishk in Helmand Province. Helmand Province was a hotbed of Taliban activity; it is also the largest opium production area in Afghanistan. Guy and Toby's mission was to destroy selected vehicles in a convoy thought to be carrying the two Taliban commanders. After take-off, Toby on receiving information from a Boeing AWACS aircraft high above them, advised Guy on both route and altitude. Receiving information from his WSO, Guy descended the Tornado into a deep valley running east-west towards their target.

The valley had high terrain on both sides, which was unfortunately occupied by Taliban forces armed with shoulder held Stinger ground to air missiles. Under missile attack, Toby released packs of high intensity flares, while Guy endeavoured to avoid the black smoke trails coming at the aircraft which indicated missile trajectories. Without warning, one of the missiles exploded near the aircraft causing superficial damage to a wing tip. As the aircraft swerved violently, Guy's reaction was, "Shit, that was to bloody close for comfort."

Guy regained control of the aircraft and then checked all systems were OK, allowing them to continue towards their target. Approaching the Taliban compound, Toby saw a convoy of vehicles just as they were leaving. The information they had received was obviously correct. Toby programmed the Brimstone missiles to hit the two leading vehicles. Once released from the Tornado, the two missiles with their pinpoint accuracy hit and destroyed their targets. Guy flew over the smoke and flames coming from the destroyed vehicles; assuming there were no survivors.

He then flew to a safe altitude to return to Kandahar. ISAF troops later confirmed the success of the mission, and predictably the Taliban reported that two Senior Commanders had died in a road accident. History reveals that American forces carried out similar missions as the war with the Taliban continued.

Nearing the end of its deployment, 617 Squadron prepared to leave Afghanistan. The Squadron had achieved a remarkable number of combat sorties, registered in excess of over 400. After three months had elapsed, the Squadron returned to RAF Marham.

The moment everyone was free, each member of the Squadron phoned their loved ones. First to reassure them they were safe, and naturally for the joy of hearing their voices before re-joining them during a week's stand down.

Several weeks later, a parade was held on which all personnel who had served in Afghanistan, were presented with the Afghanistan Campaign medal. The Commanding Officer of 617 Squadron, Wing Commander Penn Gibson. Was delighted to inform the assembled ranks, that the Ministry of Defence had confirmed that the Battle Honour of "Afghanistan," could now be inscribed on the Squadron's flag. The news being received with three cheers by all those present on parade.

That night several parties were held in various Messes. These being the Airmen's, SNCO's &WO's and Officer's Mess to celebrate the day's events. To make the day extra special for him, Guy received an unexpected phone call of congratulations from his father.

Sir Richard as always, told him how much they loved him, and how incredibly proud his mother and he were. He then unexpectedly said. "We are so thankful you are home safe, and you have no idea Guy how we truly feel deep down, our hearts could indeed burst with pride."

Guy also used the day as an excuse to telephone me, if nothing else, just to hear my voice, and to let me know he was hoping to come home for Christmas.

"Are you ready Toby, I am somewhat eager to get home, and I still have loads of things I need to do." Toby smiled, then looked at his friend before asking.

"Does Annabelle have anything to do with your eagerness?" Guy instantly replied, with a frown now across his forehead, then laughing he replied.

"How did you guess, damn it? I must admit my friend; I am growing rather fond of her." Guy continued choosing his words carefully, his voice changing having a more serious tone to it.

"Toby, I am not ready to ask any woman to think about becoming serious with me. For the present I have no idea what the future will hold, we are not exactly in a nine to five job, and what we do is damn dangerous." Guy stopped, waiting for his friend to answer him. As Toby just stood and did not reply instantly, Guy further stated. "What about you and Amanda, do you have strong feelings for her enough to eventually ask her to marry you, or do you feel for the moment she is just a passing pleasure?"

Toby smiled, then quietly gave Guy his answer. "I guess Guy, I am content. No, that is not the right word I am looking for. I am content, I am also sure I must be in love with Amanda. When I am in her company, I feel comfortable. Not just the fact she laughs at my stupid jokes, she just makes me feel complete. When she is not around, I feel the other half of me is missing, and sometimes I feel very much alone. Does that make sense to you?"

Guy gave Toby a huge smile, before saying. "Your words are indeed reflecting your heart, and yes my friend, I guess you are very much in love with Amanda. Always thought she would make a damn fine Countess."

Both men laughed at that remark before Toby answered. "Rather think Guy, Amanda will make a beautiful Countess. Mind you, even though for the moment she is senior in rank to me, as long as she understands I am the boss at home." With that, both men were once again laughing.

Toby then cheekily said. "Ready Guy when you are, come on before I miss my drive home to your house." Again, that remark left both men chuckling, and allowed the banter to continue until they were about halfway home when Toby turned to his friend and asked. "Guy, would it be intrusive of me to ask about how you do feel in regard to Annabelle. I do not wish in any way to seem rude though?"

Guy looked straight ahead and said nothing for a few moments. Which to Toby now felt like hours, allowing him to think he had asked a question which was out of place. Guy eventually did answer him, telling Toby. "Quite honestly Toby, for the present I want my cake and eat it. Should we say, I still want to taste forbidden fruit, what man doesn't. On the other hand, I would hate the thought of Annabelle allowing another man near her. I think I would kill both of them."

Toby could see the determination showing on Guy's face, so decided to hold his tongue in regard to any further mention of Annabelle.

Halfway there, Guy decided to stop to have a coffee, fill the car up with petrol and allow both men to make use of the bathroom facilities. Once having sat down at a table, out of the blue he turned to Toby taking him off guard and asked. "Toby, do you think I am being a fool. Do not bullshit me with what you think I want to hear; I just want the truth?"

Toby sat for what seemed an eternity before he answered, as he did not want to offend Guy in anyway. Trying to ease the pressure he now felt, and choosing his words carefully, he replied. "A fool about what?"

Guy knew at that moment Toby was afraid to offend him, so smiled before saying. "A bloody fool about not allowing my feelings for Annabelle to rule either my heart or my head." Before Toby did have the chance to answer and to his relief, Guy continued. "One-day Toby, naturally I want to marry. The trouble is my wife would have to be top quality, not first quality. She would have to understand and be able to support me in all my work. On top of all that, she would have to possess all the social graces people would expect of both of us. Worse still, can you imagine when that day eventually does come; she would have to pass my parent's inspection regardless that they already know her so well. Toby, you do know how they hold me in such high esteem, it would be a situation which will not be easily remedied for any girl, no matter who she may be."

Guy looked at the frown now appearing on his friend's forehead, dreading the answer Toby was about to give him.

"Your parents Guy do indeed think the world of you. That is why I am saying this to you. I feel my friend when you eventually inform them you are bringing, should we say, that special someone to meet them. They will already know two things. One you love her, and two. As they trust your judgment implicitly, they will know she will be just perfect for you."

Guy looked into his friend's eyes, smiled, and replied. "You are always bloody tactful Toby, but thank you. For the moment I will allow the future to take care of itself, must admit though, Annabelle is damn lovely."

The two men continued their journey, until at last they reached Davenport Hall. Hopkins came out to greet them, welcoming them home as usual. Then taking their cases out of the boot, he carried them into the

Hall, ensuring each would be unpacked in the respective rooms. As they stepped into the main entrance, the Hall as always looked very festive. Hopkins informed Guy that his parents were waiting for both him and his guest, and were as usual, in the small sitting room and he would bring afternoon tea in very shortly.

Greeting their son with hugs and handshakes, Sir Richard and Lady Rosalind were for the moment very relieved to have their beloved son home, they turned and then greeted Toby, making him feel very welcome.

As with most years, the rest of the house guests started to arrive the following day. First this year, were Sir Hugh and Lady Lucille Barrington Sandford. They informed the others while looking directly at Toby, that Amanda would also be joining them, though unfortunately, much later in the day. After lunch it was the turn of my parents to arrive, and like Amanda, I would also be arriving later in the afternoon...

Hopkins brought in afternoon tea, which gave both ladies time to chat, with Lady Rosalind stating she would miss Deri and Craig Langton terribly this Christmas, and hoped to go to America to visit them later in the New Year if possible; already having put her holiday on hold, due to Guy going to war.

Amanda arrived fairly late looking a little tired from her long journey. Greeting first her parents then the rest of the company, smiling deeply as she did so by telling them, she really was looking forward to a shower and a change of clothes.

Toby's eyes lit up when Amanda first walked into the room, something which had not gone unnoticed by either Guy or the others. Holding his own council, Guy could not help also noticing the love Toby obviously had for Amanda, and the special look which passed between them. For a single second Guy actually felt a pang of jealousy, then told himself not to be so stupid. Excusing himself, Guy made his way to his bedroom. Once reaching the staircase, he took two stairs at a time, a habit he had developed when something was bothering him.

"Hello Annabelle darling." My mother greeted me, giving me a loving kiss on both cheeks. She was quickly followed by my father, who like my mother, thought that as I was his daughter; it made me the most important person in the world. Well especially to him, and quite rightly echoing my sentiments. After greeting the rest of the party, I noticed that Guy was not with the rest of the assembled guests. Being tactful as always, I did not mention it.

Hopkins gently knocked and popped is head around Guy's door. He had always had a soft spot for him since Guy had been born, which in turn had grown into mutual respect between the two men. This allowed Hopkins a great deal more licence than the rest of the staff. Hopkins with a half-smile, then told Guy. "Thought you may like to know Sir; Lady Annabella has just arrived." Without waiting for a reply, Hopkins withdrew closing the door quietly behind him, smiling as he did so.

Chapter Five

Stirring of Emotions

Guy took a quick glance at himself in his long dressing mirror and then quickly made his way back down stairs. On quietly opening the sitting room door, he stood for a moment taking in my appearance.

Having a few moments previously removed the warm winter coat I had worn, and one I particularly loved as it was very light in weight, cream in colour and matched the woollen dress I was wearing. As normal, I had chosen to wear one of the many pairs of black leather shoes I loved, matching what perhaps was my favourite black leather handbag and numerous gloves I had by now discarded. No matter what outfits I wore, I have always chosen with care, as they always allowed me to not only feel comfortable, but look as if I had just stepped out of a top fashion house.

"Good evening, Annabelle, you are looking very well this evening." Guy informed me. What he really wanted to say, he explained later was.

"How beautiful you look."

"Thank you, kind sir," I answered him, then went on to change the subject. The house party eventually ate supper, and much later everybody made their way to their respective rooms. Guy apparently, found himself unable to sleep very well and awoke the following morning feeling somewhat tired. Having a quick breakfast before the others came down, both he and Toby excused themselves having now been joined by Sir Richard.

The two men, having earlier made arrangements made their way into town to buy Christmas presents, drove off in Guy's car. As Guy parked the car, he turned and asked Toby if he have anything special in mind he wanted to give to Amanda. Guy was quite taken aback when Toby answered. "I would love to buy Amanda an engagement ring, but I doubt her family would approve at this time. So instead, I thought I would buy her a pair of diamond earrings."

Being deeply surprised by Toby's words, Guy looked at his friend as if seeing him with new eyes, before eventually saying. "Wow, you are keen on Amanda after all. I had no idea you felt that strongly about eventually wanting to marry her. How long do you intend to wait?"

"How long do you think her father would regard as reasonable." Toby asked in reply to the question, giving Guy no time to answer, Toby continued by asking.

"What have you decided to buy Annabelle.

"To be honest with you, not a clue old man. Actually, that's not quite true, I did consider buying her a diamond and sapphire pair of RAF Wings."

"You mean a sweetheart heart broach?" Toby questioned, but before Guy could answer yet another question, Toby stated. "I know you like Annabelle, but I thought you were not ready to commit to her. Giving her a pin Guy is really serious, do you think you are being fair?"

"I am very fond of her Toby, and for the moment I would be mad as hell if another man came into her life." Guy replied.

Toby with a frown now appearing across his forehead, looked at his friend and trying as always to choose his words carefully so not to offend, he quietly said to his friend.

"You know Annabelle is very fond of you, be careful how you treat her. She is after all not just the daughter of you parent's best friend, but someone you have known all of your life."

Guy remained silent due to being a little shocked at hearing his friends+ words, giving Toby time to continue. "Guy, you are not a fool. Annabelle is very beautiful, and she could have any man she chooses. The fact she is obviously very enamoured of you, should you hurt her, you are going to make things difficult all round. You do realise that don't you?"

"Damn it all Toby, actually I didn't. You are of course quite right. My parents are very fond of her indeed, and as to her father. I think he would kill any man who hurt his precious daughter. I swear even Hopkins would be annoyed with me. Damn and blast Toby, I guess even Amanda would no longer regard me as a friend, which would make our friendship difficult."

Toby remained silent for a few seconds, trying to find the answers his friend was waiting to hear. Eventually he told Guy not what he wanted to hear, but the honest truth. "You and I Guy will always be friends no matter what the future holds, naturally I cannot speak for the families, but I guess as you know them better than I do.

You also know the score in regards to their feelings towards Annabelle, and that my friend also goes for Amanda."

Toby stopped talking and waited for a couple of seconds, until at last he continued to relate further thoughts. Lowering his voice, which now had a grave tone to it, he told Guy. "Maybe you should consider giving Annabelle a different type of present, something perhaps less personal. You can buy her a pretty delightful piece of jewellery; the kind any woman would appreciate. Last year if you remember, you gave her a beautiful gold bracelet."

Guy replied, though now had a look on his face which Toby had seen a number of times before, along with that look, there was a determined note in his voice. Besides Toby it was a note anyone who knew him well would automatically recognise.

"RAF Wings are what I have decided to buy Annabelle. Should we go and see what the Jewellers have in." With that Guy jumped out of the car waiting for Toby to do the same. Toby shaking his head, followed in silence.

Christmas morning at Davenport Hall, was as usual filled with fun and happy laughter. So many funny presents as well as sentimental ones, were being given out this year. Toby hoped he would not draw too much attention to himself, though knew deep down that was an impossibility, as he gave Amanda the small beautifully wrapped box containing the diamond earrings he had purchased. Amanda was overjoyed with them, making quite a fuss as she showed her parents and the rest of the guests. In return she had bought Toby a cashmere sweater.

Guy had by this time, walked over to a beautiful carved sideboard, which was one of a pair; and had a tray laden with coffee and various small glasses of liquors. Picking up a coffee, he turned around to see me undo the ribbon around the box which contained his present. I sat there for a few moments, unable to draw my eyes away from the contents it contained. After what must have felt like a year to Guy, at last I gave a rather loud gasp before saying. "Oh Guy, thank you. You really are too kind. I was not expecting anything as lovely, you have quite spoilt me. Your gift has taken my breath away; they are absolutely exquisite." Guy said nothing, and just smiled.

The rest of the company, waited eagerly for me to show exactly, just what Guy had bought. Passing the box around, everyone was able to see for themselves. There laying on the red satin, shining like stars; was a pair of fairly large dazzling diamond earrings in the shape of bows. So many lovely comments were then made about how lucky both of us girls were. Amanda's earrings though a different shape having drops to them, were just as beautiful as mine.

Now it was my turn to give Guy his present. As I handed it to him, I said. "Guy, I thought this little present may prove useful. I do hope you like it." Guy took the present, touching my hand very briefly as he did so, then quickly let go before he went on to open the narrow black leather box. Inside, laying on the fitted black velvet material, was a classic vintage Mont Blanc fountain pen. Guy looked up into my face calmly, allowing no emotion to escape his lips, simply saying how delighted he was, and quietly thanked me. Guy was no fool, and knew just how expensive this type of pen would have been to purchase.

Though he had paid a fortune for the diamond bow earrings he had just presented to me.

Many years later, he told me that deep down he wished I had not spent that amount of money on his present. Why he felt like that, he was not quite sure. He just did and resented the thought of receiving such a pen. Naturally he also explained to me his reasons.

A number of hours later, everyone eventually made their way into the dining room. There they found the table as always, had been superbly laid. The dazzling white damask tablecloth and matching napkins set in the shape of fans, stood proud next to the various beautiful cut crystal glasses that would be used during dinner. The Georgian silver cutlery along with other pieces of silver tableware, including the antique French Louis the 14th silver gilt candlesticks which now played host to specially carved Christmas candles. Also carefully displayed, were a number of superb, crafted silver gilt containers which matched and now held the cleverly arranged table decoration.

Once everyone was sitting comfortably, Sir Richard said grace. As soon as he finished, Hopkins and other members of the staff served dinner. Sir Richard commented as he always did, what a superb job cook had performed. Lady Rosalind sat beaming, knowing full well her husband could sometimes be very feisty about his food if he felt it was not up to his standards. The atmosphere was very jovial and relaxed, unexpectedly, Sir Richard turned to Guy and asked. "Tell me Guy, what did you think of Afghanistan, I am sure our guest would also like to know?"

Guy looked at his father in astonishment, this was not a question he had expected him to ask. Certainly not around the dinner table, and certainly not while eating Christmas dinner. Before he could answer his father, Sir Richard asked. "Well Guy are you going to tell us, or must we put this conversation on the back burner for another time?"

Guy smiled, knowing he had no alternative choice but to answer his father's question. "Actually Sir, I am sure you know it is quite a historical part of the world. Sadly, with a horrific record in regard to war, and devoid of any decent human behaviour towards women and especially young girls and small boys. They actually marry the girls once they reach 12, I cannot speak here what happens to the boys as it is totally revolting.

Afghanistan, has been a country in conflict since the sixth century, having been invaded many times. Maybe due to the fact it is the crossroads of the major trading routes, known mostly as the Silk Road between China and India for over 2,000 years. That fact alone unfortunately; engendered trade disputes with many countries, due of course to the complicated geography of the land with Iran to the west, and Pakistan to the east. The dry deserts cover most of the land, and the Hindu Kush Mountain range, which is formidable, runs Northeast to Southwest dividing Afghanistan into three distinct geographical regions. The Central Highlands, roughly account for two thirds of the land. You then have the south western plateau, and last region is the northern plains, there you will find the country's most fertile soil. Many countries of course border Afghanistan. China, Iran, Pakistan, Uzbekistan and one or two other countries which I will not bore you with, I think it is six in all. The temperature varying in the different regions from -25C to 50C.

Kandahar in summer, has frequent dust storms which the locals call, "The Simoom Wind." Kabul of course, is the capital but now lays in ruins after so many wars. It was founded so the stories go, by a chap named Babur, who I was told had founded the Mughal dynasty.

The history of the place goes back a great deal further than that. Afghanistan was settled around 7,000 years ago and has been in transition for most of its history. Alexander the Great conquered Afghanistan in 330, BC. And brought the Greek language and culture to the region. Genghis Khan's Moguls invaded in the 13th century and so the wars continued. The British and Afghans as you know, fought in the 19th and 20th centuries and the Russians also tried to capture parts of the country. The Central Highlands join and become part of the Himalayan chain. I could go on, though I think for the moment I will leave it for another day. The two things I did find fascinating about the place, was that the country is rich in the vibrant blue stone lapis lazuli, which was used to decorate the tomb of the Egyptian king Tutankhamun. The other thing I found fascinating, was of course the region that leads to the Khyber Pass. This historic route connects Landi Khotal in Afghanistan, to Peshawar on the Pakistan border.

What really amazed me, was although the country is barren in some parts it could be incredibly green. There are around twenty dams, some of them are immensely huge and all full to capacity. This is due to the snows that cover the mountains most of the year, or the winter and summer rains. The people grow a really surprising range of trees and shrubs which we grow here in England including Rhododendrons. Cedar trees are abundant. Ash, Oak, and Walnut trees are also grown along with

Fir and Juniper. Many varieties of old roses are grown, also honeysuckle, as well as currant and gooseberry bushes. Would you believe that the Pomegranate, is actually the Afghanistan national symbol?"

Guy stopped and took a quick sip of his wine, and then continued by saying. "Well ladies and gentlemen I think I will leave it there. I hope I have not bored you all too much."

"Absolutely not my darling." Lady Rosalind was the first to speak. She then continued, not allowing Sir Richard to interrupt her. "Darling, the whole country seems in many ways, both very fascinating and simply dreadful. I have learned so much I did not know, but Guy as I love you, I must be honest with you. I think darling I can speak for everyone who knows both Toby and yourself, and tell you darling. We are all so very grateful that both of you retuned home safe and sound and are sitting here at this table."

Before Guy could answer, Toby thanked Lady Rosalind for her kind words. Guy then pushed his chair back and went over to kiss his mother.

By the end of the holidays, Guy was ready to return to duty. Maybe due to his emotions, as they were continuing to trouble him over Annabelle. Guy knew he was not quite being fair to her. Wanting her for himself, yet unable to fully commit his heart. Perhaps the time and space he will now have while away from her, will allow him to clarify once and for all his fears of commitment.

Returning to Marham, a letter was waiting for Guy from the Ministry of Defence.

Having previously received an identical one, as always it did not stop him still too feel a little trepidation on opening it. After reading its contents, he stood as if frozen to the spot. His emotions for a few seconds were a mixture of excitement, and then relief. The letter confirmed, he had been promoted to the rank of Squadron Leader. This was indeed news he must convey to his parents, and also to inform me.

A week later, his emotions reached even greater heights, when he was appointed as a Flight Commander in 617 Squadron. Once again, he could not wait to inform his family. A few weeks after receiving that news, 617 Squadron were warned of possible active service in Libya. Guy realised this news certainly would not be welcomed with any enthusiasm by his family, and of course myself. One of the major reasons he had decided not to allow his relationship with me, to become overly serious.

Sometimes Guy would tell me interesting things that go on behind the scenes at a Royal Air Force Base. One of the stories he told, was that at most RAF units. RAF Officers are required to perform duties such as Orderly Officer and Duty Officer. Junior Officers are Flight Lieutenants and below, while Duty Officers are normally Squadron Leaders in rank. Both duties are for periods of 24 hours, and all Officers are required to sleep in the Officers Mess.

Officers receive written instructions regarding these duties. The duties of an Orderly Officer, include attendance at the traditional Colour Hoisting (Raising of the RAF Ensign) at 8 am each morning, assisted by the Orderly Sergeant. They are also required to visit airman's dining halls in case there may be any complaints. Duties also include a check of items in the ration store, in order to confirm that food quantities in-store match the official inventory. Guy made me laugh, when he said, "How does one decide that a large item of beef weighs either 15Kg or 30Kg, will always remain a mystery."

Guy of course would take his turn as a Duty Officer, deputising for the Commanding Officer after normal working hours. His duties would be to deal with any unforeseen major problems. On two occasions, Guy was involved in unusual incidents. Late one evening, after having enjoyed dinner in the Officers Mess, Guy received a telephone call from his somewhat agitated Orderly Officer. The young Flight Lieutenant explained that he was in the Airman's' Club, where an incident had occurred, and requested for Guy to join him. Despite Guy suggesting to the young Flight Lieutenant, he should be more than capable of handling the problem. To Guy's surprise, the Orderly Officer insisted that Guy really should join him.

Taking on board the serious plea of the young Flight Lieutenant as he sounded quite distressed, Guy relented and drove over to the Airmen's Club. On his arrival, Guy discovered a drunken, diminutive Irish airman being restrained by his colleagues. One airman was prostrate on the floor, and another nursing a bruised jaw. Apparently, the Irishman had sent the two to the bar for drinks, on their return he accused the pair of stealing his change and attacked them. Guy called the Main Guardroom, and requested two RAF Policemen to take the drunken Irishman into custody. Before the policemen removed their prisoner, Guy reminded them to remove his belt and braces, along with his shoes before placing him in a cell. The Irishman was duly charged the following morning by his Section

Commander. Guy thank goodness, had no further excitement that night.

On the second occasion, Guy had received a telephone call from a tearful wife living in Married Quarters. The woman explained that she worked as a nurse in the local hospital and revealed that she was having an affair with a junior doctor. Having finished her shift that evening, her Corporal husband had turned up unexpectedly in order to take her home. Unfortunately, he discovered her and the doctor in a state of undress in the rear seat of his car. Her husband had stormed off, and she feared that he would have commenced drinking, to the point he may become violent on his eventual return to their married quarter. Wisely standing behind a very large policeman; Guy suggested to him, he knocked on the door of the married quarter. To their surprise, the husband opened the door, and very calmly in a quiet voice, apologised for the situation. He went on to tell Guy, that any thought of violence, he promised any acts of violence most certainly would not occur. Accepting his promise, Guy then deemed the matter closed and returned to the Officers Mess, smiling as he did so.

As expected, 617 Squadron was ordered to deploy to Italy to participate in Operation Ellamy. This being the codename for the United Kingdom's intervention in Libya. The operation was part of an international military coalition, aimed at enforcing a Libyan no-fly zone in accordance with a United Nations Security Resolution. The Resolution stipulated "that all necessary measures" shall be taken to protect civilians. The no-fly zone was proposed during the Libyan Civil War to prevent Government forces loyal to Muammar al- Gaddafi from carrying out attacks on anti-Gaddafi forces. Several countries prepared to take action at a conference in Paris.

Early spring and prior to full deployment, found 617 Squadron now fully prepared. Guy together with Toby, would lead six Tornado aircraft, which are capable of launching Storm Shadow missiles. Within a couple of days, the Squadron eventually were en route to Italy.

The 3000-mile flight required the Tornados to receive air-to-air refuelling. Three times on the outward flight by a Tri Star tanker aircraft, which was stationed at RAF Brize Norton. On the return flight to RAF Marham, this manoeuvre was only required once. Their destination was close to Brindisi. The Aeronautical Millitare base of Gioila del Colle which is the home of the 36th Stormo (Wing) is adjacent to the Adriatic coast, near Brindisi in the scenic Apulia Region.

History tells us, during Roman times Brindisi was connected to Rome via the historic Appian Way. Gioila del Colle opened as military base in 1915, The airfield becoming a flying school in 1917 during WW1. The British Army captured the base in WW2, and it was used by the US Army Airforce.

617 Squadron was based and used the facilities of the 10 Gruppo Caccia (10th Fighter Squadron.) They enjoyed the warm welcome given, along with the incredible hospitality of the Italian personnel.

Off duty Guy and Toby enjoyed both the Mediterranean sunshine, and the local regional cuisine. As they consumed copious quantities of local dishes such as, Pettiole, which is yeast dough stuffed with anchovies and Patani Tojedda. This dish contains rice, potatoes, and mussels. Both dishes all washed down with liberal quantities of Brindisi Rosso wine. The evidence shown by the expanding waistlines of both men.

During the following months, 617 Squadron carried out an impressive total of combat sorties over Libya and her coastline, in particular an anti-shipping patrol which prevented the import of arms into Libya. Evidence of these sorties were meticulously recorded in Guy's logbook. Just a few examples of these, included the destruction of buildings in Gaddafi's compound at Bab Al Aziza, along with the ammunition bunkers in the Sabha area of southern Libya. They also carried out air to ground attacks on Loyalist forces near Benghazi. Guy also recorded the destruction of tanks and armoured vehicles near Misrata, and the elimination of a SAM Missile site near Tripoli.

After seven months 617 Squadron was stood down. They were relieved by the French Escadron de Chasse EC 01/7 (Fighter Squadron) who flew into the Sigonella Air Base in Sicily with their Dassault Aviation Rafale fighter aircraft.

After enjoying their last Italian breakfast, Guy and Toby before departing for their return journey back to England, spent a little time making their farewells to their Italian friends. Surprisingly Toby making his in fluent Italian. Their return to RAF Marham would take them over the snow-capped Alps, which was uneventful.

As the aircraft neared RAF Marham, Guy called the tower requesting permission to land by saying, "On final approach, descending through 3, 000 feet, runway in sight."

The tower then replied. "Red One, clear to land, runway 09."

Several miles from the runway, Guy activated the instrument Landing System. The ILS assumes automatic control of an aircraft, providing precision guidance during the approach and descent to the selected runway. At around 2,500 feet, Guy was about to lower the undercarriage, when a loud explosion occurred in the port Rolls Royce Turbofan engine. Guy being unaware at the time that the explosion had resulted in the disintegration of the engine's turbine, severing fuel lines and had caused damage to certain hydraulic systems. He then made the decision not to lower the undercarriage. More importantly, with only power to the starboard engine, the aircraft swung violently to starboard. Reducing power to the engine, and establishing manual control by switching off the ILS and before further assessment of the damage, Guy called the Tower, then re-established manual control of the aircraft.

"Tower, Red One, Mayday. Have suffered complete failure of port engine."

The tower replied, "Understood. Do you wish to abandon landing and go around?"

Guy replied, "Negative. Possible damage to port undercarriage, limited hydraulic control and intend to jettison a quantity of fuel. Will attempt emergency wheels up landing adjacent to runway 09?"

The tower instantly replied, "Red One. Affirmative. Emergency services will be positioned near runway 09. Good luck."

Guy jettisoned both cockpit canopies and ordered Toby to eject. Unknown to Guy, Toby had decided to stay with his skipper. With no response, Guy repeated the order by saying, "Toby, we have a serious problem. Eject!!"

There was still no reply. Assuming a communication failure, Guy then turned his attention to landing the stricken aircraft. The Tornado's main flying controls included "Variable Wing Geometry," which allowed the aircraft's wings to be angled fully forward for landing and take-off, and angled rearwards for high-speed flight.

Instead of the conventional ailerons, to control the pitch and roll of the Tornado; the aircraft was fitted with "Taileron's" on its tailplane, together with a hydraulically operated rudder. Spoilers, Slats and flaps fitted to the aircrafts wing, were employed to reduce landing speed. An extendable panel fitted on top of the fuselage (Air Brakes) was also available to reduce speed. Guy's assessment, having confirmed extensive hydraulic failure, meant he was now faced with difficult choices regarding the various hydraulic options.

Having quite rightly jettisoned some fuel and managing to lower the flaps, using sensitive adjustments of both the aircraft's rudder and the throttle control. Guy was able to align the aircraft and crossing the threshold at 150 knots, he managed to land the aircraft if somewhat heavily: alongside the Runway 09. Fortunately, there was no fire, and the aircraft skidded to a halt after violently slewing 90 degrees to the right.

Emergency services arrived alongside the wrecked aircraft, almost as soon as it came to a halt; extricating Guy and Toby swiftly from the wreckage, as both apparently appeared not to be seriously injured.

After a preliminary examination from a paramedic, indeed showed no serious injury to either man, and both were placed in an ambulance and taken to the base medical centre for observation. Once safely in the ambulance, Toby somewhat shaken informed his friend of his thoughts and said, "Christ Guy, that was your worse bloody landing ever, and I hope you have sufficient pennies in your piggy bank to pay for that Tonca (Tornado) you have just bent out of shape.

Guy replied with a grimace. "How is your leg. The next time I tell you to eject, don't bugger about and get out understood.

Toby answered, "Eh! I think I am still deaf." Both the men then laughed, Guy then said.

"The old man is going to go mad; he will probably tear a strip of you."

A medical examination confirmed that Guy had suffered minor cuts and bruises. Unfortunately, in Toby's case, a heavy electronic monitor had been torn from its mountings during the heavy landing and had fallen on his right leg. X-Rays confirmed thank goodness, there had been no fracture, he was though treated for severe bruising. The men were eventually discharged from the medical centre with Toby having been given a large quantity of pain killers. The medical staff warning him against the consumption of alcohol, naturally celebrating their escape in the Officers Mess bar that night Toby completely ignored the warning.

The following morning Toby was summoned to the CO's Office. An initial enquiry having established, there had not been a communications failure between the Tornado's front and rear cockpit. Penn Gibson after issuing Toby with a formal reprimand and with difficulty trying to conceal a smile, said, "Toby, the next time you are ordered to eject, get your miserable arse out of the aircraft." Penn Gibson then added. "Annoyingly, it pains me to admit that you are considered more valuable than a Tornado. Dismissed."

Toby suitably chastened and hiding a smile, left the office. After making a full recovery, the two men returned to normal flying duties with 617 Squadron. A few months later the following notice appeared in the London Gazette.

"Squadron Leader Guy Davenport is awarded the Air Force Cross (AFC) for skill and airmanship in successfully landing a severely damaged aircraft after engine failure; saving the lives of both the Pilot and Weapons Systems Officer."

The late summer of that year would prove to be one of great change for both Guy and Toby in a number of ways. As part of career development, RAF Officers were often required to attend a Court Martial as "Officers under instruction." Guy was ordered to attend a Court Martial which had been convened at RAF Waddington near Lincoln. Normally, such events could not be described as being humorous; in this case that statement was proved incorrect.

One particular weekend, a group of junior NCOs from an RAF Regiment Squadron based in Norfolk; decided to visit a local brewery. They spent most of the day drinking copious amounts of the local cider, known as "Scrumpy." Not satisfied with all they had managed to drink so far, they returned to their base with a "borrowed" milk churn which was filled to capacity with cider.

Taking the churn with them to the Corporals Club, the group continued drinking merrily until later in the evening, the call of Mother Nature came into play for one of them. Standing on a table and removing his trousers, he proceeded to urinate on a portrait of a senior member of the Royal Family, who just happened to hold the post of Commandant General of the RAF Regiment. Hence the reason for a Court Martial.

During the procedure, a young airwoman, was called having on the particular evening in question, been a witness to the events that took place. Giving her evidence, she informed the court that the accused had removed his trousers and his "shreddies." The President, a senior officer from the Legal Branch, leaned forward, and spoke aloud, "Shreddies??"

Immediately, the Clerk of the Court, who was an RAF Sergeant. Leapt to his feet and in a loud clear voice said, "Underpants Sir."

"Mmmm," said the President, and then added, "Presumably, you saw his genitalia."

Just for a few seconds, the silence in the court room was such, that one could have heard a pin drop to the floor. The Sergeant nodded to the airwoman, giving her a signal to answer. Looking a little confused the airwoman said, "Beg pardon, Sir, what's that?"

Before the President had time to answer, the Clerk of the Court once again jumped to his feet and loudly said.

"John Thomas, airwoman."!!

For several minutes, the courtroom was convulsed with laughter, before order was restored. The accused's Commanding Officer in mitigation; informed the court that the accused had been commended several times during operations overseas. Hearing this, the President informed the court that the accused would receive a severe reprimand rather than a prison sentence. Guy returned to RAF Marham having enjoyed his first experience of a court martial.

617 Squadron was ordered to participate in Operation Shader, which was the code name given to

the UK contribution to the military intervention against ISIS. The UN, following a request from the Iraqi Government, had authorised air strikes against ISIS in Syria and Northern Iraq. ISIS is a jihadist terrorist group aiming to establish a Caliphate, or an Islamic Muslim State in certain regions of Iraq and Syria; after having driven Syrian Government forces from several cities in the region.

Commencing 617 Squadron's involvement in Operation Shader. Six Tornado aircraft accompanied by a RAF Voyager Tanker aircraft, flew from RAF Marham to RAF Akrotiri in Cyprus. The island of Cyprus, is situated in the eastern Mediterranean, providing easy access for combat strikes against ISIS. Forty-eight hours after their arrival at RAF Akrotiri, Guy as their Flight Commander, led a section of three Tornado aircraft in an attack against the Omar Oil field. Armed with Paveway laser-guided bombs, they destroyed several of the huge oil filled storage tanks. The Omar Oil field, was one of the largest sources of revenue to ISIS. All crews returning to Akrotiri feeling utterly delighted at their first combat air strike. The next day the attack was repeated. Only this time by Tornado aircraft armed with Brimstone Missiles. This sortie was intended to destroy the large mobile cranes, having been brought onto the site to repair the previous day's damage.

Several hundred successful sorties against ISIS, continued for many months. These included the ISIS capital Raqqa, which the RAF considered the most important of their sorties. Among the many other targets were, ISIS rocket launchers at Sinjar and Kisik. The RAF managed successfully to slow the ISIS encroachment on Bagdad, by attacking Haditha in western Iraq. After completion of their successful deployment, the Squadron returned to RAF Marham. They attributed the success of their three hundred missions to the quality of the Tornado aircraft, and the magnificent efforts of the maintenance personnel.

Shortly after returning from operations against ISIS in Syria; personnel at Marham, were excited to learn that 617 Squadron had been selected to represent the RAF, at the annual Exercise Cope Tiger in the Far East.

Cope Tiger is a multi-national exercise involving the air forces of Thailand, Malaysia, Singapore, USA and the UK. The objective being, to enhance operational ability and co-operation between air forces. Later in the month, six Tornados led by Guy and Toby departed RAF Marham. Supported by tanker aircraft, their long flight, via Italy, RAF Akrotiri in Cyprus, Bahrain, RAF Gan in the Maldives and RAF Tengah in Singapore took them to Don Muang, the Royal Thai Air Force base at Bangkok.

After a 24-hour rest, recovering from their long flight and crossing many time zones; the Squadron attended an impressive opening ceremony. The Commander of the RTAF, Air Chief Marshall Pralin Jintang; gave a welcoming speech. After the ceremony, Guy and Toby commenced their first sortie in Cope Tiger. They were tasked with surveillance of the Thia-Myanmar (Burma) border. Flying at low level, they overflew Prachuap Khiri Khan, Potharam and Mae Hong Son, landing at RTAF base Chiang Rai. After refuelling, Guy and Toby flew on a reverse course back to Bangkok. The same sorties were repeated several times during the first week, contributing to making Cope Tiger a success.

Guy and Toby were stood down for a couple of days. They agreed that after their long outward flight, and the number of sorties they had just completed, they would prefer to spend the next couple of days resting by the swimming pool. By doing so, it would give them chance to re-charge their batteries, even if sightseeing in Bangkok was tempting. Feeling fully re-freshed after eating, swimming, and sleeping, Guy and Toby returned to duty.

Once again departing Bangkok, they flew to RAMF Butterworth, and then on to Sultan Ahmad Shah Airport at Kuantan. Landing and immediately re-fuelling, Guy and Toby had been briefed before leaving Bangkok about what their duties were to be. They were to perform a simulated low level strafing attack on Pulau Tiomon Island, followed by a similar attack on Sultan Mahmoud Airport on the northeast coast of Malaysia. After several sorties they returned to Bangkok via a stop at RAMF Butterworth.

Two weeks later, Cope Tiger closed with a final ceremony. The majority of 617 Squadron's crews returned to the UK, however, Wing Commander Penn Gibson, who was still the Commanding Officer of 617 Squadron; decided that Guy and four of the Squadron's pilots, should take the opportunity to undergo Jungle Survival Training (JST) in the Malaysian Jungle. At the JST Staff briefing, Guy was horrified to learn that he and his group would be expected to "Live off the jungle." This required him and the others to kill, trap and eat various snakes, vermin and birds. Guy's solution though illegal of course, was to secrete several bags of sweets in his flying overalls; hoping to escape discovery.

The four pilots and Guy were airlifted from Bangkok to a remote clearing in the dense Malaysian jungle. Once they arrived, it was to be their home for the following seven days. The site housed several primitive shelters built from tree branches and palm fonds, affording some protection from the incessant tropical rain. The JST helicopter crew, also carried a container for the five men to use. This housed axes, a number of other tools, it also included various materials sufficient to construct snares and traps for small animals. The container included two vital items. One being a small mobile radio in case of emergencies, and the other item was a first aid kit.

Shortly after their arrival the helicopter they had arrived in left, with the crew wishing the men good luck. Once the helicopter was out of sight, the men felt somewhat lonely and nervous. Taking a look around, the men noticed a small river running alongside which would provide them with fish; (should they be able to catch them), and water to drink (if suitably boiled). Unfortunately, during the third night, one of the pilots was bitten by a large spider. The wound became infected and extremely painful. This caused the pilots leg to swell to the extent he was unable to walk.

Guy made the decision to use the mobile phone and contact JST Headquarters. A helicopter arrived, airlifting the wounded pilot to hospital in Bangkok. After seven the days, the same helicopter returned to pick up the rest of the group and fly them back to RMAF Butterworth. On their arrival, it was noticed they had indeed lost a little weight, with Guy returning minus any of his sweets.

As a respite from conventional military operations, the United Kingdom welcomed an invitation to join Exercise Maple Flag. This is an advanced military exercise hosted by Canadian Forces based in Cold Lake

Alberta, the home of RCAF 409th Tactical Fighter Squadron.

617 Squadron had been nominated as the United Kingdom's representative, leaving Guy delighted that he and Toby, together with one other Tornado crew received orders to fly to Canada.

The exercise uses the extensive Cold Lake Air Weapons Range (CLAWR.) The range straddles the Saskatchewan-Alberta Province border along the 55th Parallel, and is considered one of the very best ranges in the world.

Departing Marham, the two aircraft landed initially at Prestwick in Scotland, taking on extra fuel in readiness for the North Atlantic crossing. Thule airbase in Greenland, being 2134 miles from Scotland was Guy and Toby's first transit stop. There they enjoyed the hospitality offered them by the USAF 821st Air Base Group. 24 hours later, and after a flight covering 1950 miles, the two Tornados landed on Canadian soil at Gander in Newfoundland.

After enjoying a good breakfast the following day, Guy and Toby set off on the final leg of their journey, arriving at Maple Flag HQ, CFB Cold Lake Alberta. The men were given a 48-hour rest period, during which both men attended a briefing. Afterwards Guy and Toby commenced Maple Flag sorties.

Over the next week, they flew several simulated high level bombing attacks at 15000ft AGL. The locations included Wabasca, Loon River and Bitument. During the second week, the high tempo continued with low level, simulated bombing attacks at 500ft AGL, on locations at La Loche, Buffalo Narrows and Agnes Lake.

Before departure back to the United Kingdom, Guy and Toby each received commendations from the senior officers at Maple Flag HQ. Having completed saying their goodbyes, both crews flew back to Marham feeling highly satisfied with their efforts in their first Exercise Maple Flag.

Prior to Guy's departure to the RAF Staff College; the Yemeni President was ousted from power, by the anti-Government Group Ansar Allah, who were known as Houthi rebels. The Saudi Government, in response to this action, headed a coalition of Arab States and launched air strikes against the rebel forces using the Tornado aircraft which they had purchased from the UK; operating them since 1989.

The Saudi Government requested assistance from the UK Government, in order to support the Saudi Air Force, enabling them to use the Tornado's in the air attacks. 617 Squadron received orders to deploy six Tornado aircraft from RAF Marham. Guy and Toby this time, found themselves flying to Saudi Arabia. Their destination was to be the King Abdulaziz RSAF base at Dhahran.

The base was occupied by the RSAF 29th Squadron, operating Tornado aircraft. Having operated these aircraft for several years, meant that all facilities and maintenance personnel were already available and ground personnel were not required to travel to Saudi Arabia from RAF Marham.

On their arrival, Guy and Toby including the other aircrews from 617 Squadron, were warmly welcomed by Group Captain Saud al-Qahtari, the Base Commander and Wing Commander Fayadh Al Saud, the officer commanding RSAF 29th Squadron.

48 hours later, after appropriate briefings, Guy and Toby commenced sorties in Operation Decisive Storm against the Yemeni rebels. Their sorties included air to ground attacks on rebel camps responsible for insurgencies across the north Yemen border with Saudi Arabia, at Al Bough and Saadah. Mobile rocket launchers at Marib and Al Hazam, were attacked with conventional bombs, and rebel forces at Taiz, with Mauser cannon and Brimstone missiles. After six weeks of intensive operations, 617 Squadron aircraft flew back to RAF Marham, enabling them to celebrate another successful deployment.

Unfortunately, the RAFs involvement in the Yemen provoked loud protests from several far-left Human Rights groups. The groups contention being. That the use of UK aircraft and munitions, may well cause significant casualties in the civilian population. The UK Government's comment was.

"That the sales or assistance to a foreign government, for military equipment is always given careful consideration. Secondly, the avoidance of collateral damage to civilians or non-military facilities is always a priority. These protest groups, should realise that the sale of all military equipment remains an important economic need to this country."

Not long after returning to RAF Marham, Guy received a telephone call from the appointments section of the Ministry of Defence. The Officer at the other end of the phone, informed Guy that he had been selected for study at the RAF Staff College.

Chapter Six

Promotion

Guy was thoroughly delighted with this news, followed very quickly by the realisation of it, which became tempered with sadness that his partnership with Toby would draw to an end. Guy decided his father must be the first person, to be made aware of this news; then with a heavy heart, he would go on to inform Toby. The men continued their duties until the night before Guy left. Guy had asked Toby if he would join him in the Officers Mess, where at the end of the evening Guy said an emotional farewell. Not just to his Weapons Systems Officer who had now become an intricate part of his life but someone who he would continue to remain great friends during all the years to come. Should Guy eventually decided to marry Annabelle, this would enable Guy and Toby to see each other more frequently than normal friends may do. Toby eventually would leave the RAF and take up his seat in the House of Lords.

The following morning straight after breakfast, Guy said goodbye to his fellow Officers, everyone in return wishing him good luck. Toby walked with Guy to his car, the two friends shook hands and said their final farewells. Toby stood firm until he was unable to see Guy's car any further. As he turned around, he thought the wind must have made his eyes water just for a second, then realised there was of course no wind.

Selection for the RAF Staff College was intended for Officers considered to have shown the potential for senior rank. Thus, graduates from the college could expect accelerated promotion. Guy's course at the college was to be the Intermediate Command and Staff course for RAF Squadron Leaders. The curriculum included such topics as Air and Space Power, War Fighting and Planning, and Command Leadership and Management.

Arriving at the staff college, Guy as expected, quickly settled in. Most evening after studies and alone in his reasonably comfortable room, Guy later told me his thoughts invariably turned towards his feelings for me. He was trying to equate to himself, "was he falling in love," or perhaps more likely, he was just infatuated. As he still felt unsure, perhaps a better word would be to describe his emotional feelings as they were somewhat trapped, even a little confused in which direction he wanted to go. After giving it a great deal of thought, and being relatively close to where I now lived having at last acquired an apartment for both myself and a couple of my work colleagues in St John's Wood. Guy decided he would make the effort to see a little more of me.

The next day, straight after having finished breakfast, Guy phoned my office. Unfortunately, he was informed I had already left to attend court but would be back at around four. The receptionist having first asked his name, politely then requested if he would like to leave a message. Guy informed her no, but he would phone back later. Thanking her, he replaced his receiver. As he did so, he surprisingly said out loud to himself, "damn it."

Regardless he had a great deal of work to occupy his mind, Guy felt the hours seemed to be dragging unmercifully. Unable to excuse himself until his study class drew to an end, he became more and more frustrated. Thankfully at precisely 4-00pm, Guy was able to rush to his room and at last phone me. Returning to the office after lunch, the receptionist informed me that a gentleman by the name of Guy Davenport, had phoned early that morning and stated he would phone back later.

My first thought being, how unusual it was for Guy of all people to phone, and wondered what it was he wanted. Ensuring I was available to take his call, regardless of who else wished to contact me. It was just a little after 4-00 pm when sure enough the phone rang out, with Guy on the other end. I politely said, "Hello."

"Hi Annabelle, it's Guy." His reply made me smile, but he was not going to allow me time to speak as he continued. "Annabelle I am just wondering if you are free on Saturday evening, and if so. I was wondering if you would care to join me for dinner at an Italian restaurant named Topogigos." I remained silent for a moment, quite taken aback by Guy's invitation. "Hello, are you still there," Guy asked quickly.

"Yes, I am still here Guy," I answered.

"Will you join me then." Guy said sounding a little impatient.

Answering his question politely, I calmly said without sounding overly eager, "Thank you, Guy, dinner would acceptable."

Guy then arranged that he would pick me up at my apartment at 7-30. "Perfect, thank you. I will not keep you waiting if I can help it." I gently laughed at his reply. I knew Guy hated being late for any appointment. He continued the conversation for a further few minutes by asking, how had my day gone. Replying to his question, again I calmly informed him of the day's events. Guy went on to tell me about his own day, while I sat patiently listening before he eventually informed me, he needed to go. "See you Saturday evening then, bye," and with that Guy replaced the receiver.

He continued to sit for a while going over the conversation we had just had, thinking to himself that unlike other women he had asked out; I never flattered him, or said over enthusiastically, "Oh Guy, that would be simply wonderful Guy. Or something like, I would absolutely love to join you Guy. Even, how marvellous of you Guy, I cannot wait to see you."

Guy later informed me, he actually thought for a few moments. Maybe Annabelle does not actually fancy me. We have after all, known each other forever. The time we spent up in Elgin when we kissed, was fun. Maybe Annabelle may have liked me somewhat then, now, I wonder if I may have got it wrong. I know she loved the earrings I bought for her at Christmas, but then most women love diamond earrings. Damn it all, now I am not so sure if she does fancy me or not.

The rest of the week continued to drag on, and for no apparent reason Guy found it hard work giving his full attention to his studies. At last Saturday arrived and having already packed his overnight bag the previous evening rather than one of his many suitcases, he drove up to London immediately after breakfast. Until now, he had left purchasing the type of RAF Pin he had in mind, which he had previously intended to buy last Christmas. Now he felt the time was right, and so made for one of the famous jewellery stores in London. Once there if they did not have one in store, he knew they would order or have one made to exactly his specifications.

By the time he had reached the store last Christmas, he had once again changed his mind. Now he was indeed ready to buy this special sweetheart the pin and present it to me when the perfect moment arrived.

Guy booked himself into the RAF Club in Piccadilly, then made his way to the jeweller's shop. While there, he had decided to also buy a gold charm for the beautiful charm bracelet which my parents had bought for my sixteenth birthday. Each year, most friends and family would purchase a charm for it, as well as very kindly giving me other presents. Taking a last look in his bedroom mirror, ensuring as he always did he was turned out perfectly. Guy quietly closed his room door and made his way downstairs.

Arriving precisely at 7-30, more by luck due to the London traffic. He was able to see me waiting for him just inside the large glass elegant porch of the apartment block. Stepping out into the street, I hoped this evening Guy would think how elegant I looked, I had after all taken a great deal of time and care in choosing exactly what I would wear. This evening I had chosen a lightweight red wool coat with black satin lining, matching the large black buttons. Under the coat, I had on a matching red silk dress, both coat and dress as always, coming from Paris. My shoes and handbag this evening, were as usual in black patent leather and the matching gloves in black kid leather, all of which came from Italy.

Guy having previously decided he would leave his car at my home, ensured a taxi would be waiting to pick us up. The taxi arrived exactly on time as I joined him. Guy immediately opened the taxi door for me, smiling as he did so, he commented.

"You are looking very smart, in fact quite sensational. Ready then, I hope you are looking forward to going to this particular restaurant."

"Thank you," I replied, smiling to myself at his compliments. Once in the taxi, I then told him. "I have not actually been to the restaurant you mentioned, do tell me a little about it."

Guy smiled and seemed rather pleased for some strange reason at my reply. I found out later, he had often dined there, and occasionally took other women. So why it pleased him that I had not accompanied other men to this restaurant, he had no idea. Feeling more relaxed than he had done most of the day, Guy went on to inform me a little about Topogigos.

"The restaurant Annabelle, is in Soho, and belongs to an Italian family. They have been there many years. The food is wonderful, and I am sure you will love the ambience of the place. I think one could say, it is both warm and welcoming for both the young, the elderly, and even lovers."

I sat in silence as I thought Guy may have felt a little uncomfortable at that last sentiment. A little later, he said I was indeed right in my thoughts. On arriving at the restaurant, Guy was greeted by Signor Fattorini and two of his very handsome sons.

"Good evening Luigi, how are you and your wonderful wife this evening?" Guy inquired politely, then waited for Signor Fattorini to answer him before he continued.

"As always Signor Davenport, we are both keeping well. As you see, my sons also are very well, and soon, we hope to have another new grandchild."

A huge smile crossed both of the men's faces. Guy conveyed his congratulations, along with his good wishes for the new parents.

After pleasantries had been exchanged, Signor Fattorini turned to look at me. Guy giving me all sorts of information later in our relationship, told me. Apparently this was not something Signor Fattorini normally did when he brought a woman in with him, but being Italian Signor Fattorini must have known by the way I was dressed, there was something different about me. Signor Fattorini later told Guy, compared to all the other women he had accompanied to the restaurant, I was in fact very different...

Guy smiled to himself and thought why not, and decided he would indeed introduce me to the restaurant's owner. Something of course he would never normally consider.

"Luigi, allow me to introduce you to Lady Annabelle du Beauchene Willoughby. Annabelle this is Signor Luigi Fattorini."

I proceeded to shake hands with Signor Fattorini and both of his sons, but like all Italians, I found to my delight instead of shaking my hand, they kissed it gently displaying all the charm Italian men know exactly how to. After pleasantries had been completed, the eldest of the Fattorini sons, escorted Guy and I to the best table in the restaurant, which conveniently had a reserved sign displayed on it. Signor Fattorini, then asked his other son to look after the front desk for a few minutes, enabling him to speak to his wife who was in the restaurants ultra-modern kitchen, amazingly so different from the romantic old fashioned dining area.

Walking quickly and entering the kitchen, Luigi quickly went to tell his wife that a very special lady was dining this evening with Signor Davenport. "I swear Maria this is the one, she is so beautiful and a real Lady. Her manners are charming, and you should see her clothes, I swear they have come from Paris."

Maria Fattorini laughed, before telling her husband. "You are always swearing, about this and that, what do you know of Paris fashions. Italian yes, but not French clothes."

Signor Fattorini kissed his wife on the cheek, then asked, "Maria, please come. I will introduce you, then you will see for yourself."

"Very well Luigi, but if you are wasting my time, I will not be pleased," she replied. Maria removed her apron, then quickly tided her hair, before she followed her husband into the dining area of their restaurant. Signor Fattorini walked over to where Guy and I were sitting. Excusing himself profusely for interrupting us, he then asked if he may introduce his wife to me.

After introductions had once again been made, on returning to the kitchen, Maria told her husband. "The next time I need a new outfit, remind me to fly to Paris." Maria further told him. "I feel Lugi, you could very well be right, this Lady is indeed very different from all the rest of the women I have seen with Signor Davenport, we must wait and see."

Glancing through the menu, Guy asked if there was anything in particular, I would like. Calmly I gave him my reply, before continuing to ask. "No thank you Guy, it all looks so inviting and I am very spoilt for choice. Do you recommend a particular dish?"

Guy answered by informing me. "Maria is such a good cook, it would not really matter what a person chose to eat, it would be cooked to perfection, and taste simply delicious."

After a few more minutes, both Guy and I had at last decided on what food we fancied and related our order to the eldest of the Fattorini sons. Once having done so, Guy excused himself as he needed the bathroom. This gave me a chance to take in my surroundings. Guy was of course quite right; the restaurant indeed had a lovely atmosphere. On the warm red brick walls, hung a number of beautifully painted scenes of Italy. The majority of them were of places I recognised having already visited them. Along with the paintings, hung empty Chianti bottles scattered here and there, adding to the ambiance of this warm and inviting room.

The tables were covered in the usual red under cloth, and a pure white linen damask tablecloth over it with matching perfectly folded napkins, that one sees all over Italy. The tables had been set with silver Italian cutlery and crystal glasses, along with a crystal water jug. On each of the tables stood a further Chianti bottle, each holding a candle. Every bottle was covered in candle wax that I loved.

Due to the type of lighting in the restaurant, this in turn gave the appearance as if both glasses and jug were covered in diamonds. Guy returned to the table just as a bottle of wine he had ordered, was being brought over. One of the many young waiters that worked in the restaurant, opened and served the wine smiling as he did so, then discreetly walked away. Dinner was not long in following, with both Guy and I having chosen as our preferred dish, spaghetti bolognaise which smelt and tasted wonderful.

"I see we like the same type of food," Guy said, idly trying to make conversation. Smiling to myself I could sense his embarrassment, though why I was not sure, having of course known him since being a child.

I began to ask various question I thought he would enjoy talking about, which in turn helped both of us to enjoy the rest of the evening. As our meal came to an end, Guy unexpectedly pulled out from his jacket pocket, the box which contained the charm he had bought. He looked directly into my eyes and said, "Annabelle, I know a man may usually buy his dinner date flowers or a box of chocolates, I hope you do not mind. Instead of either of them; I bought you this little present."

With that Guy handed the beautifully wrapped box to me. Taking the box gently from him, carefully opening the lid, there laying on the white satin cushion, was an exquisite, jewelled charm which took my breath away.

I sat for a moment or two before quietly saying. "Guy it is beyond lovely, how very thoughtful of you. I shall enjoy adding and wearing it along with the other charms that mean a great deal to me." Guy smiled, but this was not the reaction he was hoping for. What reaction was he hoping for, he later asked himself?

We sat until at last, we had emptied our wine glasses while talking about nothing important. Guy then asked if I was ready to go. He indicated he wanted the bill, but before leaving, we made a particular point of saying goodbye to Signor Fattorini and his wife who were indeed so gracious. As we waited for a taxi, Guy looked at me and asked. "Have you enjoyed the evening."

"Very much so, thank you. I would love to go there again if you have a free evening sometime." Came my matter of fact reply.

"Do you mean that, or are you just being polite." Guy heard himself ask. His voice had now taken on a cold note that was unusual when he talked to people, he liked.

"Yes, I do mean that, and yes, I am being polite." I answered calmly.

"Very well, I will take you at your word Annabelle. How about next Saturday evening, that is unless you have something else planned?"

Once again, I informed Guy what he wanted to hear.

"I have nothing planned, and I shall look forward to joining you."

Guy never spoke for a few seconds, then out of the blue, he surprised both of us by raising my hand to his lips. After gently kissing it, he looked down into my eyes, and before either he or I had time to say a word, he swept me up in his arms. His kisses at first were soft and gentle, then became more demanding until I could barely breath. As he released me, conveniently our taxi drew up. Without a word passing between us, I carefully stepped into the taxi as Guy gave instructions where we wanted to go.

Both Guy and I still sat without a word passing between us, until eventually the taxi reached my apartment block. I alighted and walked up the few steps to the doors of the glass foyer while Guy paid the taxi. Just as I reached them, Guy caught up with me. Strangely, he once again quietly asked if I had enjoyed the evening, and would I still join him next Saturday evening? I suspect the unusual phenomenon of feeling nervous had once again overtaken his emotions.

"Yes, I am looking forward to next Saturday, and are you?" I asked, with a well-shaped raised eyebrow.

"Very much so," he replied. Then impulsively once again he took me into his arms and kissed as lovers do. How long we stood there in the cold night air kissing, neither of us would ever remember.

As the weeks progressed into months, Topogigos became our favourite haunt. During one of those romantic evenings, Guy finally decided to give me the magnificent diamond and sapphire jewelled RAF Wings sweetheart pin he had bought the day before he had first taken me to Topogigos.

Guy said, he found his feelings towards me were becoming more intense. What he did not at the time tell me, he was still not one hundred percent sure about how deep his emotions actually were. Unfortunately, with not knowing where his future career would lead him, he was still being very cautious.

Chapter Seven

Commander's Dinner

My father, Sir John Edward du Beauchene Willoughby KCBE. DSO. MC, was a member of the Gurkha Regimental Association. The Association held Commander's Dinners, were held with the intention to commemorate regimental anniversaries and other events. A dinner had been planned for late October, which my father had been invited to as its Guest of Honour.

As a Brigadier, my father had commanded the 5th UK Infantry Brigade, which was part of the UK Land Forces in the Falkland's War. The Brigade included the 1st Battalion 7th Duke of Edinburgh's Own Gurkha Rifles. He had also previously served in the Brunei Revolt with the 1st Battalion of the 2nd Gurkha Rifles.

The Ghurkhas have served the Crown for over 200 years. The history of the Brigade stems from its inception during the early wars between the Honourable East Indian Company and the city state of Ghurkha. Situated on the hill-principality Gorkha kingdom, which eventually the Kingdom of Nepal expanded. The khukri, is a forward-curving knife the Gurkhas are well known to carry, and is as fearsome as the men themselves.

A former Army Chief of staff once said, "If a man says he is not afraid of dying, he is either lying; or he is a Gurkha."

The Gurkhas have served with honour in a great many wars, just a few of them are. Afghan Wars, also two World Wars. The Malaya Emergency, the Borneo Confrontation, the Falklands and the Balkans. We must also include the Gulf Wars and of course, Afghanistan. The battle honours include 26 Victoria Crosses, and Two George Crosses. Prior to 1997, the Brigade's base was in the Far East. Following the handover of Hong Kong, the Ghurkhas moved to the United Kingdom. After partition of India in 1947, four of the 10 Ghurkha Regiments opted to transfer to the British Army to form the Brigade of Ghurkhas, eventually amalgamating to form the Royal Brigade of Ghurkhas. During the final battles of the mountains around Port Stanley, the Ghurkhas took Mt William. The Brunei revolt was a short-lived insurrection in the British Protectorate by the Brunei Peoples Party. The party was opposed to the Monarchy, and its proposal to join the Federation of Malaysia.

As a young Captain, my father had been involved in the rescue of the Sultan of Brunei from his Palace, which at that time was being besieged by the rebels. For his leadership during this action, he had been awarded the Military Cross.

Now as the Guest of Honour, my father had been given the privilege of inviting a number of personal friends apart from mummy and myself. He had asked Amanda's parents Sir Hugh and Lady Barrington Standford, but sadly they were unable to attend. My father therefore decided to bring with him their daughter Amanda; especially as he knew she was not only my best friend; she was the daughter of mummy and daddy's best friends. Daddy had asked Guy's father and mother as well as Guy, if they would honour him by attending to what he hoped would be a pleasant evening.

Once Amanda and I had been informed we were to be included as guests, predictably the two of us made arrangements to fly to Paris, enabling us to purchase the latest evening gowns and take the opportunity to see Amanda's parents. Sir John also extended an invitation to Toby, the newly promoted, Squadron Leader the Earl of Portland, who of course at present, still remained in the RAF.

The summer warmth quickly dissipated, and one could feel the chill of the autumn air. The Commander's Dinner which was to be held at the Dorchester Hotel in Park Lane, had at last arrived. Every suite and room available in the hotel had been booked which was not surprising. As the guests made their way downstairs, either by lift or slowly descending the beautiful grand staircase, allowing them the first chance of observing the gowns the ladies were wearing, as well as how smart the serving Officers looked in formal Mess Dress. Along with serving Officers, were the retired Officers in their dinner suits, all proudly displaying their miniature medals.

On entering the foyer, the guests were graciously shown by a number of the smartly turned-out hotel staff, into a charming medium sized room for pre-dinner drinks. Once in the room, mummy and daddy were very quickly joined by Toby and Amanda, Guy and myself.

Amanda and I having ensured our trip to Paris had been well worth it, as we both looked as if we had stepped out of a Paris fashion magazine. Amanda had chosen to wear red satin, a colour she loved; and I decided this evening on black sain. Both our gowns were fitted to perfection, showing off our gentle curves. Amanda's gown had a huge black satin bow set to the left side of her waist, with the tails nearly reaching the floor. My gown had also been adorned with a huge bow, the material used for this accompanying bow, was white satin. The bow was so huge, it entirely covered the left narrow shoulder strap. The effect of both our gowns, one would describe as being very dramatic. This left anyone who knew very little about couturier clothes, to wonder where we had purchased them, though obviously correctly guessing they came from Paris.

No sooner had Toby joined Guy, Amanda and myself, we were then followed closely by many of the guests. After pleasantries had been exchanged, Guy raised my hand to his lips and told me how beautiful he thought I looked, and that he was the luckiest man in the room. Kissing my hand in public for the first time, gave everyone in the room to assume he was making a statement, allowing in turn a bit of tittle tattle to take place by those who just loved to gossip.

Once all the guests had gathered and enabling them the time to enjoy a pre-dinner drink, a discreet signal was then given that dinner was about to be served. The guest filed through double glass doors into the adjacent dining room, there they were greeted by the President and the Chairman of the Regimental Association.

As my friends and I followed my parents, Guy proceeded once again to take my hand, kissing it gently, then slipped it through his arm as we walked with the others into the dining room. My father quickly found the table that had been assigned for him and our party.

Dinner was served impeccably by the very well-trained staff, the food itself one could only be describe as superb. With everyone in top spirits, the atmosphere in the room was extremely relaxed. Dinner eventually drew to an end, which was then followed by a short break, allowing those who wished to stretch their legs, or use the luxury restrooms provided. Once the guests returned and settled themselves down, the speeches could begin. First from the President, followed by his guest of honour who was of course my father.

The evening drew to a close, after which most guests then made their way to the hotel bar or lounge for a nightcap.

The following morning, after saying goodbye to his family, friends and myself, Guy made his way back to the Staff College for his final term.

Formal studies ended at the beginning of December and were then followed by examinations. The results of these exams would be published in late December, just before the Christmas holidays. Not unexpectedly, Guy graduated at the top of his group. As anticipated, he received accelerated promotion to Wing Commander.

After an eventful year, Guy left the Staff College, but before doing so, he ensured he said goodbye to his fellow students, knowing he would not be returning after Christmas.

During Christmas dinner, with everyone thoroughly enjoying the wonderful meal cook had prepared, Guy suddenly put his knife and fork down and started laughing quite heartily. Lady Rosalind looked at her beloved son's strange behaviour as it was something as far as she could remember, he had ever done before, and asked, "Guy my darling, may we all know what has distracted your attention away from your food and left you to laugh so much."

Guy continued laughing for a few more moments excusing himself, before informing those present what he had found so funny, looking at his mother he went on to explain, "I was just thinking about traditional dining in nights at an Officer's Mess, and although extremely formal, it often produced humorous incidents. I can remember when I was at RAF Lossiemouth on one such occasion. The thirty Officers seated with me at a long refectory table, managed to position our knees, enabling all of us to shuffle the table further along the dining room towards the door, until that is, the Mess President intervened and spoilt our fun. The hilarity continued when the Mess Servants came to remove the table napkins, only to find the ends had been tied together like a long washing line."

Guy started laughing again and was quickly chastised by Lady Rosalind telling him, "Darling, you and our guests are not going to behave like that at my table." Lady Rosalind gigging, before further saying. "Anyway, my table is far too heavy and far too precious for such behaviour."

At that last remark, everyone present started to join in laughing. Sir Richard then decided he also would add a funny tale and went on to relate an incident which took place when he was serving with 43 Squadron at RAF Leuchers. He started by saying, "My Commanding Officer at the time, was an afficianado of carpet bowls, in fact he was an addict. Once the loyal toast and speeches had been given after dinner, the Mess Servants would clear and move the dining tables to one side. They would then lay a strip of green baize along the dining room floor in order for members to play this damn game. The majority of us were required to stand, absolutely bored stiff, while the CO showed his skill. The CO proceeded to throw a perfect bowl which nestled alongside the white jack, producing the obligatory polite applause from the bored onlookers. I was standing next to Lofty Thomas, who had played rugby for the RAF. Before I could intervene, Lofty having consumed a fair amount of alcohol, marched across the carpet, and kicked the jack through the open French doors. The CO's face changed to a wonderful colour of puce, as he ordered Lofty to leave the Mess and report to him at 09-00 the following morning. The act cost Lofty a week's Orderly Officer Duty, which everyone agreed was well worth it."

"My goodness darling" Lady Rosalind interrupted, and gently said. "You have never mentioned that tale to me before, how amusing."

Sir Richard was just about to reply, when Toby not to be left out, asked. "May I also tell you about an incident that occurred at one of my dining in nights?"

"Of course, please go ahead," Sir Richard answered.

Toby pretended to clear his throat which brought a smile to everyone, and then proceeded to tell his tale.

"While undergoing training at No 1 Air Navigation School at RAF Hullavington. My friend Daniel and I, who was a fellow student, had purchased a vintage upright piano from an antique shop in Chippenham; being the nearest town. The relic was delivered to the Officers Mess in time for the next dining in night. After dinner, Daniel and I placed two Thunder Flash grenades inside the piano, before wheeling it into the dining room. (The Thunder Flash naturally is used by the military. After being triggered, it explodes to produce a blinding light and extreme noise, disorientating opponents.) Once in position, a fellow Officer and pianist agreed to play the wreck. His first touch of the keyboard, then triggered the first Thunder Flash. Producing a blinding light and explosion which blew out the back of the piano, much to the merriment of all in the room."

Listening to Toby's tale, everyone started to laugh. They knew the rest of it would indeed be very funny, so quickly everyone settled down and Toby was allowed to continue telling his tale. "At the time, the Commanding Officer of No 1 ANS, was Group Captain David Mills, an ex-Bomb Disposal Officer. Before I could intervene, the CO ordered everyone to stay clear and approached the piano. Unfortunately, as he lifted the top of the piano lid, the second Thunder Flash was initiated. This time, in addition to the noise and blinding light; the front of the piano disintegrated, covering the CO in black soot and dust. Daniel and I fled from the dining room and took refuge in the games room; pursued by a very irate Group Captain.

The following morning Daniel and I received extra duties and we were presented with a dry-cleaning bill, plus another bill for the damage that had been done to the dining room carpet. Despite this, both Daniel and I did eventually graduate."

"Why am I not surprised." Sir Richard informed Toby, allowing the rest of company to continue laughing.

The Christmas period sadly was drawing to an end. Just before the end of his leave, Guy received a phone call with orders to report to RAF Uxbridge. The caller also notified Guy that his next duties would be as an Air Attaché, he did not for the moment state where. Guy was absolutely thrilled at this news, and immediately went to tell his father of this new appointment.

On arrival at RAF Uxbridge, Guy contacted the Mess Manger to arrange for his accommodation etc. The following day he visited the Air Secretary's Branch at the Ministry of Defence, where he was provided with details of his required induction training. The training included a short course at the Joint Military Attaché School, together with several briefings at the MOD, the Foreign and Commonwealth Office and MI6. At the end of his training, Guy was informed that his first assignment would be as the Air Attaché at the British Consulate in St Petersburg in Russia.

As an Air Attaché in a foreign country or a Commonwealth country, he would perform a variety of diplomatic, advisory and analytical duties. These duties were performed by observing, and reporting on military activities, which he would then report back to both the MOD and politicians in the UK.

Now being in London, it ensured Guy and I could see a great deal more of each other, enabling us to spend most weekends doing what two people in loved doing. Well, I hoped we were in love, and doing the normal things lovers do such as going shopping, or go for a coffee. The other things we enjoyed together from going to the theatre to see a show, or enjoying helping each other to choose small presents for friends and family for either birthdays or anniversaries. Frequently we would return to Topogigos, as it had now become our favourite restaurant.

Much to my disgust, and because I loved Guy, I allowed him to take me to Lords Cricket Ground. Being a woman, watching twenty-two men bat and chase a ball, I felt I was being tortured, especially having to sit for hours and watch the grass grow. Of course, I was well aware of Guy's cricketing skills. He had obtained a Cricket "Blue" while at Cambridge University, he was then selected to represent the RAF College in fixtures against the Royal Naval Collage at Dartmouth, and the Royal Military Academy Sandhurst.

His performances in those games earned him selection for the Royal Air Force XL, also playing at Lord's against the Civil Service. A well-known fact is that in a military career, excellence in a sport may enhance one's promotion prospects. As far as Guy is concerned, this was in no way an exception.

At the beginning of Autumn, having completed his induction training, Guy was given orders to travel to St Petersburg in Russia. While the news was expected, Guy for the first time in his life felt sad, even a little distraught at the thought of being separated from both his family and myself, especially as he would also miss Christmas. Not knowing how long he would be away, made him feel even worse.

On the day of his departure, I went with him to Heathrow Airport to say goodbye. Before doing so, Guy asked me if I would wear the RAF Sweetheart Pin he had bought. He did not tell me when he had actually purchased it. That along with many other thoughts and feeling, would eventually come to light, but those days were still far into the future.

As he made himself comfortable in his business class seat, he looked out of the window wishing I was at his side. For the first time, Guy was experiencing pangs of sadness and other emotions he had not felt before, that were to go on to change his life. The British Airways flight landed three and a half hours later at Pullcovo Airport in St Petersburg. Immediately after landing, a second British Airways aircraft also landed. This second aircraft taxied to a position some distance from the terminal building.

By this time, Guy was walking down a corridor towards the diplomatic channel, and could see quite clearly through the floor to ceiling terminal windows. He noticed that a police vehicle had parked next to this second aircraft. To his surprise, stairs had already been attached and two Russian policemen entered the BA aircraft. Within moments, the pair re-emerged, accompanied by a handcuffed female passenger. The woman was placed in the waiting police vehicle, which then drove away at high speed. Intrigued by what he had witnessed, he addressed a question to a member of the airport staff who was aware of Guy's diplomatic status. The staff member explained the reason for the apparent arrest of the female.

The British Airways aircraft was carrying a Chinese National being deported from the UK. For security reasons, the man had been seated alone in an empty row of seats. Shortly after take-off, a young female passenger had left her seat and for reasons unknown, attempted to approach the Chinese man. The cabin crew intervened but were unable to convince the female to return and remain in her seat. The Captain having been advised of the problem, made the decision to divert to St Petersburg and offload the troublesome female.

Guy smiled to himself, thinking perhaps he had witnessed diplomacy in action for the first time.! He continued his arrival via the diplomatic channel without further incident. Another tale to tell his family on his return. With all the usual formalities completed, Guy went to collect his luggage. After that he was met by a driver from the British Consulate, who drove him directly to the Pushka Inn Hotel in central St Petersburg.

After once again going through various questions as normally happens in Russia, he was taken to a very pleasant suite of rooms. The Pushka Inn Hotel was originally a home which belonged to a very old noble family as long ago as the fifth century. The last owner had been a man called Ivan Pushchin, who had been a great friend of the great Russian poet Alexander Pushkin.

Guy immediately unpacked his suitcase, as he wanted a shower and change of clothes before dinner. Before doing so, he made himself a cup of coffee. Taking it over to the balcony he looked out onto the stunning view of the Winter Palace now fully lit. Guy decided there and then, he would like to see a great deal more of this beautiful city and its historical architecture.

The following morning having enjoyed a fairly decent breakfast, Guy ordered a taxi to take him to the British Consulate. There he was warmly greeted by the female Consul General, Kathryne Cummings CMG. He was pleasantly surprised to meet such an attractive lady, considering she was in her early forties. Offering him coffee and taking the time to chat, she then proceeded to show him to his office. After a few weeks and getting to know the ropes of the job, the Consulate found him a pleasant apartment on the Admiralty Embankment,

SQUADRON LEADER ROY HANDLEY AND DENISE LUNT

facing the river Neva within walking distance of the British Consulate.

During off duty hours, Guy took advantage of exploring the picturesque city as well as acting like a tourist by taking a trip on the river Neva. Having taken the time to do a little research about the history on St Petersburg, which Guy would describe to his family and myself when he returned home. He found it a beautiful city, one that was full of history and tinged with a great deal of sadness.

St Petersburg was founded in 1703 by Peter the Great. The city's beginnings were very humble with a fortress being built close to the mouth of the river Neva. Peter the Great, so history tells us. Loved this part of Russia, and therefore built not only a port, but an entire city with beautiful palaces employing between 20, 000 to 40, 000 people in its construction. He called it "paradise" but for many it became their cemetery.

Catherine the Great, also loved St Petersburg. During her reign the population grew to 160,000. She had more palaces built in the city and spread out to the suburbs. Catherine not only loved the finest clothes to wear, they say her wardrobes were immense, and she was both very kind and generous, giving a huge number of beautiful gowns away to her servants. She also became a huge collector of art and precious object's d'arts. Her collection was so vast, that most of it, later ended up in the Hermitage Museum.

St Petersburg enjoyed the status as the Russian capital for over 200 years. Lenin moved the capital back to Moscow when the Bolsheviks came into power after they murdered the Czar and his family. They also renamed St Petersburg, calling it Leningrad, but only until after Lenin's death.

During WW2, by some miracle, Leningrad withstood a 900-day siege by the Nazis which decimated the city's population, and the infrastructure of the city itself. After the war the city was quickly rebuilt, though the treasure of the Amber Room has so far never been found.

For its 300th anniversary in 2003, the city was given a complete face lift. There are now estimated to be around 5,000,000 people living in and around the city and its islands, which are connected by 300 bridges. After the collapse of the Soviet Union, Leningrad was once again renamed St Petersburg, it is the second largest city in Russia. As he was born in St Petersburg, the current President of Russia who is of course Vladimir Putin, pays special attention to his hometown.

Guy later described winter in St Petersburg, as pretty brutal. He was more than delighted as spring arrived, and even then it still felt pretty cold. At Last summer arrived, and it was on a warm summer's night while walking along the city's beautiful embankment, Guy found it was truly an experience never to be forgotten. There would be times during the months ahead, Guy romantically told me on his return home. He often wished I was with him, in this the most romantic of cities; known as the Venice of the North.

After several months enjoying his work, an event occurred which radically changed his career.

Sadly, the Air Attaché in Beijing, was killed in a road traffic accident leaving the post vacant. The MOD knowing of Guy's performance in his career to date, together with his capability in fluent Mandarin Chinese. Now considered him as the ideal candidate to fill the vacant position in Beijing. Unfortunately, Attachés for the coveted post in Beijing, Berlin, Paris, and Washington were required to be no lower in rank than Group Captain. The only solution the MOD had, was to promote Guy to Acting Group Captain. Guy was given permission to return to England and take a week's leave. He was then required to report to the British Embassy, to take up his new post as Air Attaché in Beijing.

Looking around checking he had packed everything before zipping his case, Guy made himself one last cup of coffee, then walked over to the balcony to take a final look at the scene in front of him. His thoughts apparently quickly drifted to me, as he wondered if I still loved him or had someone closer to home entered my life. He also had to admit, he was very pleased he did not have to suffer another winter in Russia.

Boarding a British Airways aircraft, he doubted he would ever return to Russia, even though he had enjoyed the few months he had spent there. After having eaten, Guy opened the English newspaper that was offered to him by one of the cabin crew. Time seemed to have passed very quickly as the captain's voice came over the intercom informing his passengers about the weather in England, and to please fasten their seat belts as the aircraft would shortly be landing.

Guy was unusually excited to be home, he had made a momentous decision and wished to talk it over with his parents. Once having quickly gone through all the formalities of entering England that are required when returning from Russia, he collected his luggage.

THROUGH ADVERSITY TO THE STARS

Guy quickly found the hire car he had ordered to take him directly home.

As he sat in the back of the cab, Guy smiled to himself wondering what Hopkins would say to him once having related his personal news to him. As Guy stepped out of the limousine, Hopkins greeted him warmly, and instantly went to retrieve Guy's suitcases. Even though it was now quite late, both Sir Richard and Lady Rosalind had stayed up to see their beloved son. Hopkins as usual brought a plate of Guy's favourite biscuits, as well as his goodnight drink. Guy decided as he was fairly tired, he would leave his news to the following morning when everyone would feel so much more refreshed. Hugging his parents as well as kissing his mother goodnight, all three made their way to their respective rooms. On reaching Guy's bedroom door, Lady Rosalind before wishing him goodnight, once again told her precious son how much she loved him and was so pleased he was home safe and sound.

As Guy stepped into his room, whether it was because he was very tired, once again he found himself questioning his emotions. He knew that before he mentioned anything to his parents, he must be one hundred percent sure of his feelings knowing his decision would affect not only the rest of his life, but that of the people he loved.

The following morning still looking tired and drawn, Guy quickly showered and dressed, then made himself a cup of coffee. Walking over to his bedroom window, he drew back the heavy chintz curtains and stood looking out onto the beautiful manicured lawn and flower beds below, and then beyond to the parklands that belonged to Davenport Hall. By the time Guy turned around to go down for breakfast, he had allowed his coffee to go cold. Just as he was about to replace his cup back onto the saucer, Hopkins knocked and gently opened the bedroom door.

"Good morning, Sir, enjoyed being back in your own bed?" Hopkins asked with a smile.

"Good morning to you, Hopkins," Guy replied, further informing him, "Yes and No, Hopkins." Then out of the blue Guy asked.

"Hopkins, would you be offended if I asked you a personal question?" Hopkins gave a small laugh, replied, "Depends Sir what it is you wish to know, though as far as I know, I do not have any unwanted children." Both men smiled broadly and found themselves chuckling.

"No, not about unwanted children, but you are getting warm,." Guy replied still smiling, he then asked, "Hopkins, did you ever consider settling down, or did the right lady never come along?"

Hopkins looked at Guy, a very wide smile gradually crossed his face before he answered, " I had lots of ladies I could have married, but at the end of the day Sir, I decided I preferred working for your father. When your parents married and then you came along, I just somehow felt content. Your family became mine, and I have no regrets. I hope you do not mind me saying so Sir, Lady Annabelle seems perfect." With that Hopkins turned away leaving Guy astounded, subconsciously asking himself, how the hell did Hopkins know he was thinking about Annabelle.

Guy made his way downstairs to the small inviting morning room which was adjacent to the large kitchen that had been modernised and brought up to date, making it into a rather ultra-modern kitchen, though still maintaining its old fashioned structure. On clear dry days, the entire morning room would be flooded with natural welcoming sunlight.

As Guy entered, Sir Richard and Lady Rosalind greeted their beloved son, so happy he was once again able to join them. Guy helped himself from the various dishes that were laid out on the overly large sideboard, all of which he loved. Sitting himself between his parents, he went on to answer a great number of questions they delighted in asking and listening to all he had to say about his trip to Russia. Once breakfast was over and before everyone left the table, Guy asked his parents if they had time to have a serious talk with him.

Chapter Eight

Engagement

"Darling, your father and I always have time to talk to you." Lady Rosalind replied, she then asked, "Guy, is there something wrong you wish us to know about in regard to your health?" Lady Rosalind now questioned anxiously.

"No mummy, I am perfectly well, thank you." Guy replied.

Sir Richard then looked at his son and in a grave voice asked, "Guy do not pretend with me. You are my only son, and if something is wrong, I insist you tell us right now?"

Guy smiled, his father had always been loving towards him, and very rarely had reason to be firm. Now he was seeing a tiny glimpse of how strict his father could well have been had the need to be ever occurred. Immediately Guy went to answer him, but before he could, his father continued.

"Guy if you are sure, you are completely well, then has something happened in regard to your work?" Again, Guy smiled, and answered his father, his voice taking on a lighter tone, "No Sir, I am well, work is excellent, but thank you for asking.

Sir Richard always having had a placid nature where his beloved son was concerned, which did not necessary always apply in respect to others. With Guy being his only child, he worried more about him than he would ever admit to anyone, especially in regard to the well-being of his precious son. Once again Sir Richard asked, only this time with a sharp tone in his voice, "Then if you are well, and work is going well, what the hell is bothering you?"

Guy was just about to help himself to another cup of coffee when Sir Richard immediately said, "Never mind the damn coffee Guy, just tell your mother and I what is on your mind."

Guy looked from one to the other, smiled, then calmly said, "I am considering asking Annabelle to marry me. I wanted your thoughts, or I should say, actually you're blessing."

For a few moments the silence in the room was deafening, enabling a person to hear a pin drop. Lady Rosalind was the first to speak, she rose from her chair and went over to give her precious son a kiss on his cheek, then told him her thoughts while doing so, "My darling boy, I could not be happier for you both. Annabelle is a wonderful girl; you could not have chosen better."

Before she had time to say another word, Sir Richard rose from his chair and offered his congratulations and thoughts, shaking his sons hand at the same time. "Your mother is quite right Guy; I will be very proud to have Annabelle as my daughter in law. I must admit, your mother and I have noticed for some time that you were quite smitten with her. Have you spoken to her family?"

Guy then answered sounding very surprised, "Have you really, I had no idea you were aware of my feelings for Annabelle." He then answered his father's questions. "No Sir, not yet. I wanted to hear how you felt first."

Sir Richard then asked. "Guy before you do, I want you to be absolutely sure that you are in love with Annabelle. Not just the fact we are very old friends of the family, plus the fact she naturally comes from the perfect background for you. You know full well her family and ours, have been friends for generations, and as much as I love you Guy. I would hate to see you hurt her."

Guy saw the serious look on his father's face. He knew Sir Richard would never interfere in his life; he also understood the wisdom of his words. Guy smiled at his father before saying, "I must admit; I was not sure I wanted to settle down with anyone as my career in the RAF means everything to me. Over the last number of months in St Petersburg, maybe due to the fact I was on my own and I had quite a lot of time to think. I found myself frequently thinking more and more about Annabelle. Naturally there were plenty of very beautiful women to tempt me, yet strangely not one ever did."

Guy stopped and turned to look out of the window onto the garden he loved, now obviously in deep thought as he remained silent for a few minutes.

His parents were wise enough not to interrupt him, giving him the time he needed, until at last he turned around to face them and then told them how he felt. With his voice now filled with emotion, something which his parents were not expecting, Guy stated. "I think deep down I have always loved Annabelle. I would walk along the Neva when I had the chance to do so, and found myself constantly thinking of her wishing she was at my side. More than just thinking about her as a friend. Towards the end of my visit, I knew I wanted to share my life with her."

Sir Richard was not a man anyone could fool, and certainly not by his beloved son. As both he and Guy looked at each other, Sir Richard nodded, smiled deeply and proceeded to say, "I am so happy for you. Not just happy, but deeply proud of you Guy in everything you do. I am sure Annabelle and yourself will be very happy as long as you love each other. Now you must of course go and ask her father for her hand in marriage. I am more than sure you will have his and Arianne's blessing." Sir Richard then asked before Guy had a chance to say a word. "Tell me, have you bought a ring as yet? Maybe you would like Annabelle to have one of our family rings, or had you something more modern in mind?"

Guy thanked his father, and told him he had intended to go to Gerrard's to buy a certain type of ring. One he had particularly liked when he bought Annabelle her earrings. Should it have been sold, then maybe they would have something similar or be able to re-order the one he liked. Guy then asked his father, when did he feel would be the right time to go and see Sir John and Lady Arianna. Sir Richard with a chuckle answered, "There is no time like the present my boy, go and phone and see if they are at home and will receive you."

Guy thanked his father, and was about to walk to the door. Just as he was about to leave the morning room, his mother once again gave him a hug and kissed him on the cheek, and in a very small voice full of emotion, she told him how much she loved him. Guy smiled at her and said, "I hope, I will not be long. Once I have spoken to Sir John, I will come and tell you both instantly what he had to say." Guy gave a final smile and walked from the room leaving his mother with the need to wipe away a tiny tear.

Guy was shown into the small cosy though elegant sitting room, which Sir John and Lady Arianna used during the day, especially when only the family were at home. Sir John welcomed his guest by saying, "Hello Guy, how very nice to see you again, please do come and join us." Guy politely returned the greeting and gave Lady Arianna a kiss on the cheek, and proceeded to take a seat in one of the comfortable armchairs. Sir John then asked Guy if he would care for a coffee or perhaps something a little stronger.

"No Sir, but thank you. I do not require anything for the moment," Guy replied, then waited for Sir John to ask him why he wished to have a word with him; which in fact was Sir Johns next words.

"First let me say, it is very good to see you home. We are all so pleased you have returned safe and sound, I am sure your parents are thoroughly delighted. Well now young man, may I ask as to why you wished to speak to Arianna and myself. Must be something important?" Before Guy could answer, Sir John continued now wearing a frown across his forehead, before he asked in a serious tone of voice, "Your parents are both keeping well I hope, as they never mentioned anything to me when we last spoke?"

"Yes Sir, my parents are both in good health." Guy replied, leaving Sir John to give a sigh of relief before he continued.

"Excellent Guy, Arianna and I are very pleased to hear that. Then may I ask dear boy just what does bring you here?"

Guy stood up, which surprised both Sir John and Lady Arianna, and in a quite calm voice he gave his answer. "Sir John, Lady Arianna. I have come to ask for your permission and blessing, in allowing me to marry Annabelle."

Guy could feel his heart pounding, as he waited for what seemed an eternity for Sir John to answer him. Sir John half closed his eyes, and then in a grave tone of voice, asked, "Have you already asked Annabelle to marry you?"

"No Sir, not yet. I have though spoken to my parents, and now to you. I did not want Annabelle to be upset in case you do not approve of me."

With that answer, Sir John beamed and surprised Guy with his reply. "Many congratulations my boy. We could not wish for a better husband for our beloved daughter. Annabelle as you know means the world to us, and we could not find a better son in law. I know you will take great care of our precious daughter and continue to make all of us very proud of you."

Sir John walked over to where Guy stood and shook his hand. Lady Arianna followed by also walking over and proceeded to give Guy a hug, going on to gently kiss him on both cheeks. Something she had always done each Birthday and Christmas since Guy had been just a small boy, but this time it was so different.

"Thank you both very much, Guy replied, then went on to say, "I love Annabelle with all of my being, and promise I will indeed do my utmost to ensure she has as a wonderful life with me, just as she has had with you. Now I must go and make arrangements at our favourite restaurant for Saturday evening, as I would like to propose to her there."

As Guy reached the door he stopped for a few moments, turned and quickly added, "I know it is rather unusual, but as Annabelle and I are both only children, I was actually wondering if you would care to join us for dinner; that is after I have proposed." Feeling a little embarrassed Guy chuckled, Sir John and Lady Arianna followed suit chuckling with delight. Guy then suggested, "Would around 8-30 sound reasonable to you? I will inform my parents as soon as I return home, as I dare say they would love for all of us to be together."

Sir John could not have been wearing a bigger smile had someone paid him to do so. He jovially thanked Guy for this most welcomed of invitations, informing him he regarded it as the very best invitation of the year.

As Guy drove back to Davenport Hall, he could not help but smile at Sir John's warm wishes towards him. Even though he had known Sir John all his life, he knew Sir John, like his father, did not tolerate fools gladly or rarely showed personal emotions. Where his beloved daughter was concerned, that was a whole different ball game. He would not be surprised if Sir John were to kill someone, while protecting her from harm.

Arriving home, Guy related to his parents all that had been said, and how happy Sir John and Lady Arianne were. He also told his parents of his instant decision to ask Sir John and Lady Arianne if they would like to join us all for dinner, but only after he had of course proposed to Annabelle. Lady Rosalind looked at her beloved son and said, "Oh, my darling Guy, how wonderful. Your father and I would be thrilled to join Annabelle and yourself as well as her parents, on this most very special occasion. Thank you darling, that is so very kind as well as very thoughtful of you." With that she walked up to Guy, and as always hugged her precious son. Sir Richard then added his thoughts to that of his wife, and told Guy he felt exactly the same as Sir John.

Guy decided he would go up to London the following day. First to buy an engagement ring, then to go over to Topogigios and make his wishes known to Luigi and Maria.

Stepping into Gerrard's, Guy was met with all the politeness he expected from such a well-known establishment. What he did not know and would never be revealed to him; was that his father had phoned them earlier.

Having been an old customer for many years, Sir Richard had ensured that no matter which ring Guy should choose, Gerrard's would agree to sell it at the price Guy stated he had considered paying, Sir Richard would then pay the difference. Guy being his only child, and one he loved dearly as well as being incredibly proud of, Sir Richard intended to try to give his precious son as much as he could while he was still alive; particularly in this case and with all the discretion required.

After choosing a magnificent pear-shaped diamond ring set in platinum. Guy was surprised how reasonable the price appeared to be, and politely asked the assistant to just check the cost he had quoted was correct. The assistant smiled, and then excused himself. Quickly returning wearing the same smile he previously had worn, the assistant informed Guy the price indeed was correct.

"Excellent, thank you. I must admit, I am thrilled at the price," Guy replied. He then happily told the assistant he would take it.

Placing the ring carefully onto the white satin lining, which covered the interior of a small blue leather box. The assistant then placed the box into an elegant gift bag that matched and proceeded to hand it to Guy. Taking the bag, Guy presented his bank card while thinking to himself how lucky, and how very pleased he was that he had managed to purchase such a beautiful ring at such a bargain price.

After leaving the jewellery store, Guy drove over to Topogigios. On entering the restaurant, Guy observed there were already a number of people enjoying lunch. Luigi Fattorini greeted Guy and admitted he was surprised to see him at that time of day. Guy gave him a huge smile, then proceeded to ask, "Luigi, if Maria and yourself are free to talk for just a few moments, would you kindly join me, as I have something I wish to discuss with you both."

Luigi Fattorini had known Guy for many years, yet not once had he been requested by him to sit and talk. Instantly his first thought being, was Guy in some kind of trouble? With lines now appearing on his forehead, he answered Guy, telling him in his best English, "Yes, Senor Davenport. Maria is always free to talk with you, as I am also." He then asked, "You are well, yes? Perhaps you have problems you wish to talk about, as I am happy to help if I can?"

Guy burst out laughing and then apologised for doing so, going on to say, "No Luigi, I am very well, and do not have any untoward problems, but thank you so much for your concern. Now please if you would be so kind and ask your beautiful wife to join us."

Senor Fattorini relieved at Guys reply, with the lines on his forehead disappearing as quickly as they had first shown, he then showed Guy to a table and politely excused himself to fetch his wife.

Guy watched Luigi disappear into the kitchen, giving him time to imagine how they must have looked when they were both young. Even today, Luigi Fattorini though somewhat a little overweight, was still a handsome man for his age. He still had a head of dark brown, almost black hair with just a little grey now showing through, which matched that of Maria's. Like Luigi, Maria if a little overweight, was still very attractive. The first thing you noticed about her, were her enormous brown eyes and long eyelashes. Within moments Maria and Senor Fattorini entered from the kitchen and joined Guy at his table. Guy stood up to greet Maria, taking her hand and kissing it. Both happy to greet each other, Guy then asked them both to please sit down while he related to them, the reason he had come and wished to talk to them.

"Luigi, Maria, first I want to tell you that I have decided to ask Lady Annabelle Willoughby to marry me. Secondly, I wish to propose to her here in your restaurant, as it now holds a very special place in our hearts. Next, I hope that after Annabelle accepts me, our families will join us for dinner and make the evening very special,"

The look of astonishment on both Maria and Luigi Fattorini's face's, could only have been described as pure joy. Luigi Fattorini was the first to give his congratulations, quickly followed by his wife. Luigi Fattorini then said, "Senor Davenport, I promise we will make it a night to remember, you just leave everything to Maria and I. I cannot express as my English is not that wonderful, how happy and pleased both Maria and I are for you and the beautiful signorina. We wish you every happiness."

Guy sat patiently listening to all the kind sentiments Senor Fattorini and Maria had to say, until at last he was able to reply, "Thank you both for your very kind wishes; and your English Luigi is outstanding. I know we could have a big engagement party, but, as Annabelle and I being only children, I wanted to make it a very special family night. I am sure you can understand my feelings, and our parents have already stated they are greatly looking forward to joining us."

Plans were then further discussed, ready to be put in place the following Saturday evening. By the time Guy arrived home, his parents were so excited having wondered most of the afternoon, about what kind of ring their beloved son had chosen. On opening the box to show them, Guy then related to his parents.

"I have been incredibly lucky in regard to the price. I was very concerned when the assistant first informed me how much they were charging, so asked him to check the cost as I felt there had been some sort of mistake. Apparently, there had been no mistake, so immediately purchased the ring. I still feel it should have cost twice the price I paid."

After taking a quick glance at the ring and passing a comment, Sir Richard excused himself and walked from the room. He would never allow anyone to see the emotion he now unusually felt, or the fact that he had ensured Guy had been in a position to purchase any ring he wished.

After carefully popping the ring into his bedroom safe, Guy phoned to ask, would I join him for dinner at our favourite restaurant on the Saturday evening. He arranged to pick me up a little earlier than normal, and in a serious voice which I was not normally used to, he said, "Annabelle, I want to talk to you about something very important that will go on to change my life."

I was a little taken aback at his words, even somewhat unnerved. As I looked out onto the rose garden which I loved, my thoughts began to become uneasy. Maybe Guy no longer loved me and had found someone else he preferred, or maybe he is going overseas once again, and wished to simply break up in case he meets another woman.

With a heavy heart I prepared for the worse, as best as I could. The next couple of days seemed long and never ending. Having loved Guy all of my life, I dreaded to think what my life without him would be like.

On the Saturday evening as I waited for him to arrive, normally being a very calm controlled person, I now unusually felt totally on edge. I wished whatever Guy needed to tell me; he would do so quickly. Now more than ever, I wished we were not going to our favourite restaurant with all the happy memories it held, and then for Guy to go ahead and give me bad news.

Not having slept well, I felt emotionally tired and drained. I prayed once Guy gave me the bad news, I would be strong enough not to embarrass myself and cry in front of him and just able to say goodbye graciously, and walk away still friends.

Guy arrived on time feeling strangely nervous, immediately I could sense there was something amiss. Not just amiss, in fact I felt something was very seriously wrong was indeed bothering him. I turned and calmly asked him, even though that was far from how I was really feeling.

"Guy obviously as you have already mentioned, I know there is something important you wish to tell me, and I feel it could be serious."

Guy seeing the look on my face and hearing my tone of voice, smiled broadly, and replied, "No Annabelle there is nothing wrong, but I do have something very important I want to say to you, in fact something rather wonderful."

Guy then changed his mind and stated, "No, actually that is not quite right. I actually want to ask you a question, but I want to wait until we reach Topogigios."

Guy drove the rest of the way in silence which made me feel even more anxious. At last we arrived at the restaurant and to the surprise of both of us, the whole place was decked out in flowers. Senor Fattorini greeted us as normal, not wishing to give the game away. Once having been shown to a table and the menu quickly brought over, Guy was then able to tell me what he wished for me to know. Lifting my hand to kiss it, but before he did so, Guy said, "Annabelle I am going to be brutally honest with you. You know I love my life in the RAF, you also know it is fraught with danger and I never know where I will be sent or even if I will be killed."

I thought this is where Guy is about to say goodbye, at least I had prepared myself mentally for this moment. Strangely, I found hearing those words, even though they were very true; they still hurt deeply. As I sat stony faced my heart beating so hard, I thought it would burst. Still not having replied, Guy then continued, "Annabelle, I love you deeply. I am praying even under the circumstances of my job; you will honour me by becoming my wife."

Pulling the beautifully wrapped box out of his jacket, Guy went on to kiss my hand and opened the box. Still I continued to sit without moving a muscle, stunned at what Guy had just asked. His question being a million miles from any of the thoughts he may have said to me. Taking the ring carefully out of its box, he slipped it onto my engagement finger. My thoughts and emotions left me to still not say a word, it was left to Guy to ask, "Please Annabelle, say you will marry me? I could not imagine my life without you at my side."

At long last, I managed to collect my thoughts and gave Guy the answer he longed to hear. Telling him in a soft gentle voice how in return, I loved him very much, and how incredibly beautiful I thought the engagement ring was. Immediately, Guy stood up and came over to my side. Pulling me into his arms, finding my willing lips, he began to kiss me passionately, not bothering about the other guests in the restaurant. To our surprise everyone started to clap, at that same very moment, our parents entered the restaurant to join us.

Senor Fattorini and Maria came over to the table, bringing with them a present of six of the finest bottles of Italian champagne money could buy. Maria had ensured our evening meal had been cooked to perfection, allowing everyone happy memories of a wonderful evening.

Chapter Nine

China

Within two days, Guy and I drove to Heathrow airport. Before he disappeared into the departure lounge, he asked, "Annabelle, are you sure you still want to wait for me to return home and marry you."

"Yes, my darling I am definitely sure, now kiss me before you go and have a safe journey. I will always love you Guy Davenport."

With that Guy pulled me into his arms and kissed me passionately the way I loved. He then gently kissed my ear as he pulled himself away to open the door, saying as he did so, "I love you Annabelle with all my heart."

With that he stepped out of the car, turned and walked quickly away with neither Guy or I, having any idea when we would be together again.

After boarding a British Airways Boeing 747, taking his seat in business class, Guy settled himself down. Looking out of the window, already he felt a pang of homesickness as well as a tinge of excitement, wondering what this new adventure would bring.

After a short delay, the aircraft left London in the late afternoon. As the weather was clear, it gave the passengers a perfect view of Windsor Castle. A Castle that had stood for 1,000 years, and which represented everything that was England. Solid and beautiful.

Guy had a number of books, as well as newspapers to occupy him during the long flight ahead. Enjoying the evening meal that was on offer, also breakfast that was later served, along with managing to consume a number of drinks as and when he wished. After a long ten hour flight, his aircraft arrived at Beijing Airport early the following morning.

With Diplomatic Immunity and a brand-new diplomatic passport, Guy moved effortlessly through immigration. Entering the arrivals area, Guy was met by a very polite Chinese driver from the British Embassy. He was then driven to the magnificent five-star Mandarin Oriental Wangfujing Hotel. After signing in, the hotel receptionist asked for his passport. When all the usual formalities had been completed, Guy was escorted to a small suite of rooms. Feeling hungry he decided to take an early lunch within the hotel, but first needed to unpack his suitcase.

Once lunch was over, Guy returned to his suite, showered, and decided to take a nap. Not something he was used to, or would normally ever do in the afternoon. Having just flown halfway across the world, he felt at liberty this time to make an exception. After a couple of hours and feeling more refreshed, he dressed and decided to have an early dinner, Guy though again decided to stay within the hotel. Even though he had managed to enjoy a couple of hours of deep refreshing sleep, having endured sitting in one position during what is regarded as a tiresome journey as well as having flown through several time zones, Guy surprisingly found he was still very tired and obviously suffering from jet lag. Therefore, straight after dinner, Guy once again returned to his suite.

Making himself a last cup of coffee, and being a man of habit, he took his coffee cup over to the balcony. On opening the balcony doors, he was treated to a superb view just as the sun was setting over the Forbidden City. Instantly, he thought of Annabelle and promised himself, one day he would bring her here enabling her to enjoy this amazing sight with him.

The following morning having had an undisturbed night and feeling completely refreshed, Guy quickly showered and practically ran down to breakfast now feeling very hungry. Straight after having enjoyed an enormous breakfast, Guy went to find the driver who would take him to the Embassy.

The driver who had met him at the airport, once again came to pick him up, and drove him directly to the British Embassy, which was situated in the Chaoyang District of Beijing. On arriving at the Embassy, Guy was met in the foyer by John Truscott who was the First Secretary.

The British Embassy is the largest in Asia, and occupied the space of two large houses, set in a walled garden. After a tour of the facilities Guy was then taken and introduced to His Excellency Sir Hugh Maitland-Browne KCMG, the British Ambassador, who warmly welcomed him. After having enjoyed a light lunch with the Ambassador, the two men took the opportunity to discuss many things, including Guy's future responsibilities as the Embassy's Air Attaché.

Two weeks after his arrival in China, the Embassy Facilities Manager, handed Guy the keys to a fully furnished luxury apartment. The apartment chosen, was in a newly built high rise building within walking distance to the Embassy. As the apartment was on the 23rd floor, it allowed a person to have a superb view of the city. Unfortunately for Guy, there were only a few "Blue Sky Days in Beijing."

The term was used to describe the days when the city was not enveloped in its notorious smog. The heavy smog often smothering Beijing, with visibility down to less than a hundred metres at ground level, with the tops of the tower blocks vanishing into the sky. Air pollution in the capital, often reached levels considered hazardous to human health by the World Health Organisation. (WHO.)

The WHO had listed China as one of the sixteen cities in the world, with unacceptable levels of air pollution. Emissions from the ever-increasing number of vehicles and the effluence from coal burning factories around Beijing, were the culprit's causing smog. The yellow grey smog was responsible for causing respiratory diseases and an increase in the high mortality rate.

The British Embassy advised its staff to wear surgical masks at all times when outdoors. On his journey to the Embassy each day, Guy never ceased to marvel at the transformation of the new Beijing. The Chinese Government had now adopted a new policy of Capitalist–Communism. The evidence of this policy, was the profusion of new high-rise buildings, including western style department stores, along with a great many fast-food outlets. This policy saw the emergence of affluent classes of Chinese which was demonstrated by numerous automobiles, including prestigious Rolls Royce and Mercedes vehicles on the streets of the capital.

Historically, the China Aviation Company, due to a lack of knowhow and production facilities, was unable to manufacture modern military aircraft. China solved the problem, by purchasing aircraft for the People's Liberation Army Air Force (PLAAF) from Russia.

The Mikoyan (MIG) Company, and the Sukhoi Company, provided fighters and fighter bombers for the PLAAF. As an Air Attaché, Guy was permitted to visit PLAAF bases in the Central Military Command. Being a jet fighter pilot himself, Guy enjoyed visiting fighter bases.

Two PLAAF bases were relatively close to the capital. The 7th Fighter Division at Zhangijakou, was equipped with the Chengdu J7 "Fishcan" aircraft, and the Shenyang J11 "Flanker" aircraft. The 24th Fighter Division at Hualien, flew the Shenyang J8 "Finback" aircraft. Both units were easily reached by road from Beijing. For bases further afield, Guy was allowed to travel by Ilyushin 76 aircraft provided by the 34th Transport Aviation Division which was based at the Beijing Nanjuan Airport.

One visit Guy took advantage of seeing, was at the Peoples Liberation Army Air Force base "Z26" located at Harbin, the capitol of Heilongjiang Provence. Harbin was the largest city in the Japanese puppet state of Manchukuo. Japan having invaded China in the 1930's gaining control of north-eastern China.

When the second Sino-Japan War flared again in 1937, there was a continuing conflict with Japan attempting to take control of the whole Chinese mainland. That war continued until the end of WW2 in 1945 when Japan surrendered to China.

Guy's visit to the notorious ex Japanese Unit 731, situated in Ping fang 15 miles from Harbin. Unit 731, also known as the Kamo Detachment, which had been a covert biological and chemical warfare research unit of the Japanese Army. The unit was responsible for some of the most notorious war crimes by the Japanese armed forces.

Experiments on humans included disease injections, controlled dehydration and amputation. Thousands of men, women and children were subjected to vivisection, often performed without anaesthesia; even after inflicting them with various diseases. The unit were also involved in research and development of epidemic-creating weapons. Plague-infested fleas, bred in laboratories, were then spread by low-flying aircraft over the coastal cities of Ningbo and Changde. These operations which included the release of bubonic plague, Cholera, and anthrax plagues, are estimated to have killed half a million civilians. The site of Unit 731, is now a museum. Before returning Harbin, Guy left a suitable message in the visitors' book.

Once having established a close rapport with PLAAF Senior Officers. Recognising him as a fellow pilot, they invited him to spend time with them in their Officers' Mess, often enjoying a drink of the local fiery rice wine. Establishing this important excellent rapport, or as the Chinese would say, "Oiling the wheels." Guy continued to enjoy the traditional Chinese hospitality on offer during his visits. With the many Diplomatic missions in the Capital.

As an Air Attaché, Guy was required to attend an interminable round of Embassy receptions and Government functions. Due to the fact the Chinese loved gargantuan multi course banquets, Guy eventually managed to cope with exotic dishes such as green bear bile, which they also use for medicinal purposes. Along with the bear bile, they drank turtle's blood. However, he drew the line at fried bird's feet and scorpions on rice. Guests were also required to listen to numerous boring speeches, each one toasted with the fiery rice wine. Guy became adept at the use of chop sticks and his fluency in Mandarin Chinese increased rapidly.

Later in the year rumours surfaced in diplomatic circles, revealing that the Chinese Aviation Company had produced a new stealth bomber. This was known as the Xinjiang H20. Previously to that, PLAAF had relied on modified Tupolev passenger aircraft as their bombers. Eventually, the Chinese Government, announced that the new Xinjiang H20, (translated into English means) Fire Dragon stealth bomber, would be unveiled at the China International Air Show. The show to be held at the Zuhai Aviation Centre located at Guangzhou near the Hong Kong border. Keen to obtain a view of the new aircraft, and information about it. Guy made arrangements to travel to Guangzhou, flying by Air China.

On his arrival and having previously made a reservation into the 4-star Marriott Hotel Tianhe, Guy booked in after having been requested to hand over his passport. Once the receptionist was satisfied with his documents, he was then shown to his small suite. The following morning immediately after breakfast, Guy requested the receptionist to call a taxi. He informed the receptionist he wished to go directly to the International Air Show at the Zuhai Aviation Centre. This centre was the only location endorsed by the Chinese government for International Air Shows.

Guy joined the assembled Diplomats and Press along with a very large crowd, all waiting eagerly for the bat wing shaped H20 aircraft to arrive. However, although the aircraft arrived on time, everyone was to be deeply disappointed. The aircraft they had all hoped to see, did not land. Instead, it merely performed a number of low-level passes across the airfield.

The following morning, feeling somewhat frustrated at not having any important information about the H20, Guy decided to return to Beijing. On reaching Beijing, his mood improved considerably on learning that his rank had been confirmed as Group Captain.

During the following week, the Chinese Government released a statement in which it was claimed. The new stealth bomber armed with Cruise Missiles, was able to reach and penetrate the USA seaboard, without the need it seemed for in-flight refuelling. The US Central Intelligence Agency (CIA) was deeply concerned about the Chinese claim, but more concerned about the fact that their own stealth bomber, the Grumman Northrop B2 was in production, but would not be ready to enter USAF service until 2025.

The UK Ministry of Defence on its part, was concerned that the Chinese, now having a stealth bomber meant that the balance of military aviation air power in the world; would be changed. Western concern increased when India announced its intention to purchase the H20 aircraft. She intended to replace the Indian Air Force's ageing Jaguar fighter bomber, with the Chinese stealth bomber. The Chinese Government readily agreed to allow the purchase of this aircraft. They decided that the new H20 aircraft, would carry out a sales tour of India's Air Force Bases.

The CIA's reaction at this news was heightened, causing it further concern at this new development. The Agency's solution was to convene a high-level meeting in London. Participants included, the USA Department of Defence, the UK Ministry of Defence, and the Foreign and Commonwealth Office. The unanimous decision was to convene a meeting at Lancaster House the following week. With personnel from the United States Department of Defence, and the Central Intelligence Agency.

On their arrival in England, having flown directly into RAF Northolt in an aircraft belonging to the USAF and having Diplomatic Immunity, they were met and driven immediately to the American Embassy. The following day, meetings commenced as arranged at Lancaster House. After several days of discussion, a final solution was agreed upon. The agreement being that Special Agent Duff Dawson, and Group Captain Guy Davenport should travel incognito to India. Their mission was to observe and hopefully obtain fuller information about the new Chinese stealth bomber.

Guy having been made aware of the decision at the London meeting, which would require him to first visit the Central Agency's HQ, in the USA. He flew with Northwest Airlines across the Pacific from Shanghai to San Francisco. From there he boarded a United Airlines flight to Dulles-Washington airport. Passing rapidly through the diplomatic channel, he was met by a CIA driver, who then drove him to Langley in Fairfax County to CIA HQ. The building being located in the George Bush Intelligence Centre.

Guy was made welcome and shown to a room for a meeting which had been arranged. There plans were discussed for a visit to India with the CIA Deputy Director, Chuck Tannenbaum, and Special Agent Duff Dawson. Arrangements had been made for Guy to stay overnight in the Sandman Signature Hotel.

The following morning after having an early breakfast, Duff met Guy in the hotel foyer, both men were then driven to Dulles-Washington airport to catch a British Airways flight to London.

Once having arrived in England, a CIA car drove them to the hotel that had been booked for them. The Hotel in question was the Edwardian Radisson airport hotel to await further orders. This gave Guy the time to phone his parents and Annabelle.

Recent intelligence obtained by the CIA, indicated that the Chinese aircraft would commence its sale's tour within the next seven days in India. Once receiving this information, Duff and Guy were given immediate orders to leave for India once arrangements had been made. They flew out the following morning, departing from Heathrow at 0800 hrs with Air India. They arrived at New Delhi Indira Ghandi Intentional Airport at 2000 hrs the same evening.

Arriving at their destination, and after having gone through the normal procedures that tourists must comply with; something which had become unfamiliar to Guy. Leaving the airport they took a taxi to the Oberoi Towers Hotel, some sixteen kilometres drive to the centre of New Delhi.

After booking in, Guy and Duff were then shown to their respective rooms. On entering his room, Guy could not help but notice how palatial it was as befitting an international five-star hotel. The unique carved dark wooden wall panels, providing a superb contrast to the contemporary ultra-modern furniture. There were several exquisite floral displays, which had been carefully arranged in tall silver embossed vases, all tastefully placed around the room. Arranged against one of the walls, stood a heavily carved antique wooden table. On the highly polished surface of the table, a huge copper bowl had been placed, containing an enormous selection of fresh fruit. Discreetly hidden in a large cabinet, stood a drinks refrigerator. Matching the cabinet, were large floor to ceiling wardrobes, providing plenty of space for anyone travelling with a great number of suitcases. Ceiling fans and a modern air conditioning system maintained the room at a comfortable temperature.

Guy noticed the windows were double glazed, obviously in an attempt to keep out the continual noise of the traffic. The windows were dressed with both curtains and blinds, all matching the silver and white silk counterpane of his bed. The highly polished wooden floors throughout his room, were covered with several expensive and very beautiful designer Jaipur rugs. The thought struck him, that maybe he would buy one for Annabelle, as he was sure she would enjoy owning one.

After a long journey and slightly jet lagged, the two men decided to order room service, and eat in Guy's room, rather than visit one of the hotel's many restaurants. Both men agreed they needed to shower and have a change of clothes. Once Duff eventually joined him, Guy proceeded to telephone for room service. Almost immediately there was a gentle knock on the door. On opening the door, Guy was greeted by a tall turbaned waiter, resplendent in his a red and gold hotel uniform. Greeting Guy most politely, the waiter then requested permission from Guy to allow him to wheel the dinner trolley carrying their evening meal into the room.

After enjoying what Duff described as an excellent meal, along with a few drinks, the waiter returned to remove the trolley. Just as he was leaving the room, he politely wished both men goodnight. Duff decided he too would call it a day and followed the waiter out of the room, stating before he left, "I will join you Guy at 0900 hours in the morning for breakfast, if that is OK with you."

Having enjoyed an excellent breakfast, leaving both men a little fuller than they had anticipated, they continued to discuss what lay ahead while enjoying their coffee. During his short visit to the United States, Guy had been informed of the plan which involved India. It was during that meeting, Guy had remembered a fellow Indian student and friend by the name of Samir Mukarjee who he had met while at the RAF College, Cranwell. Guy was also aware that Samir Mukarjee, had now become a Squadron Leader in the Plans and Programmes Division at the Indian Air Force's Head Quarters in New Delhi itself. Knowing this fact, Guy and Duff agreed that Squadron Leader Samir Mukarjee, could well be of assistance to them. They decided to invite Samir to dinner, in the hope he would be able to provide them with some information, which they required about the stealth bomber. Once having agreed to this plan, Guy accordingly picked up the phone, in the hope it would be possible to speak to Samir directly, and if not; to then try and find out when he would be available.

As luck would have it, Samir was in his office and delighted to hear his old friend's voice. After a prolonged chat, Guy eventually invited Samir to dinner should he be free for the following evening. Guy explained he was of course with his friend. To protect Duff's CIA identity, Guy though hating to do so, informed Samir that Duff was a fellow diplomat at the Embassy in Beijing. Later he thought to himself, what a dirty business spying was. Samir informed Guy he was delighted to have the opportunity to meet both Guy, and his friend after such a long absence and willingly accepted Guy's invitation. After replacing the receiver, Guy made the necessary reservations for dinner in the hotel's finest restaurant. Once having completed that task, the two men then decided they would make full use of the hotel's spa and indoor swimming pool, enabling them to relax for the rest of the day.

At precisely 7-30pm, Samir's taxi pulled up to the hotel. Paying the driver and dismissing him. Samir walked into the hotel's elegant foyer, there to be greeted by Guy and Duff. After introductions had been made, the men found their way into the plush cocktail bar and found a quiet corner with comfortable armchairs. Guy called over one of the many waiters and ordered pre-dinner drinks. Having enjoyed an hour chatting, the men slowly made their way to the restaurant. Samir was delighted to guide them through the intricacies of an Indian menu which produced a superb meal; enhanced by a magnificent couple of bottles of red wine.

A few of hours later, the trio retired to one of the hotel's luxurious lounges and ordered coffee. Possibly due to his consumption of red wine, Samir was unexpectedly voluble. One could say; even to the extent of being overly keen to discuss the Indian Governments' potential purchase of the new Chinese stealth bomber. Guy and Duff were both surprised and delighted, that Samir had revealed the expected arrival time of the bomber at the Indira Gandhi International Airport.

Guy's delight increased significantly, when Samir aware of Guy's career as both a fighter pilot and currently being an Air Attaché; suggested he may enjoy a visit to an Indian Fighter Squadron at the Maharajpur IAF Base in the Western Command. The base being situated 10 Km northeast of Gwalior in the Madhya Pradesh region. Samir went on to inform the men, "Coincidently the base was due to be the first destination in the stealth bomber's sales tour."

The men continued to talk of other things, until it was time for Samir to leave. Before leaving, Samir smiled and told Guy, "I will be in touch with you in a few days' time my friend. I will let you know by telephoning to advise you when the visit will be possible."

Guy thanked him and told him, "I will indeed look forward to seeing you again." With that the men shook hands before saying their goodbyes.

After Samir had left, Guy and Duff on reflection, realised that due to Duff's connection with the CIA, it would be unwise for Duff to accompany Guy on this visit. Now being aware of the date when the stealth bomber was due to arrive in India; Guy and Duff decided to assume the tourist role by occupying their time sightseeing.

Old and New Delhi had a wonderful selection of ancient buildings for them to discover. These included the Red Fort, built in 1648, which was the seat of Mughal (Mogul Empire) until 1857. The Fort with red sandstone walls, was set in an area of two square kilometres. The grand magnificent Delhi Gate having been used by the emperor on ceremonial occasions. Another amazing site for the men to visit, was the beautiful 12th century Temple of Qutur-Minar. This temple included India's tallest minaret, which even today is a World Heritage Site. Finally, they decided to make their last visit to the 18th century Gurudwara Bangla Sahib, a most important Sikh place of worship with its famous gold dome and flagpole. To enable them to visit the various places they had chosen, the United States Embassy provided them with an Embassy driver of Indian origin, and an unmarked car.

The following morning after breakfast, Guy and Duff tossed a coin to choose which of the historic buildings they should visit first. As Duff won the bet, he decided he would actually like see the Red Fort first, which Guy found amusing. After spending a number of hours looking at all that was on offer, and feeling somewhat tired and dirty, they decided to make their way back to the hotel spending the rest of the day relaxing by the pool.

The next day straight after breakfast, the same procedure happened again, and at Duff's instigation they tossed a coin which once again Guy found highly amusing. As they had already chosen to see the Gurudwara Bangla Sahib Sikh Temple on the third day. Duff realising his mistake, also found it highly funny. The men left the hotel in high spirits and once more enjoyed another day of great interest, remarking how amazing it all was.

This second visit was not as prolonged as the previous day, so the men decided on their way back to the hotel to take in a local bazaar. Guy thought he may find a little something of great charm to give to Annabelle. Taking a slow walk through the bazaar and their presence being highly noted, they eventually came across one of the many tiny open fronted stores. The man was selling all sorts of beautifully made jewellery boxes, along with many other examples of tempting Indian jewellery. After an interesting haggle, Guy handed over several rupees for a superb silver jewellery box, which had been decorated with mother of pearl, and embossed tiny roses and leaves.

Duff looked at Guy and said, "Your lady must be very special."

Guy gave him a huge smile and answered. "My fiancée is indeed very special, and a real titled Lady."

Duffs next words took the wind out of Guy sails by replying. "Yes, I know, I do work for the CIA remember, and would not be with you if I did not know what colour of underpants you wear." Both men then laughed heartly and went to look for something Duff felt he would like to take home for his wife Judy. Once having made their purchases, the men returned to their car and drove straight back to the hotel.

Guy was the first to go down to breakfast, on entering the dining room he noticed it was still quite empty. Sitting eating his breakfast and left alone with his thoughts, he began to feel a little anxious as this was now day three and he had still not heard from Samir. Guy decided to hold his own counsel for another day or so, yet he knew that Duff could well be thinking the same thing. Finally, Duff joined him and apologised for being a little late.

"Nothing to apologise for, we are after all on holiday," Guy informed him.

At that remark Duff roared with laughter and remarked, "I love the way you Brits think." He then continued laughing for a further couple of moments before stating, "No tossing a coin today, is that OK with you?" This time it was Guy's turn to laugh. Once having finished their coffee, both men made their way to the foyer to find the driver of their car waiting for them as usual.

Today of course, they were going to visit the 18th Century Gurudwara Bangla Sahib Sikh Temple, which both men were looking forward to, particularly being able to seeing the golden dome.

Even from some distance away, they were able to see the gold of the massive dome glistening in the morning sun. The men found themselves actually enjoying this trip out, and were sadly reluctant to leave. Having clambered back into their car, their driver started making his way back to the hotel. As they entered an area of New Delhi called Dr Zakir Hussain Marg, they encountered one of the ever-present notorious traffic jams which characterised New Delhi. Both men being seated in the rear of the car, Guy found himself dozing. Duff was seated on the offside behind the driver. As the car slowed to a standstill, a motor cyclist with a pillion passenger, slowly moved alongside the stationary vehicle and stopped.

Being a CIA Special Agent, and realising the possible danger, he shouted to Guy to get down and began drawing his Glock 9mm pistol from his shoulder holster. Unfortunately, before he had drawn the pistol fully from its holster, the pillion rider pointed a semi-automatic Beretta pistol firing a volley at the car, the bullets shattering the car windows also the windscreen.

One of the bullets hit the driver's arm, causing a superficial flesh wound. Having finally managed to draw his pistol, Duff fired a couple of shots at the assailant, hitting him below his helmet in the neck and chest, causing him to fall into the road alongside the car.

The number of bullets fired from both guns, drew attention of those around them including the police and security forces who arrived rapidly on the scene. The assailant was immediately pronounced dead by one of the police officers, and a member of the security forces turned to Duff to question him. After showing his credentials, the officer then informed Duff he fortunately recognised their assailant and identified the man as a member of a terrorist group called Lashkar-e-Taiba, or as it was called "Army of the Good." The security officer, then continued to tell Duff.

"This group is the largest Islamic military organisation in Southeast Asia, and was originally funded by Osama bin Laden. The organisation is accused of a recent attack on military targets, including a military convoy and an Indian Air Force base. This current attack obviously indicates that the Army of the Good, remained opposed to the Indian Government's purchase of the Chinese stealth bomber. The police officer told the men, "Take my Advice and be constantly on the alert, as you never know when they will strike." After the removal of the dead terrorist's body and their driver had received first aid, Guy and Duff were allowed to continue to return to the hotel.

They chose to go via the American Embassy, where Duff briefed the US Ambassador on the afternoon's events and were then returned to their hotel. Arriving at the hotel Guy and Duff decided they needed a stiff drink, so headed for the cocktail bar. Sitting themselves down Guy then asked his companion, "Duff what the hell was that all about, why would they target us and who the hell are these people. I know we were told they belonged to a terrorist organisation, but again why us, after all we are not in uniform?"

Duff looked at his friend and told him, "Buddy I have no idea who the bastards were, at least we are safe for the moment, or so it seems." The men continued talking and then went into dinner. Strangely for some unknown reason, Guy appeared to have lost his appetite. After the first course, he told Duff he was calling it a night. Duff smiled and obviously realised Guy was still a little shaken and replied, "I guess flying a fighter jet in a war zone, is safer than the streets of New Delhi." Guy smiled and wished his companion good night.

The following morning Guy still felt somewhat uneasy. To his relief, his thoughts were disturbed by the bedroom phone ringing. Picking up the receiver, Guy was very pleased to at last hear Samir's voice with some very welcome news.

After a polite greeting, Samir then told Guy what he wanted to hear. "Guy, the Chinese stealth bomber is due to arrive at the Indira Gandhi International Airport the following morning." To Guy's further delight, Samir also added, "I have received permission for both you and I to visit the Maharajpur Base should you care to join me." Samir then suggested, "I think Guy, you should meet me at the Hinan Airforce Base on the outskirts of New Delhi, at 1100hrs in two days' time." Samir continued to enlighten Guy by telling him, "We can then fly north to visit No1 Indian Fighter Squadron; (The Tigers,) is that ok with you and if so; goodbye for now and see you in a couple of days?" Guy informed his friend that would be perfect, he then thanked him and made his goodbyes.

Replacing the receiver, Guy's excitement increased by several degrees, any thoughts or worries he had of yesterday's events instantly dissipated. Guy being aware from previous CIA information that he had been given, that the first stop of the sales tour for the Chinese bomber, would be at the Maharajpur Base. Immediately he went to inform Duff of his conversation with Samir. The two men then made their plans for the following morning, Duff wishing this was one trip he would love to have been included in, especially with Samir and Guy going to the Maharajpur Base.

As they stepped out of their hotel the following morning, the American Embassy ensured there was a car waiting for them. While driving to the International Airport, both men were naturally being extremely vigilant in case of a repeat attack. They were more than quite relieved when at last they arrived safely at the airport, without any further incident having taken place.

Guy was now feeling a little more relaxed, though in Duff's case that did not apply. The men made their way to a coffee shop, which was situated on the first floor of the terminal building. Sitting at a table next to a row of huge floor to ceiling glass windows, they were provided with an excellent view of a number of aircraft, as well as unused passenger ramps. At precisely midday the Xinjiang H20(Fire Dragon) aircraft landed. Fortunately, the aircraft taxied to a ramp immediately below them. Duff's reaction was.

"Cool man, that's some god dammed aircraft. At this moment in time, I sure as hell would love to be a pilot."

Guy smiled and replied, "I agree; it certainly is a very impressive aircraft."

Shortly after the stealth bomber's arrival, a second Chinese aircraft arrived. An Ilyushin 18 aircraft, from the 34th Aviation Transport Division at Nayuan Base in Beijing. Guy guessed that the second aircraft was probably carrying maintenance personnel, spares and munitions to support the stealth bomber's sales tour. Even though a large crowd had now gathered, Duff and Guy continued watching as both aircraft were being refuelled.

Two hours later, the two aircraft taxied towards the main runway and eventually took off to the north. As the aircraft disappeared, and although at this time they had not amassed a massive amount of information about the stealth bomber, they were pleased to have been afforded a close up view. Guy asked Duff if he would like another coffee, Duff replied, "No thanks buddy, I am swimming in the damn stuff, how about we return to the hotel and clean up." Guy was more than happy to go along with Duff suggestion and quickly made their way out of the airport to their waiting car.

The men decided to have dinner and retire early. The following morning during breakfast Guy apologised to Duff once again, stating he was sorry he would not be accompanying both Samir and himself to visit Maharajpur Air Base. With breakfast over, Guy asked the receptionist if she would please call me a taxi. Duff walked with Guy to the foyer door and stated, "Best of luck buddy, take care. I hope you are able to see all we need to know."

With that the men shook hands and Guy jumped into his taxi. Settling himself into his seat, he asked the taxi driver to take him to Hinan Airforce Base on the outskirts of New Delhi.

On arrival at the base, Guy paid his taxi driver and got out. Samir having notified security personnel at the Main Gate of his visit and was immediately directed to the Movements Section where Samir was waiting for him. Samir escorted Guy to a C130 Hercules aircraft from the Indian 44th Squadron which they boarded immediately for the 170-mile flight to the Maharajpur Air Base.

After a thirty-minute flight, they arrived at the IAF base, where a car was waiting in readiness for them. Once they disembarked, they were then driven directly to the Officers Mess. Stepping into the Mess, both men were given a warm welcome by the Commanding Officer No1 Squadron, Wing Commander Aadash Tagor, (his names fitted him perfectly as they meant Command and Hero.) who was also a graduate of the RAF College Cranwell. A welcome cup of coffee was ordered, as they walked into the Officers lounge. Finding a quiet spot, the men sat down and chatted until coffee was served. Once the waiter departed, Guy then explained to Aadash, "Aadash the prime reason for my visit, is to obtain information about the Chinese stealth bomber. I am however as you can appreciate extremely interested in seeing the operation of an Indian Fighter Squadron. Particularly as yours is the oldest in the Indian Air Force." Guy continued with a smile to say, "What a pity you are flying the French Dassault Aviation Mirage 2000., with them all being single seater aircraft, I will miss out on a flight." All three men found themselves laughing at that remark.

Aadash went on to reply, "I do understand; Guy do please feel free to stay with us for as long as you wish."

Guy giving Aadash a huge smile, answered, "Thank you my friend for your kind invitation, it is very much appreciated, but on this trip my time is limited."

Dressing for dinner, Guy was looking forward to spending a convivial evening meeting officers from the Indian Squadron, many of whom had also undergone training at RAF College Cranwell. As Guy entered the bar, Aadash came across and asked Guy, "Would you like to be introduced to the Pilot and Co Pilot of the Chinese stealth bomber."

Guy nearly fainted, as he could not believe his luck and naturally accepted with delight the opportunity afforded to him so unexpectedly. Aadash and Guy walked over to where the Chinese Pilot and Co-Pilot were sitting, Aadash was delighted in making the formal introductions, stating, "Guy, may I introduce you to (Zong Xiao) Lt Colonel Wu Faxian, who is the Pilot of this amazing aircraft, and to (Scao Xiao) Major Liu Yalou, the Co Pilot."

The Chinese Officers shook hands, and were very impressed with Guy's fluency in Mandarin Chinese, in fact quite amazed. As they continued making polite conversation for quite a number of hours, that amazement also applied to Aadash, as it was something he was not expecting of Guy. French, Italian even Spanish, but most definitely not Mandarin.

As the evening wore on, and after the Chinese Officers had consumed a fair amount of alcohol allowing them to feel at ease in Guy's company, they became keen to talk about the features and performance of their new aircraft.

The next morning, Guy spent a considerable time on the Squadron's Flight Line. Parked there were several

Mirage aircraft: along with the stealth bomber. Guy was more than delighted to be able to carry out a close examination of the Chinese aircraft. Overall, the aircraft's Batwing, or as often referred to as a flying wing configuration, was similar to the USAF's current B2 stealth bomber. This configuration was known to provide exceptional range and further reduce the aircraft's radar signature. Guy also noted the curve and rounded surfaces of the aircraft which were intended to deflect the radar beams. To ensure its stealth role, the engines were buried deep within the wings, and were equipped with large fans to minimise thermal activity.

To reduce optical and visibility during daylight operations, the aircraft was also painted in a special reflective paint. In addition Guy was able to observe the Chinese maintenance personnel, as they were unloading and re-loading munitions into the aircraft. Unlike most contemporary aircraft, the bomber did not have provision for the mounting of missiles under its wings.

The aircraft though did have a large internal bomb bay, which was capable of housing conventional iron bombs, laser–guided bombs, and importantly for Guy's interest, air stand-off cruise missiles. All in all, Guy felt he indeed had had a most informative day.

Unfortunately, although not allowed into the cockpit, he enjoyed watching the stealth bomber perform several take offs and landings together with refuelling operations.

At the end of a serious useful, though tiring day, Guy retired to his room and decided he would now return to New Delhi straight after breakfast the following morning.

Once Guy had said his goodbyes in particular to Aadash, he then met Samir at the Movements Section, who had previously made arrangements for one of the IAF aircraft to return them back to New Delhi. Aadash had decided he would escort the men back to the aircraft, allowing him a little extra time with Guy. As they boarded the aircraft Aadash waved goodbye to the men, calling out to Guy not to leave it too long before he visited again.

Guy could feel his excitement growing, as he had become eager to divulge to Duff, all he had seen and heard. The return flight seemed interminable, until at long last the aircraft landed. Samir being very efficient had previously arranged a car to meet them, taking Guy back to his hotel, and himself back to Air Head Quarters.

Going into breakfast, Duff was already in the dining room enjoying his first meal of the day. Wearing a large smile across his face, Duff instantly knew Guy had a great deal to tell him.

"Good morning, Buddy," Duff greeted Guy in his familiar American way. "Everything O.K. How did things go?" he asked.

Guy being English, he replied in his rather cool reserved laid-back manner. "Terribly well actually."

Duff sat back and roared with laughter and answered, "Love your style Buddy. O.K. Come and eat first, and at least tell me about your flights." Guy enjoyed his breakfast while he told Duff about Aadash and Samir.

Once they had finished eating, the men made their way into one of the small lounges and chose a quiet corner away they hoped; from being overheard. After ordering a pot of coffee, Guy informed Duff of everything that he had seen and heard during his trip away.

Several hours later, Guy and Duff had complied a report, and having agreed its contents, they then saved the document on their respective laptops. The men took a break and ate a very late lunch, during which Duff told Guy, "I need to get this information back to America ASP. I will miss you Buddy, but I really must report in with this information. Once we have eaten, I will pack my bag and be on my way. Should you ever need my help, here is my card. You know Guy, it has been great meeting you and I really am sorry to say goodbye, you are a great guy."

With that Duff finished his meal, stood up and shook Guy's hand. Guy quietly told Duff, "You have made this part of the job fun, and maybe when I visit America, you would allow me to look up both you and your lovely wife, if that is O.K."

"You bet its O.K. You will always be welcome. I am sorry, but I really must go. Goodbye my friend and good luck."

Guy returned to his room, strangely feeling a little despondent at having to say goodbye to Duff, having thoroughly enjoyed his company. Making himself a cup of coffee, taking it over to the window where a comfortable armchair and a small table had now been placed. On the table stood a tiny vase containing a rather exotic flower and an onyx telephone. Guy laid his cup and saucer on a pretty place mat that matched the décor of his room. Picking up the phone, he asked the receptionist to connect him with the hotel's travel agency, which they did within seconds. A very well-educated voice answered, belonging to a young woman who spoke excellent English. She pleasantly asked,

"How may I help you Sir."

Guy went on to explain to her what he wanted. "I require flight reservations for tomorrow from New Delhi to Kuala Lumpur with Air India, and a connecting flight from K.L. to Beijing, with Malaysian Air Services." He then quickly added, "I would prefer a morning departure."

The lady confirmed the details and informed Guy she would send the revised tickets up to his room. Finishing his coffee Guy went to pack his suitcase less the personal things he required until the next morning.

Having returned to his room after breakfast, at last completing his packing, Guy called for a porter, and following him down stairs went directly to the reception desk to check out. Placing the cases into a waiting hotel taxi, Guy gave the man a good tip before climbing in to take his seat. Once having done so, the taxi drove him back to the Indira Gandhi International Airport. After waiting in the departure lounge for a while, at last his flight was called, he then boarded a Boeing B747 "Palace in the Sky" of Air India to Kuala Lumpur. A Boeing 767 of MAS took him on the final leg of his journey back to Beijing.

Arriving during the evening and tired after his long flight, Guy took a taxi direct to his apartment, although he really would have preferred to have presented his report first to the British Ambassador.

Attending to his daily routine with meticulous attention, something he normally did to ensure he looked perfect before stepping out of his apartment, Guy walked the short distance to British Embassy. Before leaving, Guy checked he had placed all the documents he required from his room safe, putting them carefully into his briefcase. Stepping into the

Embassy and walking to his office, Guy waited impatiently until later that morning, when he was at last able to meet up with H.E. the British Ambassador, and hand over his report with some relief.

"Thank you, Guy, I will ensure the Ministry of Defence receives your report, which I will send immediately in the diplomatic bag to the UK." The Ambassador then continued, "Glad to have you back and thank you for your efforts in this matter. By the way, did you manage to meet anyone of interest, and not a woman." A remark that made both the men laugh.

Guy still smiling, replied, "Actually, Sir I did, which pleasantly surprised me. He went on to tell the Ambassador about Aadash Tagor. "The Commanding Officer of No1 IAF Squadron, is Wing Commander Aadash Tagor. He turned out to be an ex-RAF College Graduate like myself, it was indeed very fortunate I met up with him." Guy continued to relate what had taken place. The Ambassador asked Guy if he would care to join him for coffee, before going on to ask other personal questions about Guy's future. Guy was delighted to accept the Ambassador's offer and accepted the comfortable chair which the Ambassador indicated.

No sooner had the men made themselves comfortable in the two chairs situated either side of a highly polished coffee table, when a gentle knock came on the door. A member of the Embassy staff quietly opened the door, carrying in a tray laden with exquisite China including a pot of Darjeeling tea, accompanied by a plate of chocolate biscuits. He walked across to where Guy and the Ambassador were sitting, and carefully placed the tray on the coffee table, smiling as he did so. Before leaving the room, he asked if there was anything further needed. The Ambassador replied, "No thank you," and informed him, he would ring should he require anything later. The Ambassador then turned to Guy and said, "I understand Guy your tour ends just before Christmas; both the staff and I will miss you. I hope you have enjoyed your time with us here in China."

"I have indeed Sir, more than I had expected to. The tourist sites one normally visits, I found to be deeply interesting, particularly the Great Wall. I had hoped to see the Terracotta Army, but decided to save that for when I return with my wife, maybe as part of our honeymoon." The two then continued to chatter, enjoying their coffee for a further hour, until it was time Guy for to return to his office.

The months slipped away until just a couple of weeks before Christmas, when Guy unexpectedly received both interesting and personal news. The Indian Government confirmed they had purchased several Chinese stealth bombers. Apparently, it was intended that the new aircraft would replace the Mirage 2000 aircraft of No 1 IAF Squadron at Maharajpur. Guy was also delighted to learn that Aadash Tagor was to be promoted to Group Captain, also that Aadash would be appointed as the new Commanding Officer of the new Chinese bomber Squadron.

Personal news, also brought a huge smile to Guy's face. He had received notification from the Ministry of Defence that with effect from 1st of January, he would be promoted to Air Commodore.

As normal, the Embassy held its traditional Christmas dinner allowing the Ambassador to say a few welcomed words to members of his staff, and to thank them for all their efforts and hard work during the past year. This year after his speech, the Ambassador presented Guy with a gift. The gift was a beautiful Chinese Cloisonné clock, in recognition of Guy's service during his tour as an Air Attaché.

Guy stood for a few moments, while taking a last look around the apartment that had been his home for the last two rather exciting years. Checking once again he had packed all his possessions, particularly from his bathroom as he had a habit of leaving his razor behind. Guy closed the door behind him for the last time, and made his way downstairs to the waiting Embassy car which would take him to the airport. Just before saying goodbye to the driver, he handed over the keys to his apartment and thanked him, wishing him all the best.

After checking in, Guy did not have long to wait for the 10am British Airways flight to London. Ensuring as he normally did, Guy had brought with plenty of reading material to occupy in helping the time to pass. He was wise enough to know he would need it during the long 10-hour flight to Heathrow.

Settling himself down in his business class seat, and after having enjoyed the meal on offer served by the ever-smiling cabin crew, Guy turned to the reading material, including a quiz book which he fully enjoyed doing. Even having read and done a number of quizzes, the time still seemed interminable just as it normally did on all long-haul flights.

Feeling at peace he eventually drifted off to sleep, only to be awakened a couple hours later by one of the pretty cabin crew, who went on to inform him they were approaching Heathrow and the Captain was preparing to land his aircraft.

Guy smiled and thanked her, and quickly made his way to the bathroom knowing there would still be a few minutes to spare. Ensuring everything around him was in place, he then fastened his safety belt. Once he felt the aircraft touch down, out of habit he glanced out of his window to assure himself that the aircraft was indeed slowing down until eventually the aircraft drew to a halt.

Quickly going through diplomatic channels, which Guy found most welcoming, as he was eager to go home and see his family. He had decided this time not to inform them he would be returning for Christmas, as he knew how much his family would be thrilled to see him.

Although he had bought Annabelle the pretty silver jewellery box in India, plus a beautiful polished cherrywood trinket box which he had purchased near the Great Wall, he wanted a more substantial present for her. After being away so long, he now had every intention of marrying her, that is of course if she would still have him. He hoped if Annabelle agreed, they could then marry within the next few months.

Chapter Ten

Promotion

Entering the gates of Davenport Hall, Guy's excitement grew. His home looked like a magical palace in the cold light of the winter sun. He knew his taxi would have already been picked up by the security cameras and that Hopkins would be the first person to greet him, which indeed was the case. "Welcome home Sir, this will indeed bring a smile to your parent's face," Hopkins said with a touch of familiarity which Guy did not mind, as he knew how devoted Hopkins was to his parents, and in particular to his father.

"Thank you, Hopkins, so good to be in England, especially at Christmas. Are my parents home?"

"Yes Sir. Your father is in his study, and your mother is with Lady Willoughby. That is Lady Willoughby senior." Hopkins replied with a knowing smile.

Guy paid the driver, then went directly to his father's study leaving Hopkins to bring in his suitcases. Gently knocking on the door and opening it before his father had time to answer, Guy briskly walked over to his father, stretching out his hand as he did so.

Sir Richard was so completely overjoyed at seeing his son, he quickly stood up and shook Guy's hand, then threw his arms around him. Unashamedly hugging his beloved son rather tightly, something which of course he would never do in public. Eventually letting his son go, stating as he did so, "Guy my boy, I cannot find the words to express how happy I am at seeing you here. Marvellous, simply marvellous. We must go and see your mother instantly; she will be ecstatic. We have missed you so much, more than either of us thought possible."

Guy and his father continued chatting as they walked towards the small drawing room where his mother was entertaining of course, my mother. As Sir Richard opened the door, both Lady Rosalind and my mother looked up to see who the brave intruder was, who had dared have the audacity to disturb them. Both ladies being deep in discussion about the upcoming activities, and who would be staying with whom during Christmas and New Year with Guy being away.

Sir Richard allowed his beloved son to enter the room first, knowing the reaction his presence would bring from both ladies. He was indeed quite right, as both his mother and my mother quickly rose from their chairs. Lady Rosalind was so taken aback; she could barely speak before managing to quickly pull herself together, and with a huge smile lighting up her face, she said, "Oh, my darling boy, how wonderful to see you. You could not have given me a better Christmas present or any present for that matter; than having you with me at this moment."

Guy by then had reached his mother's side, kissed her gently on both cheeks and then hugged her. Once Lady Rosalind released him, he then turned to my mother and politely kissed her cheek asking as he did so, "How are both Sir John and yourself keeping?" Before my mother had time to answer, Guy instantly went on to say, "How is Annabelle, is she still up in London?"

"Yes dear," came my mother's reply, as she gave out a small token laugh, then continued to answer Guy's questions. "Annabelle is fine my dear, and yes she is still in London. I am sure Guy she will be delighted to hear your voice."

Sir Richard was the next one to talk by asking his son, "How long will you be staying?"

Guy replied with a huge smile, "I am taking three weeks' annual leave, during which time I expect to be notified of my next posting. I do though, have a number of things I need to do; which means I must go up to London."

Guy's parents were naturally very pleased, Lady Rosalind then made everyone laugh when she turned to Guy and stated, "Do you realise dearest; you have just upset everyone's meticulous plans in the most wonderful way. I cannot express how thrilled and happy we are all feeling, now that you have arrived home safe and sound; especially as it is Christmas."

Guy gave his mother another loving hug, going on to having a further chat, though making it brief before excusing himself. Sir Richard took the opportunity to return to the privacy of his study, leaving the ladies once again to talk happily of various things, though knowing full well, they will now be planning some event or other to celebrate Guy's return home.

Once in the privacy of his room, Guy made a quick call to Gieves and Hawkes, having already previously ordered his new dress uniform complete with Air Commodore rank insignia.

SQUADRON LEADER ROY HANDLEY AND DENISE LUNT

The cultured voice of the gentleman on the other end of the phone, informed Guy his uniform would be ready to collect, or if he preferred; they would be happy to send it to his home. Guy informed the assistant he would be coming up to London the following day and would like to try it on. He then added, "I would be most grateful if you would indeed send it to the Hall afterwards."

Replacing the receiver, Guy redialled having every intention of phoning me. Instead, he replaced the receiver and practically flew downstairs. Thankful at finding his mother still with my mother, he interrupted them to ask, "Lady Willoughby, have you informed Sir John, or Annabelle I am home?"

"No dearest, not as yet" she replied, then informed him, "Sir John is due to arrive very soon. Your parents have asked us to stay for the weekend, and I was under the impression you were now going to inform Annabelle yourself."

Guy was delighted to hear this information and told her why he had asked. "I would like to give Annabelle a surprise, do you think you could persuade Sir John not to say a word, and ask Annabelle to meet you at Topogigos tomorrow for lunch."

Both our mothers looked at Guy and were delighted to hear what he had just told them, leaving them to laugh at the same time until my mother said, "My goodness Guy you are going to give my daughter a heart attack, but I will do my best and let you know." Mummy answered.

Guy then told her, "I have no intention Lady Willoughby of doing that. I do though have every intention of telling Annabelle how much I love her, and feel it is time she thought seriously of marrying me."

"Oh, Guy my darling boy, are you really serious about marrying shortly?" Guy's mother asked before anyone else had a chance to say anything.

"Yes, very much so," Guy answered, before his mother once more put her loving arms around her precious son.

My mother then said, "I am so thrilled Guy to hear this wonderful news. Jolly good job Sir John will be here shortly. I know he has been quite concerned about Annabelle settling down with someone he trusts, and we both know how much she loves you. We must of course tell him the moment he arrives."

Guy conveyed to both our mothers, that he had better go and tell his father or he would be in deep trouble with him. Once having done so, he also wished to order a hire car to take him up to London. Guy left the ladies, who he knew would no doubt now start to plan his and Annabelle's wedding. He walked to his father's study and knocked, before popping his head around the door as he always did, saying as he did so, "Are you busy Sir, I have something important I would like to tell you."

Sir Richard smiled and answered with a pleasant tone to his voice, "Come in Guy, would you like a drink?"

Guy thanked his father and informed him he did not require any refreshment; he then went on to tell him what was on his mind. "Sir, I do need you to sit down, as I have something important to tell you, and then I must go and take a shower.

Instead of sitting down again at his desk, Sir Richard stood up and walked from behind the desk over to one of the two armchairs close to the open burning log fire.

Settling himself down in one of the comfortable large armchairs which were placed either side of the fireplace, enabling Guy to join him in the other armchair. "Well, my boy what is it you wish to tell me." Sir Richard asked, wearing a little frown across his forehead, eager by now for his son to tell him his news.

Guy looked direct at his father, and totally out of character, Guy instead of saying Sir; he said. "Dad." At that very moment, Sir Richard knew his son was about to convey something momentous, allowing a smile to cross his face as his son continued. "I want to tell you; I have decided to ask Annabelle to marry me as quickly as possible."

Sir Richard rose from his chair before Guy could say another word and shook his hand, telling his son he could not feel happier even if it was possible. Sir Richard then said, "Have you informed Annabelle's father, and have you spoken to Annabelle since you have been home?"

"No Sir, to both questions," Guy replied. He continued saying, "Lady Willoughby informed me that Sir John was expected later today, as they were staying here for the weekend. Once he arrives, I will tell him then. I have arranged with mummy and Lady Willoughby to ask Annabelle to meet them up in London, but not to tell her it is me she will be meeting her, not them. Cannot wait to see her face."

Guy and Sir Richard both laughed at that thought. Sir Richard then told his son, "Guy I could not ask for a lovelier, more suitable daughter-in-law. You know your mother and I are deeply fond of Annabelle. We wish you both every happiness." With that Sir Richard could not resist the temptation of giving his beloved son another hug.

Sir John arrived in time for afternoon tea, by which time the two conspirators in the form of Guy's mother and my mother had done their work by phoning me. They had successfully made arrangements for me to meet them for lunch the following day. Once Sir John arrived, Hopkins had been instructed to show him into Sir Richards study, enabling Guy to inform him in private about wanting to marry as soon as possible. With that formality over, Sir John and Guy joined the others to enjoy afternoon tea, before going to dress for dinner.

Straight after breakfast the following morning, the hire car Guy had ordered had already arrived a few minutes earlier than expected. Guy greeted the driver and asked him once they reach London, would he please take him to Savile Row. On arriving and paying off the taxi, Guy then stepped into the store. After a final fitting, Guy signed his account and asked the assistant when could he expect his uniforms. The assistant informed him they would be with him in the next twenty-four hours. Guy thanked him and then asked, "Would you be so good as to call a taxi," Guy politely requested, going on to say goodbye and immediately left the shop, and waited outside until his taxi arrived. By this time Guy was feeling a little excited, knowing it would not be long before he would meet up with me once again.

Entering Topogigios, Luigi could not believe Guy was standing right there in front of him. Greeting him with a huge smile and a welcoming handshake. He went on to tell him how happy he was to see him back. The two men spent the next five minutes or so chatting exchanging news until eventually Guy told Luigi, "I am hoping Lady Annabelle will be here shortly, as both our mothers had arranged for her to meet them here, not knowing she was actually going to meet me."

Should it have been possible, Luigi could not have been more delighted that Guy had taken him into his confidence. Luigi very kindly told Guy, "Please, I show you a to a private corner. When your beautiful lady comes, I will just direct her to where you are sitting, then I bring you Champagne. Yes?" Guy smiled and thanked Luigi for his understanding and kindness. Later in the evening, Guy told me of all the plotting and planning the family had gone too, including how Luigi was so delighted to see him and was pleased he did not have long to wait until I entered the restaurant.

Not expecting to see Guy I was still in my business suit, though of course looking exceedingly smart as the white silk blouse I was wearing, set off the black outfit perfectly. Luigi directed me towards my table, thinking of course I would be meeting up with my mother and Lady Davenport. As I neared the table, I saw there was a man sitting at it with his back towards me. Guy of course had deliberately chosen to sit that way, in case anyone other than myself may have approached him. As I drew alongside, I quietly said, "Excuse me, I am so sorry, but I think."

"What do you think?" Guy asked.

"Oh Guy, oh my darling how wonderful to see you. When did you return home?"

Guy was in no mood to answer questions, instead he stood up and took me in his arms, and passionately kissed me. Time it seemed stood still until eventually I could by now barely breath and said, "Guy please everyone is watching us."

Guy replied, "Are they darling, how wonderful." He then proceeded to kiss me all over again. After another long passionate kiss, Guy slowly released me from his arms and pulled the chair away from the table enabling me to sit down. Stretching his arm across the table, he took my hand in his and in a voice full of emotion said, "Darling I have missed you so much. Annabelle being away from you so long, has given me the time to do some serious thinking. Darling I want you to marry me as soon as possible."

Before I could answer him, Guy continued, "Annabelle, I want to spend the rest of my life with you. Unfortunately, you know full well marrying someone like me, means moving around from place to place, country to country. Do you feel you are prepared to do this, as it is not always easy living out of a suitcase and being away from our families and home?"

"Guy Davenport, have you already forgotten I am the daughter of a Major General. One who had the need along with my mother and myself, to move all over the world practically." This statement made him laughed for a few moments, until in a firm voice I informed him, "We Willoughby women go where our men go, and do not forget that Group Captain Guy Davenport." Guy once again lifted my hand to his lips and kissed it, at the same time, he could not help but smile to himself, as he found himself longing to tell me of his promotion.

Luigi walked across carrying with him a bottle of Champagne, having tactfully given the lovers a little time to themselves. Little food was consumed, even though as usual it was superb. Guy and I just sat and talked about our future, until at last we decided it was time to go. Guy had asked Luigi to call a hire car

SQUADRON LEADER ROY HANDLEY AND DENISE LUNT

company, first to take me back to my apartment, and then on to Davenport Hall.

Once the hire car pulled up outside my apartment block, Guy escorted me in. Taking me once more in his arms he found my lips, kissing them gently to start with. His kisses became more and more demanding. I in return found myself responding to each and every one, until eventually Guy let me go as he said, "I love you so much my beautiful future wife, if I do not stop now, I will not be responsible for my actions. I will see you when you arrive at the Hall tomorrow my darling." I gave him a smile and told him how much I loved him.

Once Guy walked back through the glass door, I practically ran up the stairs to tell my friends who I shared the apartment with. I was so eager by then, to inform them of my wonderful news.

On arriving home, Guy jumped out of the hire car and paid the driver, giving him a generous tip while doing so. Hopkins opened the Hall door to greet him, then gave a gentle quick cough before saying, "A large box Sir was delivered for you a little earlier this evening, it did have on who had sent it. So, I took the liberty of opening it and ensured after pressing the contents, everything is now hanging in your wardrobe." Before Guy could say a word Hopkins continued, "May I be the first to offer my congratulations, your father is going to be extremely pleased."

Guy gave Hopkins a huge smile then in a serious voice he said, "Hopkins, under no circumstances whatsoever must my father, or anyone be told about my promotion until after midnight on New Year's Eve. I will excuse myself for a few minutes before, and on the first stroke of midnight I will re-join the others.

Annoyingly, there is a method in my madness, as that is the moment my promotion takes effect. You do understand."

"Perfectly Sir, "Hopkins replied, then further said, "You are going to start the year off well for everyone, as I know everyone will be absolutely delighted."

Hopkins words were of course to prove correct. This Christmas everyone appeared to be in high spirits. The fact that Guy and I were engaged, and we had now decided to marry at last, may well have had something to do with it.

As usual at dinner, various stories were told which made all present laugh. When it was Guy's turn, and with no prior warning, he was about to unleash a very sad gruesome tale. Maybe it was something he needed to get off his mind with his father present. As he laid down his cutlery, Guy looked around the table as if considering should he, or should he not express his thoughts.

After a few moments, he quietly said,"Allow me to first explain that, The People's Liberation Army numbers in excess of one million. The Chinese Government, in order to occupy its troops, allows the troops to operate various commercial activities, even car washes. While on en route to the Great Wall, I discovered a firing range where tourist for a small fee, could fire a selection of PLAF weapons using live ammunition. I opted to try the AK 47 automatic rifle. My efforts were to say the least, not impressive and I managed to miss most of the target."

Sir Richard was about to make a comment, when Guy politely stopped him and told his father there was another part to this tale. Sir Richard grinned, then indicated with a gesture of his hand for his beloved son to carry on.

"Not too far from the Great Wall, my driver slowed the car down just as we were passing a field which had a group of men and several armed police officers. The men were blindfolded, kneeling, and handcuffed with wooden boards strapped to their backs. Painted on the boards, were several Chinese characters. I asked my driver to explain just what was going on. He informed me that the men were convicted criminals and awaiting execution with a shot to the back of the head. My driver also told me, that the family of those men each received a bill for the bullet used and had no choice but to pay up. I was horror stricken, my immediate thoughts being, there was indeed a darker side of the modern China we know today."

Sir Richard noticed Guy biting his bottom lip for a second or two, a habit he had done from being a child. This told him his son was in a little discomfort. Instantly he enquired if there was more to this story, and if so; he would like to hear it. Guy looked direct into his fathers' eyes, and then replied, "No, not about what had taken place in the field, and yes, when at last I arrived at the Great Wall."

Sir Richard nodded without saying a word. Guy knew this as a sign for him to carry on, so continued.

"My driver arrived at a section that was still intact. The wall truly is an amazing structure. I found as I was climbing the steps, just how steep they actually were, so one has to be reasonably fit before attempting to climb them. Once I reached the top, I decided to walk for a couple of kilometres, enjoying the views as they were quite stunning. Everyone eventually then has to return via the same steps. The area around the steps, you will find there are dozens of souvenir stalls.Out of curiosity I bought a copy of Mao's "Red Book" that had been published during the Cultural Revolution, something all tourists do. Of course, one of the presents I gave to Annabelle if you remember, was the beautiful polished cherrywood trinket box, which also came from the Wall."

Sir Richard spoke first and asked, "Guy is there anything else you wish to tell me about that awful experience, or are you just fine with it now?"

"Thank you, I am fine. I just thought I would mention it, something different to relate, perhaps I should have left it for another time."

Sir Richard tactfully replied, "I am pleased you decided to tell us, it has made our dinner conversation very interesting, and we are all deeply impressed about what you have seen and the way you have handle things."

Sir Richard unusually winked at his beloved son. Guy knowing it was such a rare action for his father to do, told him very clearly of his father's deep understanding and the love he had for him.

The highlight of the festive season this year at Davenport Hall, was to be a large New Year's Party. Invitations had stated this was to be a black-tie affair. The ladies arriving in beautiful evening gowns, and the gentlemen looking extremely smart in dinner suits.

After dinner, the guests gathered in the elegantly appointed drawing room to await the arrival of New Year. Guy after mingling with the guests, slipped away unnoticed, then on the first stroke of midnight, he reappeared as Hopkins opened both doors for him. As he stepped back into the room, conversation and laughter suddenly stopped. For a few moments there was a stunned silence as Guy stood there resplendent in his new Air Commodore's uniform.

The first to break the silence was of course his father, Sir Richard rushed across to shake his hand and embraced him exclaiming, "Guy how marvellous, I am so proud of you attaining the rank of an Air Officer in the Royal Air Force. You know Guy, it really is a magnificent achievement, and in your case well deserved my boy!"

By this time Lady Rosalind and I had reached Guy's side. Lady Rosalind hugged her beloved son, and went on to tell him how she was also so proud of him. Lady Rosalind then made everyone laugh as she said, "My goodness, it has been a long time since I have hugged an Air Commodore". She then stepped aside to allow me to give Guy my congratulations, along with a rather passionate kiss, to which the guests then applauded.

On the last stroke of the exquisite French Louis XIVth clock, which had pride of place on top of the fantastic carved fireplace. Everyone applauded, going on to do what everyone around the world does by giving kisses and hugs. After all the good wishes and congratulations had been given, everyone joined hands in a circle, breaking into the famous words of Auld Lang Syne. The evening continued into the small hours of the morning.

By midday Davenport Hall was now quiet, with all but my family and I having departed. Guy took the opportunity to take me to one side to ask if I would agree to allow both families to make plans for us to marry in spring.

"Darling that would be wonderful, how thoughtful of you," I replied, and then told him, "Guy, I would love to marry at St Clement Danes in London, but only if it would make you happy as well?"

Guy told me he thought that was a wonderful idea, and we should now ask our parents what they thought about the idea. Guy and I found both sets of parents in the small cosy sitting room as usual. Sitting down to join them for a scrumptious afternoon tea, Guy spoke for both of us. First, he informed our respective parents of our wishes to marry at St Clement Danes, we continued and asked both our mothers, if they would like to ensure all of the arrangements for our wedding would be just as it should; simply perfect. A question which left Lady Rosalind and my mother were thrilled to bits about.

While still on leave enjoying the delights of being home, even though it was early January with the ground covered in snow. Guy received notification from the Ministry of Defence of his new appointment as the Officer Commanding the RAF's 17th (Reserve) Squadron. He stood perfectly still and practically dropped the letter, as his emotions began to take over. They ranged from being amazed and delighted, in fact, somewhat stunned. Then nervousness crept in when he realised the enormous responsibility of this appointment.

Gathering his wits, he quickly went to find his father who was still reading his newspaper in the morning room. Showing his father the letter, Sir Richard practically jumped out of his chair to shake his son's hand and told him with a smile, "Guy you will have to excuse me, as I keep repeating and enjoying saying, how incredibly proud I am of you and well done." Lady Rosalind follow suit adding her usual affectionate kiss.

Guy was aware of 17 Squadron's long and illustrious history which had commenced with the Royal Flying Corps in 1915. The squadron had also served with distinction at both home and overseas during both World Wars; particularly in the Battle of Britain in 1941. Before its disbandment several years ago, the squadron had served as the trials and evaluation unit for the Tornado and Typhoon prior to those aircraft entering operational service with the RAF.

A week after his appointment letter arrived, Guy was summoned to a briefing at the Ministry of Defence in London. It was general knowledge that the Lockheed Corporation of America, had recently won a competition to provide the USAF with the latest generation of stealth fighter. The UK Government had made the decision to purchase several of the new Lockheed Lightning II F35 aircraft. There were several variants of the aircraft and the UK had decided to purchase the F35B. The "B" version was the Short Take-Off Vertical Landing aircraft (STOVL); and was intended to operate from the UK's new aircraft carriers HMS Queen Elizabeth and HMS Prince of Wales which were nearing completion.

On arrival at the MOD, Guy was informed that 17 Squadron would be re-formed and its name changed to 17th Trials and Evaluation Unit (TEU.) Guy was amazed to learn his new Command would also be deployed to the USAF Edwards base in California.

Since WW2 the huge base had been responsible for the pre-service trials and evaluation of virtually every aircraft purchased by the USAF. Guy's 17th TEU was to be embedded in 461 Flight Test Squadron which was part of the 412th Test Wing.

Chapter Eleven

Edwards Air Force Base

Sitting in the back of the hire car returning to Davenport Hall, Guy's adrenalin was over loaded with all the exciting information he was now in possession of. Totally impatient, (an emotion he normally never felt) he was eager to return home and to discuss all he had been told to his father.

Knocking on his father's study and walking in before being invited, again something he rarely did, excusing his bad manners he went on to divulge all his news. His father smiled and said, "I have to tell you Guy; I knew something was afoot having heard the rumours on the grapevine at the Ministry. Best of luck my boy on such an exciting project." Sir Richard asked, "Do you think it is too early for a drink" and then laughed as he went to reach for the sherry decanter. After handing Guy his drink, Sir Richard then asked in a concerned tone of voice, "Guy when do you intend to tell Annabelle, and of course I must ask; will she be able to join you once you are married?"

Guy took a sip of his sherry before replying to his father's questions, he knew full well they were important, stating. "No Sir, I have not as yet informed

Annabelle, but will do so very shortly. As to Annabelle joining me once we are married, of course she will, at least I hope she will join me. While I am over there on my own, I will look for property to rent. Funnily enough I was just thinking it will be our first home together, so I feel obligated to find her something terribly nice."

The two men finished their drinks, and then went to find Lady Rosalind. They entered the small cosy sitting room which strangely, was Lady Rosalind's most favourite of all the rooms at the Hall. Lady Rosalind greeted her two most favourite men in the world, giving them a lovely smile. For just a few seconds, Guy felt he did not wish to convey his news to his mother as he knew her lovely smile would instantly disappear; even though she would be very happy for him.

Once he told her his news, Guy was of course right. Lady Rosalind's smile indeed disappeared, but she quickly went on to tell her son, "My goodness Guy, that is wonderful news." Lady Rosalind's smile now having returned. She then continued and told her precious son, "I have just got you home, and now you are off globetrotting again. Darling of course I wish you every success in your new appointment." Lady Rosalind then further continued, "As always Guy, it goes without really saying, you know your father and I are incredibly proud that you are our beloved son."

Lady Rosalind then kissed and hugged not only her beloved son but her only child, as sadly she was unable to have other children. As far as Lady Rosalind was concerned, Guy had more than made up for a dozen children, and had become her greatest happiness besides her darling husband who regarded Guy in the same frame of mind.

"Good morning, Sir, welcome aboard," the very attractive airhostess greeted Guy. After asking for his seat number, she then escorted him into the first-class compartment.

Thanking her, Guy was pleased to see he had been given seat number 2, which was close to the cockpit door. He certainly appreciated the extra wide leather seats that first class accommodation afforded its passengers; he would also come to enjoy the movable footrest once he put his seat into the reclining position when airborne.

Popping his hand luggage into the capacious overhead luggage compartment, Guy took his seat and made himself comfortable, but not before the airhostess asked him if he would he care for a drink. Guy thanked her, and replied he would like a glass of Champagne.

Another very attractive airhostess, came and offered him a couple of the day's newspapers. Thanking first one airhostess, then the other, Guy fastened his seat belt and decided to watch what was going on outside until his aircraft took off. Without consciously realising it, his mind drifted towards thinking about me, and the last conversation we managed to have.

Straight after informing his parents of his new posting, Guy phoned to inform me he needed to discuss something he regarded as very important, and would I meet him for dinner at Topogigios.

After being shown to our table, I could not help but notice that Guy seemed somewhat nervous, until at last once dinner had been served, Guy went on to tell me about his new position.After conveying his news as gently as he could, explaining that he would once again be away for a few months; but while on his own he promised he would look for property to rent, as he had every intention that his future bride would be with him on his return to America.

As I drove Guy to the airport, and for the first time in his life, Guy told me how he felt quite emotional. "Annabelle not only am I leaving you and my family behind; but England. Something that has never bothered me before. I guess I must be experiencing a form of home sickness that other men have told me about, but never quite took on board."

We kissed goodbye, then Guy disappeared quickly through the airport doors. While driving home, his beautiful words came to mind, and I found myself shedding hot tears.

As it was to be another long-haul flight, Guy had chosen to fly by British Airways in a Boeing 747. Once the aircraft accelerated down the runway, unconsciously Guy sensed the aircraft reach V1 speed, and shortly afterwards V2. That being the point when the pilot would ease the nose of aircraft off the runway as it commenced the climb to a cruising altitude of around 35,000 feet. The flight thank goodness being uneventful, Guy enjoyed doing what every passenger would normally do. Eat, drink, do a little reading, even to watch a film and then tried to doze until he was informed it was time to fasten his safety belt and prepare for landing.

After a flight of eleven hours, the aircraft at last landed at Los Angeles International Airport at 3PM LA time. After passing through Immigration and Customs, Guy took the shuttle bus to the Sonesta Hotel, where he had previously made a reservation. Suffering somewhat from jet lag, Guy decided to retire early after enjoying a welcomed dinner. He awoke the following morning feeling refreshed and ready to face the day, having had an undisturbed peaceful night's sleep.

Finding the small dining room where breakfast was normally served, he then helped himself to what he regarded as an overly large breakfast, with the waitress ensuring he was provided with as much coffee as he wished to consume. Once the task of having breakfast was over, Guy went to check out, and was given the keys to the hire car which had been delivered earlier and was now located at the front of the hotel waiting for him.

The front porter carefully placed Guy's luggage in the trunk (boot) of the Mercedes 500, which Guy had decided he would like to drive. He was hoping this part of his journey would also be without incident, as his flight had been. Settling himself down for a long drive, Guy drove out of Los Angeles, and headed towards California City which was approximately 100 miles north of LA. The weather though somewhat cooler than Guy had anticipated was still pleasant, dry and clear; thus enabling him to enjoy the view of the ocean.

The colour of the Pacific was an amazing deep blue, with the white sea horses of the waves breaking gently on the long coast of the shoreline. Looking out towards the opposite side of the car, the open fields allowed Guy to see for miles. As he continued to drive, there was the odd filling station and café, he also spotted here and there, a number of deserted houses that may have been damaged by earthquakes. He was so thankful that the roads were not too busy allowing him to make good time to his next destination, which was the Best Western hotel in California City, situated in North Antelope Valley, in Kern County.

Having made good time, Guy arrived and proceeded to book in. He was accommodated in a large room overlooking the countryside. This was to be his base for the next couple of weeks until he moved into a furnished house, one he thought; I may even like would and be happy living in.

The following morning having enjoyed a good night's rest and a rather large healthy breakfast, Guy drove the short distance to Edwards Air Force Base. Edwards had helped develop virtually every aircraft purchased by the USAF since WW2, particularly as it was a military airbase, access was naturally very limited. The first major aerial activity occurred in 1937, at which time the base was known as Murco Field; in 1949 it was officially re-named as Edwards Air Force Base.

The base is next to Rodgers Dry Lake, a desert salt pan providing a natural extension to Edward's runways. There are three lighted and paved runways, ranging from 8, 000 to 15, 000 feet in length. There are 13 other official runways on the Rodger's Lakebed, covering 44 square miles. While the Rosamond Lakebed covers 21 square miles, and has two runways painted on it, both around 21 thousand feet in length.

On his arrival, Guy was directed by security personnel to the Head Quarters of the 461st Flight Test Squadron which was part of the 412th Test Wing. After clearing security, Guy was warmly welcomed by Colonel Georgina Ripley, and Lt Colonel Chris P Reynolds; they were the respectively the Commanding Officers of the Test Wing and the Test Squadron. Guy's new command at Edwards, was originally XVII Squadron of the RAF, which had been reformed at Edwards Air Force Base, as the Operational Evaluation Unit (OEU) for the new

Lockheed Martin F35B aircraft that had been purchased by the UK Government.

The OEU, was made up of RAF and RN personnel, who were tasked with the operational test and evaluation of the F35B. The OEUs responsibility, also included the ground training of members of 617 Squadron, in order to bring the aircraft and its weapons into service with the RAF. Once fully operational, it was intended that the F35B, would operate from the new aircraft carrier being built and would eventually be named HMS Queen Elizabeth. Which now of course was currently on its first operational cruse to the far east with the Royal Navy.

Soon after Guy's arrival, the OEU commenced an intensive flying program involving the RAF's new F35B aircraft. Tests and evaluation of the F35B, was scheduled to occupy at least twelve to eighteen months, prior to it being accepted into the RAF. Components of the programme also included familiarisation for aircrew in air-to-air and air-to-ground firing of the F35 weapons; air-to-air-refuelling and simulated carrier landings. Maintenance personnel from 617 Squadron were also involved. After having spent several hours in the ground simulator over a period of time, Guy was delighted to have qualified, enabling him to fly the F35B.

Unfortunately, he was not as pleased when he was informed that Edwards, along with many USAF units, did not provide sufficient married quarters for senior officers. They were like the French Air Force who also did not provide married quarters... The Base Housing Unit, advised him to obtain rented accommodation, which was already furnished in areas adjacent to the base. The BHU, also informed him that he would receive a generous financial allowance towards the cost of whatever accommodation he chose.

At the weekend, Guy located the office of a female Realtor (estate agent) who escorted him to view various properties in the better areas of California City. With Anabelle very much in mind, Guy chose a relatively new single storey, ranch style house that had been built on a large, wooded plot. The house was located in the North Edwards suburb, a few miles from the base. Delighted with the house, Guy decided to phone and ask me if I was free, and if so, would I consider joining him for a couple of weeks at Easter. He felt it was important that I liked the house, as it was to be his home for at least the next eighteen months. Signing on the dotted line and accepting the keys, Guy checked his watch, working out what time it would be in England. He wanted desperately to speak to me and inform me of his request.

Arriving back at his hotel, Guy informed the front desk he would be leaving in the morning. Returning to his room, he then immediately phoned England. Answering the phone and hearing Guy's voice, felt simply wonderful. First he went on to tell me how much he loved and missed me, and then informed me of his day's events. He then asked, would I be free at Easter, and if so, for how long? I happily told him, I had some holidays due which I could take when I wished, so would combine them with the Easter break.

Spring quickly arrived, looking out of the aircraft window, I was thrilled at the scene below knowing very shortly I would be with Guy again. My excitement grew as the aircraft came into land at LA International after having made a perfect landing. Guy had arranged that he would be at the airport to meet me, and we would drive straight to the house he had now named Davenport Lodge. On hearing that last statement, I diplomatically never said a word, but could not help and smile to myself. Once having gone through customs and immigration, then entering the main arrival's hall, instantly spotting the tall handsome and by now tanned face of my Air Commodore. Reaching Guy's side, he immediately swept me off my feet, showering me with kisses; going on to say how much he missed and loved me. Not having seen each other for so long and is often the way; we each in turn tried to convey to the another our news by asking a million questions, while we drove the hundred miles to the newly named Davenport Lodge.

I never realised how quickly two weeks can pass by, when so much in love. Eventually the time had come for me to leave, finding it hard to say our goodbyes, as we would be separated for many months into the future. Guy had ensured I had enjoyed my first stay in California. Firstly, introducing me to his new neighbours and colleagues, who would eventually become our friends. Taking in the beautiful boutiques along Rodeo Drive, also the many restaurants closer to the Lodge. We went for scenic drives along the coast, stopping off at tiny bars that provided food, or finding tiny coves enabling us to make love in the beautiful calm waters that were filled by the Pacific.

As we approached the airport, Guy said he felt a small pang of envy wishing he too could return to England with me. Obviously, he was missing his family and England itself. I on the other hand, would have been so happy and content to stay with him in our dear, modern lovely little lodge; well little compared to

Davenport Hall. Guy looked very sad as he said, "Goodbye darling, I have to be here this Christmas, which I am not looking forward to without you and the family." He went on to explain a number of other things, and then asked me if I would return to California for the festive season.

"Of course, I will my darling. I could think of nothing more wonderful than to be with you once again," I replied. Kissing me for the last time, Guy held onto to me a little longer than he normally would have done. I looked into his eyes and told him, "The months will soon pass darling. You will not even know I am missing with the trials that are coming up, and you do need all your concentration. I love you Guy Davenport and that is all you need to remember." With that I quickly walked into the main passenger building, trying desperately hard to hold back the tears I now felt I was so close to shedding.

I was indeed quite right, with the intensive tests and evaluation programme continuing, time indeed passed rapidly. Before Guy realised, the Christmas season had arrived once again. Having made our arrangements for me to join him on the Friday, luckily Christmas Day that year falling on the Monday, allowing us the joy of spending the previous few days together.

California greeted me with the most amazing decorations I had ever seen in real life, as well as a glorious winter sunset. We had been invited to a number of Christmas parties, ensuring we had lots of fun, as well as so many lovely memories to remember. I must admit, I found it rather funny as everyone was so delighted to meet a real English Lady, not something that often happened over there in service life; or so it seemed.

New Year's Eve found the majority of personnel attending a dinner and ball at the Officer's Club on base. This was a new experience even for Guy, as English personnel usually just take leave.

The RAF of course, do have both dinner dances or a ball, though normally held later in the year. With the festivities once again over, it was time for me to return to England and for Guy to start what he hoped would be the last few months of this posting. Returning to work, Guy's unit the OEU, continued the tests and valuation of the new aircraft. It was not until till mid-June, before these tests would be completed, enabling the new aircraft to be accepted into operational service with the Royal Air Force.

Later in the month in a formal ceremony, the OEU was renamed, 617 Squadron, with Guy remaining in temporary command. Then before the month ended, the new 617 Squadron was ordered to return to a newly modernised RAF Marham, becoming the first Squadron to operate F35B aircraft in the Royal Air Force.

Having made many friends and highly respected by fellow officers, Guy found himself being wished every kind of happiness and success. He was informed he would always be welcomed back; should he wish to take a holiday. Guy phoned me as he would each week, this time he told me how he much he was looking forward to seeing his family and the woman he loved, making me strangely blush. Also crossing his mind, was the thought of us getting married...

The day before he was to leave, Guy was asked to go and see the Commanding Officer. Knocking on the door, a voice answered for him to come in, but not the voice Guy was expecting. On opening the door, stood a man looking out of the window, as he turned around, Guy could not believe his eyes. The man stretched out his hand, enabling both men to shake hands, then said.

"Hello old buddy, you look very well."

Guy was stunned but quickly replied, "Am I seeing a ghost, or is it really you Duff? How marvellous to see you old chap." Guy then asked him, "What in tarnation are you doing here?"

"I was just passing, and I heard you were here, thought we could have a quick coffee together, and I like your promotion." Both men laughed at that remark and spent the next hour or so catching up with each other's news. Before saying goodbye once more, Duff requested Guy, that should he find himself in America again, let him know first, allowing their new friendship to grow...

Guy received his movement orders to travel by military transport aircraft to RAF Mildenhall, and then on by road to RAF Marham. He was delighted to return to RAF Marham, as he had many fond memories of his previous service there during his career. Soon after his arrival, Guy relinquished his command of 617 Squadron and proceeded on leave to Davenport Hall to await his next assignment.

Prior to leaving RAF Marham, the following item appeared in the London Gazette.

"Air Commodore Guy Davenport RAF AFC, is awarded the Distinguished Service Order, (DSO) for his leadership and exemplary performance in the successful introduction of the new F35B aircraft into operational service with the RAF."

On his return journey home, Guy was hoping that preparations were now well in hand enabling us to marry as soon as it was humanly possible. Damn it all, I am not getting any younger Guy thought to himself, and I dare say Annabelle's parents would like to see me make an honest woman of her, before either of us are much older.

Greeted by Hopkins, who was as always very pleased to see him. Hopkins informed Guy that his parents had company in the form of Sir John and Lady Willoughby, who were all sitting in the exceedingly large well heated conservatory. Hopkins then gave him a rather mischievous smile, before he said, "I hope you will forgive me saying, I could not help it Sir overhearing the conversation today, as it has basically been on the same topic of conversation each day these last number of months."

"Really Hopkins, rather unusual for my father to repeat the same sentences, must be something very important," Guy stated.

"Yes Sir, it most certainly is to Sir Richard and your mother, as well as the Willoughby's it seems," Hopkins replied, again smiling.

"Then dare I ask, if you will reveal what is so special, they are discussing," Guy questioned. Hopkins looked directly into Guy's handsome face and stated, "Your wedding Sir."

Guy stood for a moment then burst out laughing, he then told Hopkins what a relief it was to hear that news and continued, "Funny really Hopkins, on my way home I was wondering how far the plans had progressed. I guess, or I should say. I hope they are now in the stage of being close to completion, which suits me fine. Let's be honest, it is about time Lady Annabelle was indeed my wife. I not only missed her when we are apart, but each time I have to leave her behind, it is becoming harder. This time I really missed her terribly. I am hoping the next posting they give me; she will be there when I return home each evening."

After greeting both his parents and my parents, Guy was indeed surprised to hear how far ahead plans had been completed for our wedding. Once he joined them, Sir Richard, his mother, and my parents, sat and revealed in detail what plans had so far been made, and if he agreed to them. They also informed him that Annabelle was delighted as things stood.

"So, our wedding is to be held at St Clements Danes Church, which of course is the central church of the Royal Air Force," Guy replied.

He managed to say before Sir Richard could answer, "Delighted to hear it Sir, as it is something Annabelle and I always wished for. May I ask, was it Annabelle who informed you of this fact?"

Sir John answered this time, before Sir Richard had a chance, stating, "Of course, dear boy. Only the very best for my beloved daughter, and I rather think your parents are of the same mind when it comes to their only beloved son."

Both sets of parents then took it in turn to inform Guy of their plans, while Guy devoured a late delicious afternoon tea which Hopkins had now served.

Allowing his parents and the Willoughby's to continue without further interrupting them, Guy's mind flashed back to the information he had been given about the history of St Clements, during one of his history classes at school. Saint Clements had been built in central London, and had been re-consecrated in 1958 as a perpetual shrine of remembrance to those who had died in the service of the RAF. The church has one of the finest organs and a beautifully maintained set of bells.

Guy's thoughts were interrupted when Hopkins asked, "Could I have a quiet word with you Sir Richard."

"Of course, Hopkins," Sir Richard replied. Hopkins then informed Sir Richard, that the Reverend James Stone was on the telephone.

A few days later, Guy received a letter requesting him to visit the MOD in respect of his next appointment. He immediately went to inform his father, wondering if he had heard anything on the grapevine so to speak. Sir Richard answered informing him that for the present, he had not been given any information, but he was concerned that his son would approve of his next posting. Deep down Sir Richard was hoping that Guy's next outing would be a little closer to home, especially with plans in hand for his son to marry. On entering the MOD, Guy was escorted to the floor he required, and shown to the room he had been requested to go to, where he would meet the Appointments Secretary. Gently knocking and then entering, Guy was greeted with a warm smile and an outstretched hand of the charming man he had come to see.

"Do please sit down," the Secretary requested, while shaking Guy's hand. He then asked, "Can I offer you a cup of tea or coffee."

Guy replied, "Neither thank you. I have not long digested a rather large breakfast and untold gallons of good old English tea, making up for the months of being without while living in America."

The Secretary smiled once again, and then proceeded to inform Guy the reason as to why he had been invited to attend this morning, in order to discuss his next assignment. The Secretary looked at Guy, smiled deeply once again, and went on to tell him, "I am delighted to tell you; your new post will to be within the MOD's Procurement Division." The Secretary carried on to tell Guy that he will be required to take up the position the following week due to the imminent retirement of the current incumbent.

At this stage in his career, Guy expected such an appointment, but was somewhat disappointed at the thought of a desk job for the next couple of years. He told me later that the only bonus to this news, was the fact that when duty permitted, he would be able to spend a great deal more time with me.

This in turn meant, Guy and I now needed to look for a new apartment, something he had previously not thought about. Thanking the Secretary, Guy shook hands once more, and left the building to return home and give his father the news.

On his return to Davenport Hall, Guy immediately went to find his father, to convey to him the news of his new position. He also decided he wanted to know and would try and find out just how far his wedding plans had so far progressed. Hopkins on greeting Guy, informed him that his father was in his study. Reaching the study door and knocking before entering, Sir Richard not knowing who it was that sought his attention, called out for the intruder to come in. On seeing it was Guy he was delighted to be interrupted.

"Well what news do you have for me?" Sir Richard asked, with great enthusiasm.

Guy had decided not to tell his father of his true feelings in that he was slightly disappointed, due to the thought of being unable to fly and stuck behind a desk. Instead, Guy informed his father of all he wished to know, and then changed the subject as he asked, "Dad, when do you expect my wedding plans to be completed, a date would now be most welcome due to this appointment."

Sir Richard looked at his son, then first told him, "You know Guy, I never tire of telling you how much I love you, and how very proud your mother and I are of you." He waited a moment for Guy to say something, as he knew his son very well. He also had an idea how Guy must be feeling, regardless he never mentioned to him about having to fly a desk rather than an aircraft. As Guy made no comment, Sir Richard continued, "I must tell you Guy, I will be looking forward to you joining me for coffee when time allows, it will give me the opportunity to introduce you to other fellow officers in the MOD. As to the final date of your wedding, I think we had better go and seek out your mother, I am sure she can give you that information far better than myself."

Sir Richard did though, inform Guy that he had spoken a couple of times to the Resident Chaplain of St Clements, the very Reverend James Stone, and that a date was to be set very shortly for his wedding. Sir Richard and Guy, found Lady Rosalind as usual in her small bright, comfortable sitting room doing the Times crossword.

"Hello darlings," she greeted her husband and precious son, and then asked, "What have I done to deserve the pleasure of seeing you both at this time of day." Sir Richard was the first to reply.

"Rosalind my dearest, our son would like to know has a final date been set for his wedding?"

"I thought I told you," Lady Rosalind answered. Giving a tiny chuckle, before she continued.

"Oh dear, how remiss of me if I have forgotten, I do apologise." Lady Rosalind then turned to her son and gently asked, "Guy my darling, I hope you approve of the last Saturday in August?" Lady Rosalind then waited for her son's reply feeling a little apprehensive.

"That will be just perfect mummy," Guy answered. He then went over to his mother, giving her a hug and thanked her for all she had done, he then stated, "I am sure you have put a great amount of love and effort to ensuring the wedding will be wonderful, I love you. Thank you again." Guy then gave his mother a kiss on both cheeks, before going on to ask if she would inform him in detail exactly what the wedding plans were.

Lady Rosalind was delighted to have the opportunity to sit and discuss with her beloved son, the plans that she and my mother had made. She informed Guy that Amanda had agreed to be Maid of Honour, and Toby had also agreed stating, "I have always been your Best Man!" This remark made Guy laugh. Anabelle had asked if her friends two little girls could be bridesmaids, which seemed perfect. All the other arrangements again have been completed and there was no need for him to have any further worry. Guy once again thanked his mother profusely before giving her another hug, telling her while doing so, how brilliant it all sounded.

The following week, Guy reported for duty. As he entered the MOD, he was greeted by one of the many messengers who worked there. She was a middle-aged lady with perfect manners, and had a very lovely sweet smile, that reminded him of Raine, Countess Spencer.

After showing his ID, the lady sent for another messenger, this time a gentleman. He led the way in order to show Guy to his new office, holding open the door for him to enter once they reached it. Thanking him, the messenger proceeded to close the door, but within a second or two, and before Guy had time to look around, immediately came a knock on the door. Guy called for the person knocking to come in, he was duly greeted by a young woman who held the rank of Flight Lieutenant. Introducing herself as Susan Blake, she then informed Guy she was his personal secretary and immediately asked would he like a cup of tea. Guy accepted her offer, telling her tea would be most welcome, Earl Grey if possible, and that he was delighted to meet her.

Later that day, Guy went on to meet other members of his staff, including the Head of the Procurement Division, Air Vice Marshal Rodney Hawes, who informed him, "Delighted to meet you Guy, welcome aboard. I am sure your father is very pleased your office is just down the corridor from his. You do know he is incredibly proud of you."

Guy replied with a wide smile, feeling a little embarrassed, "Thank you, Sir, I am delighted to have been chosen to join the team, and yes I do know how much my father loves me."

The two men continued to talk for a further few minutes until Guy was called away. By mid-July, Guy applied for his accrued annual leave which amounted to 28 days. He had decided he would like to go to Peru for our honeymoon, and hoped I would agree, as it was a country he often wished to visit.

The last week of August came around incredibly fast, and it was time for Guy to return home several days

SQUADRON LEADER ROY HANDLEY AND DENISE LUNT

before our wedding. As plans had been made for the wedding reception to be held at the Claridge's Hotel, Sir Richard had made reservations for his family and a number of friends to stay at the hotel for the weekend. They drove up to London after lunch on the Friday afternoon, ensuring they were in time to partake of afternoon tea. The weather the following morning, turned out to be perfect. Even though it was midsummer, it became unseasonably warm as the day progressed, not that anyone one minded, in fact were delighted about.

Guy, Toby and Sir Richard, accompanied by Lady Rosalind, were the first to leave the hotel. They were met at the church, first by a couple of discreet photographers, and then by friends who were acting as ushers, showing the guests to their seats. Most of the men were in uniform, all looking exceedingly smart. Lady Rosalind could not help but tell her beloved son, just how handsome he looked, fighting to control her emotions, which in public was very unusual for her. The church had been beautifully decorated in numerous varieties of flowers, in particular roses, sweet peas, carnations and hundreds of lilies, all of the flowers in white and very pale pinks. The soft perfume from the assembled flowers drifted on the air, permeating the entire church, allowing the whole building to smell like an enchanted garden.

From the background, music from the organ was being played softly, allowing guest to enjoy some wonderful pieces of classical music while taking their seats. At last, the notes of Handel's wedding march were heard, the signal for everyone to stand.

As I entered the church on my father's arm, it was lovely to see everyone looking so happy.My wedding gown had been designed and made especially for me and bought in Paris, as had Amanda's, along with the bridesmaid's dresses. The gowns were all made of the finest white silk available. My gown had been sewn with hundreds of tiny handmade satin and net roses. A wide panel had been arranged up the front and then narrowed ending about six inches from the waist.

The wide panel ran along the entire bottom and along a medium size train. The panel had been heavily beaded with roses, each rose covered in real tiny pearls and Swarovski crystals, as had the entire dress. Allowing it to shimmer like the stars, as I walked towards the man I loved so much. My mother had allowed me to borrow the beautiful large family diamond tiara, hidden for the moment under the veil. The tiara had originally belonged to Catherine the Great, who had given it as a present to a Russian Princess. After escaping the revolution, she came to England and sold the tiara, which in turn had been bought by my family. The veil like the dress, was covered in the same tiny real pearls and Swarovski crystals. I loved the long trailing bouquet of flowers which smelt divine, matching the roses and flowers now decorating the entire church.

Guy told me later; he heard the gasps from the guests behind him and could not help himself and turn around. He thought when I entered the church, I looked like a goddess that had descended to earth. Mesmerised he continued to watch me walk towards him, also drawing in his breath by my appearance. Now standing next to him, Guy asked, "Darling when did you arrive on earth, I have never seen anyone as beautiful, no matter where I have travelled in the world. I love you Annabelle beyond the stars, to the planets and beyond for all eternity."

After listening to Guy's words, it took all my self-control to keep my emotions in check and concentrate on the lovely church service which took roughly an hour. As we left the church, Guy and I walked under an archway of drawn swords, provided by a Guard of Honour of Guy's colleagues from 617 Squadron. I had noticed that Guy also was wearing the same type of sword.

The photographers were amazing, they discreetly never seemed to stop taking photos, along with many of our guests. Beautiful photos we will indeed treasure over the years. We were just so thankful the weather was perfect, allowing everyone to enjoy a wonderful day.

Our reception at the hotel was fantastic, with the food naturally being superb. Guy's father and mine, ensured the speeches were kept to a minimum, which again helped to made our wedding day simply perfect. A day filled with love and treasured memories which both Guy and I will always look back on with unequivocable pleasure and remember with pure joy, all the days of our life. The day though long, was wonderful. Our family, friends and guests like Guy and I, had thoroughly enjoyed every moment. Guy had made arrangements for us to fly the following morning to Peru for our honeymoon.

When it was time to leave Claridge's, our families and friends stood waving us off as we stepped into a limousine that would take us to Heathrow Airport. Once having gone through the normal procedures, Guy and I boarded a British Airways Aircraft for the 13-hour flight to Lima the capital of Peru. The flight though very long, thank goodness was uneventful and we arrived at Jorge Chavez International Airport.

Clearing passport control and immigration, we took a taxi to the Miraflores Park Hotel, which is a five-star hotel situated adjacent to the Circuito de Playas, that ran alongside the Pacific Ocean.

Peru, is the most popular holiday destination in South America. Guy informed me it was visited by 2.63 million tourists each year, which I found quite surprising. The country has some of the greatest biodiversity in the world due to its location near the Andes. The Amazon rain forest has over 1,800 species of birds, 500 species of mammals, including the rare puma and jaguar and the spectacled bear. Believe it or not, there are an amazing 52 species of monkeys, and many species of snakes including the giant anaconda.

The day after our arrival, Guy and I decided to stay and relax in the hotel in order to alleviate the slight jet lag we found ourselves suffering, resulting from the overly long 13-hour flight from the UK. The following day, now feeling fully refreshed, we decided to make our first visit to the historic Inca site at Machu Picchu.

The 15th century Inca Citadel in the south of the country, is situated on a mountain ridge some 9970 feet high. The buildings were constructed around 1450 AD, as an estate for an Inca Emperor. They are now considered one of the new Seven Wonders of the world: becoming a UNESCO World Heritage site in 1983.

To enable us to reach Machu Picchu, Guy having spent a great deal of time researching the facts of this amazing place, informed me we would have to commence our journey with a flight with the Peruvian National Airline from Lima, to the regional airport of Alejandro Velasco Astete Airport at Cusco. From Cusco we would have to travel by rail to Machu Picchu, and then take a taxi to the hotel Sumaq, where we would be staying for two nights. Guy was looking incredibly forward to seeing this fantastic site, hoping all he had read was true, in fact more than true; making this long journey worthwhile.

Even when we had now reached the hotel, Guy smiled and said, "Our journey my darling is not quite over even now; we will have to walk for about 20 minutes to actually reach the site. Quite a journey all told, but you will think it well worth once we arrive at our destination, at least I hope you will."

I decided to hold my own council and give my opinion later. After a good breakfast, we joined the other tourist who like ourselves, had made the long laborious journey from various parts of the world, and who were now all full of high expectation as to what they would find at this ancient site. Guy and I would never forget that stunning first glimpse our eyes beheld. The hundreds of dry-stone walls are so perfect; you cannot even slip a piece of paper between them. They were built in the shape of terraces, enabling the Inca's to grow food, due to good irrigation and soil fertility. I told Guy I must do a little more research on this most incredible historic of places, now having had the joy of seeing it.

After a long and tiring day, it was time to return to the hotel and enjoy a most welcome bath and dinner. Both of us were rather sad to say goodbye but looking forward to our next adventure in this strange and wonderful land. Repeating our journey back to Cusco, Guy had previously made reservations for us to stay at the hotel Katerra La Casona, which was renowned for its Colonial Spanish décor complete with marble fireplaces, a stone decorated Spanish gallery, and its central courtyard. Having enjoyed the wonderful Spanish cuisine at dinner, and breakfast the following morning, it was time to return by air to Lima.

On our arrival, we returned to the Miraflores Park Hotel, we were delighted to be able to spend the next few days relaxing by the excellent pool provided, and to enjoy a few of the enormous number of Chinese restaurants which Lima now has.

Lima was considered to be the Gastronomic Capital of the Americas. Peruvian cuisine had evolved from the indigenous population, along with the many immigrants from Africa, China, Europe and Japan. Guy was delighted to learn that Chinese restaurants, had first appeared in in the 1940's. Not only did he want to take me to both Chinese and Peruvian restaurants, he also wanted to go to an Italian one. We were indeed very fortunate, to have enjoyed the excellent food provided by both the Chinese and Italian restaurants. Guy chuckling, told me it was now time to go and see if the Peruvian Italian restaurant that had been recommended to him, and he wanted to see; if it really lived up to its reputation of serving both countries traditional cuisine.

Once again, we called a taxi to take us to downtown Lima, and asked the taxi driver to drop us at the Trattoria El Bambino. On entering the restaurant, we were made to feel very welcome, and shown to the best table in the place. Guy explained to me, apart from any Italian dish we may decide upon, he wished to try the Peruvian national food called Ceviche. This dish consisted of salt, garlic, onions, peppers, and raw marinated fish in lime.

"My goodness Guy, that sounds utterly deplorable, I do hope the fish will not make us ill," I explained.

Guy sat back and laughed for a few moments, before saying, "Darling I am sure we have nothing to worry about." He was quite right; I was amazed the entire meal was actually wonderful.

On-going to pay, Guy assured the proprietor that we thoroughly enjoyed the Ceviche and thanked him for everything.

During the remaining few days, Guy and I visited a couple of historic sites in the city as well as doing a little shopping, enabling us to look for special presents to take home.

The first site we visited, was the Huaca Pueillana, which is a huge adobe and clay pyramid constructed on seven levels. The pyramid is located in the Miraflores district quite near to our hotel. The history of the pyramid tells us how it had served as an important ceremonial and administrative centre for the advancement of the Inca culture. Also on the site is a restaurant and bar which Guy and I took full advantage of, and again thoroughly enjoyed.

The following day after eating another wonderful breakfast, Guy and I continued our exploring. This time, we chose to make our next visit to the Plaza Mayor, located in the historic centre of Lima. Surrounding the square, were many important buildings including the Government offices, the Presidential Palace, and Lima Cathedral. During the visit, we were very fortunate to see the rather noisy, though very colourful ceremony of changing of the guard at the Presidential Palace.

While in the Plaza, Guy decided we should take advantage of the many beautiful shops and look for the gifts we would both wish to take back home. Like all women, I fell hopelessly in love with the exquisite Alpaca and silk shawls, immediately ending up buying three of them. My next purchase being, the soft leather handbags that would undoubtedly cost a fortune in England, so decided two were the order of the day. Next it was Guy's turn to buy his presents. As we walked into a side street off the Plaza, we found a small artisan workshop, selling handmade Retablo boxes. Choosing one with great care, as Guy wanted something special for his father. Guy settled for one that had a beautifully painted biblical scene on the inside, strangely with llamas rather than camels!! The outside of the box had been painted with many exotic flowers that grew in Peru. Guy was so impressed with the box, like myself, he bought three of them. One for his father, another he thought Toby may like, and the third one for himself.

The next couple of days we decided to spend quietly by the pool, and gradually we started re-packing our suitcases to return home.

"Happy darling?" Guy asked, holding me close in his arms. Just before it was time to go down to enjoy the last breakfast of our wonderful honeymoon, while holding me close, he told me at the same time, "I know one thing my darling; no man could feel as happy as I do. Our wedding was simply wonderful, and you are the most beautiful, enchanting woman in the world. I love you so much Annabelle, my heart could simply burst."

As I looked up into my husband's handsome face. I felt as if Guy had covered me in stars, and I could now feel tears welling up and my eyes becoming misty. I loved hearing Guy saying such romantic things, and no matter how often he told me he loved me, each time it felt as if it was the first. I replied in my soft cultured voice which was now full of emotion, "My darling Guy, it is wonderful to hear you are as happy as I am, and you have no regrets marrying me." With that Guy drew even closer, could it have been possible for him to do so, and began to kiss me passionately until I could barely breathe. Like all couples when the time comes to end what for Guy and I had been an ecstatic, exciting honeymoon. I felt rather sad we had to say goodbye to this enchanting country. The thought of one day we may even return, if I was being honest, sadly I doubted it.

Chapter Twelve

New Horizon

We returned to England on one of British Airways direct flights, flying in once again to Heathrow. Guy had booked a limousine to meet and take us back to Davenport Hall. There both families were waiting impatiently to greet their wonderfully happily married offspring, and as was normal Hopkins was the first to greet the returning honeymooners. While explaining to me with a huge smile, how happy he was to be able to take the new Mrs Davenport's luggage into Guy's room. Guy could not help but laugh as Hopkins at this point, was unusually blushing but tactfully said nothing. Hopkins informed Guy that he would find both families in the small sitting room and then disappeared with the luggage.

"Hello, my darlings, wonderful to see you both home safe" Lady Rosalind was the first to greet us. She was then joined by Sir Richard and my family, all echoing the same sentiment. Everyone it seemed wanted to talk at once, then started to laugh.

After lots of hugs and kisses, it was Sir Richard that went on to inform Guy and myself, that both families had found a lovely apartment for us in St Johns Wood. He then continued.

"As an extra wedding present my dears, each family had contributed and paid the first twelve months' rent, and we sincerely hope you liked it."

Guy and I were thrilled and delighted, at the kindness and thought our respective parents had shown in regard to finding us, not just an apartment, but one that was fully furnished. This of course would eventually give Guy and I time to find a house, something we had already discussed. We returned to London on the Sunday afternoon, excited that our real lives together would now unfold.

The following day, both Guy and I returned to our places of work. As Guy walked into the MOD, he was greeted with many good wishes from various members of staff while making his way to his new office. The Ministry of Defence is one of the largest, public procurement organisations in Europe. Managing some of the most complex and technologically advanced requirements in the world. Guy had been assigned to the Defence Equipment and Support Department. This department managed a vast range of complex projects, enabling it to order, buy, support, and supply vital equipment also services for the Royal Air Force to operate effectively.

Towards the end of almost two years at the MOD, and having discussed the situation with me, Guy decided to resign from the Royal Air Force.

I must admit, on hearing Guy's decision that at this stage of his life, he wished to leave the Royal Air Force after so many years, left me to feel deeply surprised, perhaps shocked would be more the word I should you use to describe my emotions. Asking Guy if he was absolutely sure this was what he truly wanted, as not only was it a job, but a whole way of life, including of course his distinguished career.

Guy informed me, his voice now having a very grave tone to it, said it was exactly what he wanted, and it was not a decision he had made lightly. So, accepting my husband's wishes, I told Guy if it made him happy, then I would stand fully behind him.

On an agreed date, Guy attended a traditional "Dining Out night" in the Officers Mess at RAF Uxbridge. As always, these evenings were pleasant, though this evening was tainted with strong emotions. After an excellent dinner had been served, the PMC thanked Guy for his service and wished him well in his new civilian life. Guy left with the ubiquitous engraved silver tankard, and a sizeable pension. On his return home Guy found me waiting anxiously for him, naturally wondering when the reality of not returning to the MOD the following morning, how would my beloved husband then feel.

"Well, how did it go?" I asked softly.

"As to be expected," Guy replied with a smile.

"No regrets?" I asked cautiously.

"None, well none at the moment." Guy laughed and gave a small chuckle before saying, "Now it is a case of trying to find a reasonable job, any ideas?"

I could not help but a raised eyebrow to Guy's words and replied, "I am sure my darling, you will find the perfect job which will make you as happy as you have always been." Guy stared at me, and for one moment for the first time in his life, he felt a little apprehensive. I immediately told him wearing a smile, "I love you Guy Davenport, and I know everything will be just fine."

A few weeks later and to his surprise, Guy received a phone call from DAVCO (USA). The caller was the Vice President of Human Relations at DAVCO Head office in America. After politely introducing himself, he asked Guy if he would consider a position with the company which was a large Aviation and Armament group in the United States? He continued by also asking that if Guy agreed, he would like to invite him to an interview in London.

Guy realised instantly he was being "head hunted." Controlling his excitement, Guy informed the Vice President he would be pleased to attend an interview. On hearing Guy's calm reply, the Vice President went on to explain, that the interview would be taking place at DAVCO'S UK subsidiary near London Heathrow the following week. Replacing the receiver, Guy came to look for me, calling me to come immediately.

"Darling what in the world is all the excitement about?" I asked. Guy went on to tell me all about the conversation he had just had, and how he thought this could well be the job he had been looking for.

Travelling up to London, Guy could not resist the rather large smile that reflected the excitement he now felt, as this was to be his first civilian interview. Entering the building and going through the normal procedures of security, Guy was then escorted to the large boardroom. On entering, he found there were a number of senior executives already present. After a good hour's interview, with refreshments having been served, Guy returned home happy with his performance at the interview.

A month later, and not surprisingly given his career to date; Guy was invited to travel to America. There he would meet the President of the company, along with the Board of Directors of DAVCO USA, for a further interview. Arriving at Dulles-Washington International Airport, and having cleared immigration and customs, Guy took the airport shuttle bus to the General Aviation terminal. He was directed to where the DAVCO business jet awaited him, which flew him the 94 miles to the city of Harrisburg in Pennsylvania. Arriving at Harrisburg airport, Guy was met by a chauffeur driven limousine that took him to the Hilton hotel where a reservation had been made for him for the duration of his stay.

Suffering as usual from slight jet lag, Guy decided to have an early dinner and retire. The same chauffeur arrived the following morning to take Guy to the DAVCO headquarters. DAVCO USA, was one of the largest of several aviation related organisations in Harrisburg. The moment Guy entered the building, he was welcomed by Carl Schaeffer the CEO of DAVCO. Guy was then given a tour of the facilities; after which he was introduced to senior executives in the first of several meetings that would be held during his stay.

During a similar meeting on the second day of his visit, Guy learned that the position under consideration, was that of Senior Public Relations and Sales Consultant. Guy was asked by the CEO, "Would you be interested in accepting this offer, and if so, we would be delighted to have you on board." The CEO continued, "Guy we are just about to take a coffee break; this will give you a little time to consider our offer." Once everyone returned to the table, the meeting was then brought to order with all eyes now focusing on Guy, when again the CEO asked, "Well Guy, have you considered if you would care to join the company."

For a moment there was deathly silence, until Guy gave one of his charismatic smiles which normally endeared him to both men and women. Taking a quick look around the table and then directing his answer to the CEO, he informed him in his calm manner, stating, "I would be delighted to take up the position you have offered me, and I hope you in turn, will indeed be pleased to have me work alongside of you."

The CEO, replied, "Guy, we all feel you will be a valuable asset to the company, and we are delighted you have accepted to join us." The CEO then further explained to Guy, that he would be based within the subsidiary of DAVCO (UK) in London, and his salary would almost double to what he had received during his RAF years.

On returning to his hotel, Guy phoned to inform me of the day's developments, and asked would I ensure a car was waiting for him at Heathrow on his return home. He then went on to tell me how much he loved and missed me and would bring me something nice on his return. I told him, all I needed and wanted, was for him to return home safe and well.

That evening, Guy was taken out to one of the finest restaurants in Harrisburg. He was told he would be going to a celebratory dinner with all the executives of the company being present and would find the evening most enjoyable. Guy was now in high spirits and his charming manner, captivated everyone. As the evening drew to a close, Guy found himself shaking hands with everyone as they wished him a safe journey back to England and hoped he would indeed enjoy working for the company.

As Guy sat in his business class seat, his thoughts drifted back to the last few days. Knowing roughly how his life and mine would now change during the coming years. He found himself praying all would be as he hoped. The flight home this time seemed even more interminable than usual. Could it be the fact he wanted desperately to discuss matters with his father, who though now was a very grand age, still remained deeply interested in his son's career? Or more than likely, could it be he had missed his beautiful patient wife who he loved dearly.

Two weeks after arriving home, Guy commenced employment at the HQ of DAVCO (UK) situated in an impressive multi-story building near London Heathrow. He was met by Robert Fowler the Sales Director, who introduced him to Dennis Brennan. Dennis being the CEO. After enjoying a welcomed cup of coffee, Robert than proceeded to take Guy on a tour of the building, after which he was then shown to his new office.

There Guy met Martha Lyon, who was a very forceful, efficient, mature Irish lady. Martha had been given the position of becoming Guy's secretary, a lady who obviously suffered no nonsense from other members of staff. Guy smiled to himself as the thought flashed through his mind, he hoped Martha would not mistake Annabelle as another member of staff, knowing full well that if Martha did, she would more than meet her match in the person of his beloved wife.

During his induction period, Guy learned that DAVCO, also had an aircraft production facility in the north of England. Lancashire to be precise. The plant located there, was currently producing the Osprey business jet. Prior to Guy's recruitment, DAVCO had made the decision to open a new production line for the Osprey MkII aircraft. This aircraft was an Electronics Counter Measures (ECM) variant of the original Osprey. ECM, includes early warning of hostile aircraft; assisting combat aircraft to suppress radar emissions from ground missile sites and the jamming of enemy radio communications.

The decision by DAVCO to open a new production line, was based on information that several air forces who were currently operating business jets, were considering the retirement of their Dassault Aviation Falcon 20, ECM variants: in particular, the Spanish and the Norwegian Air Forces. They had decided on an early replacement of their Falcon 20 ECM aircraft. Both of these countries had expressed interest in purchasing the new Osprey MkII aircraft. To further Guy's familiarisation of the new aircraft, it was decided that he should visit the DAVCO facility in Lancashire.

Guy with several members of the sales team, flew in one of company's business jets from Heathrow, directly to DAVCO's private airport in Lancashire. The flight being short but most pleasant, giving the men time to talk about what they may find on their arrival. As their aircraft landed, Guy to his surprise, felt a degree of excitement as this was going to be a new experience for him. On their arrival, the men were escorted to the Management Dining Room. They were greeted by John Ayres, who was the General Manager of the facility, together with Leslie Kemp his Production Manager.

After lunch, Guy and the sales team, moved to John Ayres' office. There, the sales team were briefed about the DAVCO facility, and the progress to-date on the production of the new Osprey II ECM aircraft. While Guy knew exactly what ECM meant, the other members of the sales team were unaware of the role of an ECMII aircraft. Aircraft fitted with Electronic Counter Measures equipment, provided early warning of hostile aircraft; also assisting combat aircraft with the suppression of ground radar defence sites and jamming radio communications. After the meeting, accompanied by Leslie Kemp, the team visited the Osprey production line. Following the visit to the production line, the team then boarded a newly completed Osprey MKII aircraft on a routine test flight.

After take-off, the aircraft headed west over the Irish Sea. Approaching the Isle of Man, Guy was delighted to be invited into the cockpit. His excitement reached unbelievable heights, when the captain of the aircraft, suggested that Guy moved into the right hand seat and take control of the aircraft. For fifteen exhilarating minutes, Guy flew the aircraft without a problem. Returning to his seat in the passenger compartment, he was greeted by sardonic cheers and loud applause by his service team. Guy gave a very broad smile, feeling a little embarrassed, though did not deny how much he had enjoyed the experience. After overflying the Isle of Man, the aircraft turned east to fly back to the mainland, making a perfect landing on its return at the DAVCO facility. After coffee in the General Manager's office, John Ayres and Guy discussed the proposed production schedule for the new Osprey aircraft before Guy and the rest of team flew back to London later that evening.

Guy arrived home happy but rather tired. I had decided to wait to join him for dinner, even though it was now a little on the late side. Feeling relaxed and while enjoying our evening meal, Guy went on to relate about the fantastic fifteen minutes he had in flying the Osprey, making a long trip worthwhile.

A few days later after returning from his visit to Lancashire, Guy was informed that DAVCO had received confirmation that the Royal Norwegian Airforce (RNOAF) had expressed a possible interest in purchasing the Osprey MKII ECM aircraft. Delighted at this news, Guy made plans to visit Norway.

The following week, Guy joined the rest of the team once again, and flew from London to Oslo. From their arrival at Gardermoen International Airport, the team took a couple of taxis to the Four Seasons Hotel, where reservations had previously been made. As the Hotel was situated in the centre of Oslo, this allowed Guy to enjoy a little of the scenery.

Early the next day, Guy and the team attended a meeting at Air Headquarters of the Royal Norwegian Airforce. (RNOAF.) Those present, included Knut Bottesland the Minister of Aviation. The Chief of the Airforce, Major General Torje Skinnarland and several other air force officers. General Torje Skinnarland to Guy's surprise, was a typical beautiful blonde Norwegian woman. Also present were a number of Government officials. After detailed discussions on finance, administration and a delivery schedule, the meeting ended, though not before everyone present agreed to meet the following day at Orland Airforce Base close to Oslo.

The next day as arranged, the team met and flew the 474 Km to the Orland Airforce Base. On arrival, Guy was welcomed by General Major Olan Ulstein the Base Commander. Accompanying General Olstein, was the

Officer Commanding the 132nd Air Wing, Brigadier Jorgen Hakon. 331 Squadron of the Air Wing, was currently operating the United States F18 Hornet aircraft and the Dassault Aviation Falcon ECM aircraft. The Norwegian Air Force, was hoping that the DAVCO Aircraft, would replace the Dassault Falcon. After introductions were completed, the team, the VIPs and Officers positioned themselves, enabling them to witness several test flights of DAVCO aircraft. Eventually the team, VIPs and Officers, were invited on board enabling them to enjoy a number of flights. All agreeing how impressed they were with this new aircraft.

The team returned to their hotel, and made an early start the next morning, where a further meeting had been arranged at AHQ... Once discussions were concluded, Guy was delighted when the Minister for Aviation, agreed to sign a Memorandum of Understanding, (MOU) confirming the Norwegian Government's decision to purchase a minimum of two Osprey MkII Aircraft.

Returning to the hotel and digesting a very welcomed evening meal. Guy decided he would take a taxi to the local stores to see if he was able to buy a present for me before returning to England.

Returning to England, and after having a good night's rest. Guy walked into DAVCO HQ, feeling in very good spirits, especially when warmly congratulated by Dennis Brennan on the success of his first sales trip. By mid-morning, Guy wished to celebrate his first successful trip, but would only do so if I was with him. He decided to phone and ask if I would like to go out to dinner that evening at Topogigios. The restaurant of course held a special place in our hearts, as it always reminded us of so many happy memories when we were courting, including the wonderful night of our engagement.

Several months later, the Spanish Government registered an interest in the purchase of the Osprey aircraft. Receiving the good news, Guy made the necessary arrangements for the sales team and himself to visit Madrid. The Spanish Air Force or Ejecito del Aire, had been established in 1939, at the end of the Spanish Civil War. Guy and the sales team, departed from Heathrow in one of the Osprey aircraft, which was flown in specially from the company's facility in Lancashire.After completing the normal arrival requirements at Madrid airport, the team were driven in vehicles provided by the Spanish Air Force, to the 5-star Vincci Capitol Hotel situated in the centre of Madrid.

The following morning, fortified by an excellent Spanish breakfast, the team were driven to Air Headquarters located in the Moncoia –Aravaca District of Madrid; to commence a number of meetings with various representatives. The participants at the meeting included Air General Javier Ruiz, who was Chief of Staff. Captain General of the Air Force, Juan Lopez. Margarita Torres, Minister of Defence, and her deputy Juan Lorraga, along with other senior members of the Spanish Government and the Air Force.

After two days of fruitful meetings, the third day was held at Torrejon Air Base which was adjacent to the international airport. The base was home to the 45th Group of the Combat Air Command which included the 472nd Squadron, currently operating the Dassault Falcon 20-ECM aircraft. Prior to the meeting, Guy was introduced to the Base Commander, Lt General

Fernando Caravaca and Julio Lopez who was the Officer Commanding of 472 Squadron. Once all meetings had been completed, the rest of the day included demonstration flights. Before returning to their hotel, Guy was delighted to be handed a signed Memorandum of Understanding, which confirmed the Spanish decision to purchase the DAVCO Mk II ECM aircraft.

Flying back to London the next day, Guy and the excited Sales team were so delighted their trip had concluded in such success, they consumed several celebratory bottles of vintage champagne. Once back in London, Guy received further congratulations from the CEO on another successful trip. During the next two years, DAVCO received sales inquiries from Thailand, Bahrain, and Denmark, ensuring the success of the new aircraft.

While Guy was delighted with and thoroughly enjoying his new career. Now in his mid-sixties he became keenly aware that he was spending an inordinate time on overseas visits which were taking him away from not only myself, but his beloved parents who themselves had now reached a grand old age. Receiving yet another inquiry, only this time from Belgium, Guy it seemed decided it was time to discuss his thoughts with me.

Guy and I, over a long period of weeks found ourselves having a great number of rather lengthy discussions, due mostly to my concern as to whether Guy should indeed decide to retire. I felt he must be absolutely sure in his own heart and mind, this was what he wanted, and that he would have no regrets once having done so. Eventually, after a great deal of soul searching, Guy and I, at long last came to an agreement. We decided, it may after all be time for him to hang up his wings as he would say.

Sadly, a tragic accident changed Guy's decision for the present to retire. An Osprey ECM aircraft on a routine test flight, departed the DAVCO facility using runway 26, adjacent to the River Ribble in Lancashire. Climbing to 2500 ft, the aircraft flew west following the course of the river. After 12 miles and overflying Preston, the aircraft departed the Lancashire coastline over the Ribble Estuary. Heading west over the Irish Sea. The Osprey, on autopilot, climbed steeply to its assigned altitude of 15000 ft. Without warning, the autopilot initiated a nose down attitude of the aircraft, forcing it into a steep dive towards the Irish sea below. Unfortunately, the pilot was unable to control the descent or disconnect the autopilot. The Osprey, nose down, plunged into the sea at high speed.

The aircraft disappeared from the screen of the UK Northern Radar, causing the Area Air Traffic Control Centre to declare an emergency. This action included notifying the Coastguard immediately, and the RAF Air Sea Rescue unit. Responding, an Air Sea Rescue helicopter was alerted at RAF Valley, also the RNLI Lifeboats were launched from New Brighton, and Lytham St Annes. 202 (SAR) Squadron at RAF Valley scrambled a Sea King rescue helicopter, with all units heading towards the possible crash site. The search for the crashed Osprey, continued all day until nightfall, but without success. A decision was taken to call off the search and resume again once there was daylight.

Since 2007, all commercial aircraft had been fitted with underwater beacons, which assisted salvage teams to locate the wreckage, and more importantly the location of the black box flight recorder. The next morning, one of the lifeboats identified a signal coming from the locator beacon, thus enabling the crash site to be identified and marked. With the crash confirmed and the cause unknown, the UK Civil Aviation Authorities issued a notice to DAVCO, informing them they must ground all Osprey aircraft until further notice. This also applied to all other Osprey operators. Once this information had been given, DAVCO immediately commissioned their UK Underwater Recovery Company, to salvage the crashed aircraft.

At dawn the company's salvage vessel the RV "Recovery II," departed Holyhead and sailed with all speed to the crash site. On arriving at the crash site, the unmanned underwater submersible was lowered to the seabed. The vessel confirmed that the aircraft fuselage was intact. Sadly, it also enabled the recovery vessel's personnel to be informed it contained the bodies of the crew. The wreckage was in comparatively shallow water and was therefore able to be hoisted onto the deck of the recovery vessel.

Once the wreckage was on the deck, the crew ensured with great care; that the bodies were removed and then carefully put on board a helicopter. With its sad cargo on board, the helicopter then flew to a main hospital in Lancashire. There the bodies after formal identification would be eventually released back to their families.

The recovery vessel sailed back to Holyhead, where transport awaited the arrival of the ship. Once the wreckage had been transferred to a specialist haulage vehicle, it was driven to the Royal Aeronautical Establishment at Farnborough. There the wreckage would be examined by the Accident Investigation Board.

Within weeks, the AIB personnel at Farnborough had established the cause of the tragic accident and published a provisional report. The culprit was the software associated with the aircraft's autopilot. This meant after take-off, with the aircraft climbing rapidly to its assigned altitude, the software "decided" that the rate of climb was excessive and fearing a stall, forced the nose of the aircraft downwards. Unfortunately, as the pilot could not override the autopilot and regain control of his aircraft, sadly this caused the aircraft to crash at high speed into the Irish sea.

The publication of the AIB provisional report, did not therefore allow the CAA to rescind the grounding of all DAVCO Osprey aircraft. A final report by all interested parties was required to lift the grounding order. DAVCO's financial situation deteriorated, with all production lines idle. Personnel unfortunately also had to be laid off; in addition, Guy and Senior Executives were also offered redundancy packages.

Then strangely enough, and to Guy's amazement; the opposite happened. Although offered redundancy, he was also offered the position of Vice President (Sales) in Harrisburg Pennsylvania with the parent company in America. Once again Guy and I found ourselves discussing the situation at length, as I had to be sure that Guy in his own mind would be happy with whatever decision he finally made.

At last, Guy decided he should accept redundancy, and retire finally from full employment.

Having made his final decision, Guy was actually excited at the thought of retiring to a life of not having to watch the clock to get up for work, along with our dogs and myself. Also, the thought he would have as much time as he wished to spend on his precious car and motorcycle delighted him. Making his final farewells to all those he had worked with; Guy left the building and took a taxi to Topogigos. There we would meet up with our lifelong friends, Amanda and Toby to celebrate. The four of us had decided to stay in town for the night at our favourite hotel.

Saying goodbye before leaving London the following morning. Guy and I drove home back to Briars; the Gentleman's Pink Cottage Guy had fallen so in love with the moment he saw it. Mr and Mrs Jenkins were already at the cottage by the time Guy and I arrived home. Once having changed, Mrs Jenkins ensured the normal routine of serving afternoon tea on the small patio was laid for both Guy and I to enjoy. We were very shortly joined by two adorable Briard puppies, which we had named Sophie and Sadie, who would grow to love our darling Shih Ztu who answered to the name of Teddy. The Briard had originated as a working sheep dog on small French farms in the 18th Century. The fields being very small demanded a dog with both speed and agility. Guy's delight when he was able to before dinner, was to walk with the puppies around the garden, and then watch their boisterous behaviour in the orchard.

Enjoying this time alone, Guy's thoughts invariably drifted back to his exciting and successful career in the RAF, both as a fighter pilot and spy. His reverie only interrupted by my call to dinner.

The life of Air Commodore Guy Davenport DSO AFC RAF (Ret'd) in real life epitomised the motto of the Royal Air Force… "Through Adversity to the Stars."

Acknowledgements

As always, I would like to thank my wonderful family for their love and constant support. The great care they take in looking after me, is amazing; including their expert technical help and guidance which I am so deeply grateful for, in regard to using a computer and allowing me the time I need to write.

Next, I would like to sincerely thank Becky Banning and Melanie Bartle of Grosvenor House Publishing, for their kindness, understanding due to me being dyslexic. Also, other members of their excellent staff.

The beautiful cover of this book has been designed by my dearest friend Mourad Dehmas, of Imagine Design. He is always so very kind and no request is ever too much. Thank you dear.

Finally, a very special and sincere thank you, the man I know only as, Squadron Leader Roy Handley. The only man in the world allowed to wear the colours, including Officers and men of the French Air Force. For once again in honouring and allowing me to tell further chapters, of his very special, amazing life. Without the hours of professional guidance, advice, and help he has given, this book and "An Precedented Life" could never have been written.

Ingram Content Group UK Ltd.
Milton Keynes UK
UKHW040625260523
422394UK00001B/10